STRAIGHT FROM THE HIP

STRAIGHT FROM THE HIP

SUSAN MALLERY

WHEELER
CHIVERS

This Large Print edition is published by Wheeler Publishing, Waterville, Maine, USA and by BBC Audiobooks Ltd, Bath, England.
Wheeler Publishing, a part of Gale, Cengage Learning.

ALL RIGHTS RESERVED

The text of this Large Print edition is unabridged.
Other aspects of the book may vary from the original edition.
Set in 16 pt. Plantin.
Printed on permanent paper.

LIBRARY OF CONGRESS CATALOGING-IN-PUBLICATION DATA

Mallery, Susan.
    Straight from the hip / by Susan Mallery.
      p. cm. — (Lone star sisters series ; 3)
      "Wheeler Publishing large print hardcover."
      ISBN-13: 978-1-4104-2062-6 (alk. paper)
      ISBN-10: 1-4104-2062-0 (alk. paper)
      1. Women—Texas—Fiction. 2. Sisters—Fiction. 3. Texas—
Fiction. 4. Large type books. I. Title.
    PS3613.A453S77 2009
    813'.6—dc22   2009030434

BRITISH LIBRARY CATALOGUING-IN-PUBLICATION DATA AVAILABLE

Published in 2009 in the U.S. by arrangement with Harlequin Books S.A.
Published in 2010 in the U.K. by arrangement with Harlequin Enterprizes II B.V.

U.K. Hardcover: 978 1 408 47726 7 (Chivers Large Print)
U.K Softcover: 978 1 408 47727 4 (Camden Large Print)

Printed in the United States of America
1 2 3 4 5 6 7 13 12 11 10 09

STRAIGHT FROM THE HIP

Chapter One

In the movies there was always a warning before something bad happened. Music swelled, the good guy promised everything would be fine now or the camera suddenly went into slow motion.

Life wasn't so tidy.

Izzy Titan sat in the window seat, as she had every day for the past month, staring out at a blurry world and feeling sorry for herself. While it wasn't a career choice everyone would make, it filled the day. She ignored her sisters' pleas that she join them for lunch or shopping or even come downstairs to dinner. Like a regular person. When it got too annoying, she pointed out she wasn't regular anymore — she was handicapped. If that didn't work, she slammed the door and locked it until they went away. She'd always given everything she had, so she was ready to become the self-pity queen, if necessary.

Finally her sisters stopped bugging her. Which should have been a really big clue.

There wasn't any warning. One minute she was sitting in her usual spot, the next, someone grabbed her around the waist, pulled her to her feet, then tossed her over a very broad, very hard shoulder.

"What the hell do you think you're doing?" she yelled as blood rushed to her head, making her a little dizzy.

"My job. Go ahead and fight me all you want. You can't hurt me."

It was a challenge she couldn't ignore. But when she tried to kick her attacker, he wrapped one arm around her legs, holding her still. Wiggling didn't help either. The man had muscles like rock and a month of immobilizing self-pity had left her girlishly weak.

"I swear," she began, as the guy turned and started walking. "Do you know who I am?"

"Izzy Titan. Hey, Skye."

Hey, Skye?

Izzy raised her head and tried to make the room focus. Unfortunately it was dark and blurry and she couldn't see any details.

"Skye?" she yelled. "Are you there?"

"Oh, Izzy." Her sister sounded concerned, but not worried. Not afraid. "We didn't know what else to do."

"We?"

"I'm here, too," Lexi, her other sister, said. "This is for your own good."

"Having me *kidnapped?*"

"Nick comes very highly recommended. You told us that your doctors wanted to put you on an antidepressant, which you wouldn't agree to. This is better."

"What?"

"You wouldn't leave your room or talk to us. It's been a month, Izzy."

"You're having me kidnapped because I wouldn't go *shopping* with you? Are you insane?"

They moved into the hallway. She could tell because the room got darker and her fingers brushed against the walls. Then they were going down, down, down into more darkness.

Each step jarred her entire body. If she'd had that lunch her sisters were so hysterical about she would be throwing it up, right about now.

"I'm not kidding," she yelled. "Stop this right now. All of you. Nick, I don't care what my sisters said, I didn't agree to this. Put me down or I swear I'll throw your ass in jail for so long, you'll actually learn to enjoy being Bubba's love slave."

9

"You signed a release," rock-guy said calmly, still moving through the house.

"What?"

"You signed a release. I've got it here in my pocket."

Izzy wanted to scream in frustration as she remembered Skye asking her to sign a few checks so her sister could pay Izzy's bills. "She tricked me. I'm *blind!* I didn't know what I was signing."

They went outside. She saw the blurry outline of trees and the welcome light and heat of the sun.

"You shouldn't sign what you can't read," Nick told her.

She could hear the humor in his voice and that really pissed her off. Seconds later, he opened a car door and dumped her onto a smooth leather seat. Before he could close the door, she pushed past him and bolted for freedom. She made it all of three steps before he grabbed her around the waist and pulled her against him.

It was like pressing against the side of a mountain. She kicked and tried to pull her arm free. Irritation turned to fury and betrayal. She turned toward the house — at least she could see something that big — and assumed her sisters were on the porch.

"How could you do this to me?" she

demanded. "You're my *family.*"

"Izzy, we love you." There were tears in Skye's voice.

Good, Izzy thought furiously. She hoped Skye felt guilty for the rest of her life.

"We didn't know what else to do," Lexi called, sounding less than sure.

"I would never do this to you," Izzy screamed. "Don't think I'll ever forgive you. Ever!"

The last word was cut short as she was tossed back into the rear of a car or SUV. She couldn't tell which. The door slammed shut before she could run again. She lunged for the door handle, only there wasn't one. Nor could she open the windows.

Seconds later she discovered a thick, mesh screening behind the seat and between her and the front of the vehicle. She was trapped.

She heard the door open and vaguely saw Nick slide behind the wheel. Then they were driving away. Her sisters had hired a stranger to take her from her home and do God-knows-what to her. They'd abandoned her. No. This was worse — this was actual action on their part. The two people she'd counted on her entire life had discovered she was too much trouble and had tossed her out like the trash.

■ ■ ■ ■

For the next three hours, Nick Hollister drove ten miles above the speed limit. He wanted to go faster, but knew he couldn't outrun the inevitable. His pretty, dark-haired passenger was staring out the window with a determination that told him she was about ten seconds from losing it.

"You can cry if you want to," he said. "It won't bother me." He'd seen a lot worse than tears.

Izzy didn't turn toward him. "I won't give you the satisfaction."

"You think I win if you cry?"

"Don't bullies always enjoy knowing they've hurt someone? You didn't win. You can't break me."

She raised her chin as she spoke, instinctively defying him. Good, he thought grimly. She was going to need every ounce of strength she had if she wanted to find her way back. Which was his job — to make sure she did.

"Break you?" he asked, ignoring that she'd called him a bully. He'd stormed into her life and taken her away from everything she knew. Hardly comfortable circumstances. He understood the fear of the unknown, although her unknown was a whole lot more controlled than his had been. "Dramatic much?"

"Hey, you're the one who tossed me into the back of a car."

"SUV."

"Whatever. This is kidnapping. I get to be however I want."

"Your sisters know where you are and what will happen when you get there."

"And I should find that comforting why?" She swallowed. "Don't even talk to me."

He heard the fear in her voice. He could see it in the way she kept herself stiff. Behind fear was terror and while he wanted her attention, he didn't need it that bad.

"My name is Nick Hollister," he said, using the same tone that calmed unbroken horses. "I run a school that teaches corporate survival training. That pays the bills. I also take in kids who have suffered a traumatic loss or been victims of a violent crime. I teach them how to survive in my world. That helps them cope with their own."

Izzy stared out the window, obviously ignoring him. He wondered how much she could actually see.

"Your sisters asked me to take you on for a few weeks, to help you adjust to being blind."

"I'm not blind," she snapped. "I have thirty percent of my sight."

"You're acting like you're blind," he told her. "You've been hiding in your room for a month."

"It's not like I can do anything else."

"Your life is over? Because of one little challenge? That's impressive."

"Shut up," she yelled. "You don't know what you're talking about. You can see fine."

"Wouldn't it be interesting if I couldn't?" He swerved slightly as he spoke. The SUV swayed. Izzy didn't bother looking up.

"Very funny."

"I thought it was," he said. "Look. They care about you. Your sisters," he added, in case she wasn't following.

This time she did glance at him, only to roll her eyes. The hazel irises were unmarred by her injury. "I'm more than capable of carrying on a conversation. I'm probably smarter than you."

"I doubt that."

"Oh, please."

"How smart is sitting on your ass, feeling sorry for yourself?"

She straightened and glared at him. "I was in an explosion," she said, speaking slowly, as if to make sure he would understand. "I could have been killed."

"But you weren't."

"I was seriously injured and I lost most of my eyesight."

"Which you could get back tomorrow if you weren't such a girl about the surgery."

He glanced in the rearview mirror in time to see her narrow her gaze.

"A girl?" she asked softly.

"Yeah. You know. Chicken. Lacking in bravery."

"That's it!" she yelled. "Let me out, right here. Let me out or I swear, I'll kill you myself. I'll rip you apart with my bare hands and feed your body to the snakes."

"Snakes wouldn't eat human flesh."

"Shut up!"

"Skye didn't say anything about you being hysterical."

"Let me out!"

"No."

She grabbed the mesh screening and rattled it, but it had withstood a lot more than a scrawny woman without much muscle on her.

"She did warn me you would be difficult," he said. "I charge extra for that."

Izzy sank back in the seat and resumed staring out the back window.

"If you won't have the surgery, then you have to survive with what you have," he told her. "That's where I come in. I teach you how to make it. You're staying with me until you can be on your own."

"What if I don't want to be on my own?"

"You think your sisters want you hanging around all the time? They have lives. You're what? Twenty-five? Twenty-six? You ready to give up so fast?"

"Go to hell."

"I've already been there."

He turned onto the familiar paved, private road and drove toward the two-story main house. He'd bought the run-down ranch nearly eight years before. Neighboring ranchers leased his pasture for their cattle, while he used the twenty acres of wilderness for his retreats. He kept a dozen horses in the big barn and had built several guesthouses where clients stayed. There were meeting facilities, a restaurant-grade kitchen that could serve up to fifty at a time and a big media room that rivaled a multiplex.

Not that Izzy would deal with much more than the barn. He planned to work her hard enough that she didn't have time to feel sorry for herself. The little he knew about her told him she would fight him every step of the way, but he didn't care about that. He would win, as she put it, in the end because he had to.

16

He parked in front of the house and turned off the engine.

"We're here," he said in the silence.

Izzy folded her arms across her chest and stared out the window.

"When I let you out, you can run if you want. We're about a mile from our closest neighbor and ten miles from the nearest town. But if you want to go looking, I won't stop you. The temperature is close to a hundred. Without water, you'll last maybe three days. Assuming you don't get bit by a rattler and die sooner."

"Oooh," Izzy said, still not looking at him. "I'm all tingly with fear. Want to threaten me with whips and chains next?"

"I don't usually work with adults, but I've made an exception for you. Don't think this is going to be easy. You'll work for your room and board. No work, no food."

She snapped her head around until she was facing him. "My sisters are *paying* you. You can't starve me."

He grinned. "I can do anything I want. I'm not the one who's blind."

"Fuck you."

"You're not my type."

If there hadn't been mesh between them, Izzy would have scrambled over the seat and gone after Nick with everything she had.

He was so smug and mean and dismissive. Didn't he know what she'd been through? She'd lost most of her sight. It was easy to be oh, so confident when you hadn't suffered. She would bet Nick didn't know anything about being afraid.

She hated him and right now she hated her sisters. It was hard to say who she resented more. Anger burned within her, making her want to lash out. The problem was there wasn't anyone she could fight. At least not yet.

Nick climbed out of the SUV and walked around to her side. The door opened. She felt the blast of afternoon heat on her skin.

She wanted to be back at Lexi's house, in the cool room with the window seat. Over the past month, the four walls had been a refuge. But her sisters had sent her away. She was on her own.

She slid out of the seat and followed Nick into a large house. The second they walked inside, the light dimmed and so did her ability to see. The world darkened until it was little more than blurry shapes.

"This is the main house," he said. "You'll be sleeping upstairs. First door on the left. There's an attached bathroom. You'll find your luggage there. You can unpack later. This is the living room. We don't use it much. Through here is the kitchen."

She knew from his voice he'd moved away, but had trouble seeing. She managed to follow him, only to bump into a table and then trip on a single step he hadn't bothered to mention. She tried to catch herself, but there was too much momentum. The ground raced toward her.

A familiar strong arm grabbed her around the waist and jerked her to her feet.

"Maybe you should use a cane," he said.

"Maybe you should warn me about stairs."

"You'll figure it out."

"That's it?" she demanded. "Let's pause for a moment, because your incredible concern is making me all teary-eyed. *I fell.*"

"I know. So what? You're going to fall. Then you're going to get up and move on. Or are you the type to just lie there, feeling sorry for yourself? Never mind. I already know the answer."

She wanted to tell him she wasn't like that. She was the one who climbed mountains and jumped out of airplanes and swam with sharks. She didn't believe in self-pity or giving up. At least she hadn't until the explosion.

"You don't understand," she told him.

"You sure about that?"

She heard footsteps, but couldn't tell the

direction. Who else was here and what would he or she want from her?

"Oh, you're back. Good. I have papers for you to sign, Nick. And you must be Izzy. I've heard so many wonderful things about you."

The man reached for her hand and shook it. His fingers were nearly as soft and smooth as Skye's or Lexi's.

"This is going to be fun. You're staying here in the house. You know that, right? Upstairs. I picked out your room myself. It has great light. Is Nick taking you on the tour? Don't you love the kitchen? I swear Norma, our cook-slash-housekeeper is going to kill me with her biscuits. I can't resist them but I *refuse* to let my jeans get any tighter. I love your hair. Are those curls natural? They're beautiful. Don't you think they're beautiful, Nick?"

"Stunning." Nick sounded more resigned than impatient as he spoke.

Izzy turned toward the enthusiastic new guy. "Who *are* you?"

The man laughed. "Oh, silly me. Introductions are essential. I'm Aaron. Aaron Levine. Two *A*'s. I work for Nick." He linked arms with her and led her into the kitchen.

"I'm his manager. I take care of all the bookings for the corporate retreats and

20

oversee the retreats from start to finish. I make sure everything runs smoothly here at the Hollister Institute. Nick takes care of the kids on his own. The man is rabid about helping those poor children. It's really very sweet."

Aaron patted her hand. "Okay — refrigerator on your right, but I wouldn't go in there if I were you. Norma's a little possessive about her supplies. There's a second refrigerator with drinks and snacks in the mudroom. I'll show you that. Table in the corner. Can you see it? There's lots of light. Norma rings a bell when it's time to eat and we all come running like dogs." He chuckled. "Don't you just love Texas? Where else can a man get away with wearing snakeskin boots and a giant belt buckle. And you know what they say about the size of a man's belt buckle."

Izzy felt more than confused. She felt lost and unsure. With the light pouring in the windows, she could actually see the outline of the tables and shapes she assumed were chairs. But who was Aaron? How had macho Nick gotten involved with charming, funny and obviously gay Aaron? Unless Nick was also . . .

She glanced in the direction he'd last been.

"No," came a low voice in her ear.

"No, what?" she asked.

"I know what you're thinking and no."

Aaron bumped her shoulder with his. "You mean is Nick gay? I should be so lucky. He has his lady friends he visits in town. It's all very John Wayne-esque. He rides into town, seduces the schoolteacher then rides off to fight another day."

Izzy rubbed her forehead. "I don't remember that movie."

"You know what I mean. Here's the mudroom." Aaron pressed her hand against what felt like a refrigerator. "Plenty of water, soda, that sort of thing. Don't track in dirt or Norma will skin you alive. And I'm not kidding. I think she collects knives."

"Aaron?"

"Yes, Nick?"

"I'll finish Izzy's tour."

Aaron stiffened. "I don't mind."

"I know, but I'll do it."

"Izzy's new. She's nervous."

"She's also standing right here," Izzy grumbled, appreciating that Aaron was trying to help, but hating the fact that they were talking about her as if she were a fern.

Nick didn't say anything. Maybe he was making violent hand gestures or maybe he was just staring. She had no way of knowing. Seconds later, Aaron let go of her arm and stepped back.

"Fine," he said with a sigh. "Izzy, whatever Nick says, what he really means is that he's really happy to have you here and that he thinks you're pretty." He leaned toward her and dropped his voice to a whisper. "We'll talk later."

Then he was gone.

"Follow me," Nick said and started walking.

Izzy started to point out, yet again, that she was *blind,* only to realize she could hear his boots on the hardwood floor. She took off after him, clipped her hip on the corner of a counter and stumbled over the threshold of a door.

They went outside. She saw the brighter light and felt the intense heat.

"You'll be working in the barn," Nick said, his dark shape moving in front of her. "Rita's in charge. Do what she says. We have twelve horses that need to be cleaned up after, fed and groomed. That should keep you busy. When you're more comfortable with your surroundings, you can start exercising them in the corrals. There's a corporate retreat in a couple of weeks. When that happens, we all pitch in, including you."

She waited until they passed into shade,

then stopped and folded her arms over her chest. "I don't know who the hell you think you are, but you're not going to tell me what to do. The only thing you're going to do is take me back to my sister's house, right now."

"Too bad you're blind, because if you weren't you could take one look at my face and know that's not going to happen. Obviously I need to convince you with my words." He took a step toward her. "No. Clear enough?"

She curled her hands into fists and started hitting the dark shape in front of her. "It's not clear. Nothing's clear," she yelled. "Don't you get that? Nothing is right. I can't make it go away. It sucks. My life is ruined and you want to talk to me about horses? About your stupid ranch? I want to go home. I want to be left alone."

She hit and hit until her arms got tired. Nick didn't bother defending himself, probably because she wasn't hurting him. Eventually, she dropped her hands to her sides.

"You about done?" he asked. "Is there more? You want to cry now?"

She hated him, then. Hated him more than she'd hated any human being ever.

"I'll find a way to crush you," she vowed.

"You'll have to find me, first. But that's

the trick, isn't it? You can't find anything. If you had the surgery, you could."

"Get off me about the surgery," she yelled. "Did they tell you it wasn't a sure thing? Did they tell you I could end up totally blind?"

"Yes, but the odds are you'll be fine. Those are odds worth taking."

"Easy for you to say. You've got nothing to lose."

"Fair enough. The barn is this way."

He just started walking. As if he expected her to follow him. As if her pain and suffering didn't matter.

"I'm not even a person to you, am I?" she asked, defeated and exhausted.

"You're a person. You're just not much of one right now. Rita will show you everything in the morning. For today, you can groom one of the horses. Skye said you've been around horses your whole life so you know what you're doing."

They were near the barn. Izzy saw the yawning darkness and didn't want to go inside. It was too black, there. Too frightening.

"I don't want this," she murmured.

"Too bad."

Maybe this was all designed to break her so she could be built up again. Maybe there was a master plan. Or maybe Nick was just a sick bastard who liked torturing people. Either way, she didn't much care.

She turned slowly, until she felt the sun in her face. It had to be late afternoon, so the sun was in the west. She thought about sitting in the back of the SUV during the drive and feeling the sun moving across her lap, warming her hands and her thighs. Then she closed her eyes and pictured a map.

They'd driven north for a while, then turned into the sun. So she had to go east to retrace the route. If she started walking, maybe she would find her way back. Or maybe just die. Right now that seemed okay, too.

She spun on her heel and took the first step. She half expected Nick to say something, but he didn't. She kept moving forward, straining to see anything that could trip her, like a fence or a bush.

"Where are you going?" he called after a couple of minutes.

"Home."

"Good luck with that."

She raised her hand and gave him the finger. The sun was hot on her back, but the heat was reassuring. It reminded her she was going the right way. That if she didn't give up, eventually she would make it.

CHAPTER TWO

Women were an inherent pain in the ass, Nick thought as he grabbed four bottles of water from the refrigerator in the mudroom. Aaron followed him back outside.

"What are you doing? Where's Izzy? You haven't lost her already, have you?"

Nick jerked his head to the right and kept on walking. "She took off."

"What?" Aaron took a half hop to keep up. "She's blind. She can't just take off."

"She did."

"What did you say? I know this is your fault. You said something mean, didn't you?"

"No."

"Then why didn't you stop her? She could get lost out there."

There was a slight possibility, but Nick doubted it. He'd given her a thirty-minute head start, so she could walk off some of her mad. He didn't want to find her for at least an hour, maybe longer. She needed time to think through her options.

"She's in the dry riverbed. She'll walk along it because it's the easiest footing."

Aaron trailed him into the barn. "What if there's a flash flood?"

Nick handed him the water and went to get his horse. "You see any clouds in the sky?"

"Okay, but what about snakes? Or she could fall."

"I'm willing to risk it."

"Is she?"

"Apparently. She's the one who took off." He led his horse out of the stall.

"She's *scared*. Jesus, Nick, the girl has been blind all of fifteen minutes. Give her a break."

"She'll have to earn that."

Aaron put the water on a worn stubby table, then planted his hands on his hips. "Sometimes you're a big pain in my ass."

"You think?"

Aaron pressed his lips together. Nick's assistant was about five-ten, thin, with styled dark hair and a fussiness about him Nick had learned to accept. No matter how many pairs of jeans he wore, he never looked as if he totally fit in. He would always be a city boy trapped in rural Texas.

Nick accepted that, as well. Aaron was

damned good at his job and loyal. But he had a way of burrowing in a topic like a tick during rainy season.

"She's a nice girl," Aaron said. "She's out of her element. As far as she's concerned, her family just rejected her. Doesn't that mean anything to you?"

Nick finished with the saddle. He grabbed the water and stuck it into the saddlebags. "She's here so we can help her. That's what matters. She's upset. She'll walk it off and then be easier to handle."

"She's not an upset cow. She's a *person*."

"You're taking this too much to heart."

"Someone has to. Give her a break."

"I'm rescuing her. Isn't that enough?"

"No. She's nice. You need nice in your life."

Nick led his horse outside. Before mounting, he glared at Aaron. "Whatever you're thinking, stop it right this second. You hear me?"

Aaron grinned. "She's pretty, too. I know you saw that. I'm not into women and even I was impressed."

"She's a client, nothing more."

Aaron rolled his eyes. "Oh, please. You think anyone believes that?"

"I don't care what you believe." Izzy was here because he was going to help her. For no other reason. He didn't get involved, certainly not with someone on his ranch. The last thing he wanted was to be responsible for someone else's emotions.

"Did you see her butt?" Aaron asked, as Nick swung into the saddle. "It's perfect. Do you think she does squats? My butt is just so flat."

All Nick wanted was a nice, quiet life. Instead he had this.

"I'm leaving now," he said.

"Okay, but be gentle when you find her. She'll be upset and she might have a little heatstroke. Maybe you'll have to do mouth-to-mouth."

Nick turned his horse toward the riverbed. "Don't you have work to do?"

"Yes, but this is better."

"Say goodbye, Aaron."

"Goodbye, Aaron."

Nick adjusted his hat. The temperature had to be over a hundred. He glanced at his watch and calculated how long Izzy had been gone. He would get close enough to see her, but not so close that she would hear the horse. Then he would watch her to see how she was doing.

It took twenty minutes to catch up with her, which surprised him. She'd gone farther than he'd expected. Despite her month

31

of shutting herself in her room, she was still in decent shape.

He reined in his horse and watched her walking. Involuntarily his gaze fell to her rear and he saw that Aaron was right — she did have a great ass. That combined with her wide hazel eyes, her long, dark, curly hair made her the stuff of fantasies. Not that he would be acting on any he might have.

He would do his best to fix her, not only because his friend Garth had especially requested that he take her on, but because that's what he did. Fix the broken, then move on. Sort of like a reverse body count. Because if the numbers were high enough — if he did enough good — maybe he could finally let go of the past.

Izzy put one foot in front of the other. The sun beat down unmercifully, burning her exposed skin. Sweat poured down her face and her clothes stuck to her. Her mouth was dry, her head ached and if there had been an extra drop of moisture left in her body, she would have actually considered crying.

As it was, she argued furiously with herself. Going back made the most sense. She should just turn around and walk into the sun. That would get her to the barn. But it felt too much like giving up.

Nick would come for her. Or send someone. She knew in her head, he wasn't going to let her die out here. Except if she kept walking, she might get so lost, no one could find her and then what? Did she really want to risk it?

"I don't want this," she said aloud. "Any of it."

Not being outside right now, not being at the ranch or being blind.

"Why did it happen to me?"

She wanted to scream at the unfairness of it all. Only that would take too much effort.

She stumbled on something she couldn't see, then caught herself. As she straightened, she heard a sound behind her. Fear tightened her chest, then she recognized the steady steps of a horse. She drew in a breath and stopped.

"You're probably feeling stupid about now," Nick said casually.

She raised her chin. "Not at all."

"Then more than your eyesight got damaged in that explosion. Are you finished making your point or do you want to keep walking? In another twenty minutes, your sunburn is going to blister. That'll hurt."

"Is this your way of convincing me to accept your help?"

"You don't need convincing. I'll give you this. You're the first blind person I know who would willingly walk into the wilderness with no idea of where she was going. I can't decide if that makes you brave or an idiot. I'll get back to you on that."

"Don't bother. I was fine."

"You were lucky. You could have fallen and cracked open your head or been bitten by a snake."

"I would have preferred a snake to you."

She heard him get off his saddle.

"Now you're just talking sweet to make me like you," Nick said. "Here."

He handed her a bottle of water. She took it and unscrewed the top. The liquid was cool and sweet on her dry throat.

"I wouldn't drink too much of that all at once," he told her.

She ignored him and kept drinking. She finally stopped, took a step, then bent over and threw it all up. Her insides twisted, forcing her to retch and gag. She coughed and did her best to catch her breath.

"Not the brightest bulb," he murmured.

"Shut up," she said with a gasp.

"Drink it slow and this time it'll stay down."

Humiliation joined the heat of the sunburn. She sipped cautiously.

"See?"

He sounded smug, which made her want to hit him. But she'd already tried that and it hadn't worked at all.

"Come on," he said. "Let's get you back." He took her free hand and led her over to his horse. "I'll get on and pull you up behind me."

"Or you could walk and I'll ride."

"Do you think that will happen?"

She saw blurry movement, then heard him settle in the saddle.

"Give me the water," he said.

She passed it up to him, then found the stirrup with her hands and put her left foot in it. He grabbed her arm.

"One, two, three."

On three, he pulled her as she pushed off the ground. For a second, there was an uncomfortable sensation of moving through nothing, then she settled behind his saddle, on the horse's rump. He pressed her bottle of water into her hand.

"Hang on," he told her.

"I'll be fine."

"Do you have to argue about everything?"

"Yes. It's one of my best qualities." As she spoke, she reached around his waist to hold on. If she didn't, she would slide off and it was a long way to the ground.

The horse moved forward.

Sitting on the back of a horse was a lot different from sitting in a saddle. Instinctively Izzy held on with her thighs and tightened her grip on Nick's waist. She rocked with the movement and found her nose pressed against his back.

He was warm and his shirt still smelled like soap and fabric softener. Underneath that was the scent of male skin. Her fingers encountered nothing but muscles at his midsection. She might not know much about the guy, but based on how he'd swung her over his shoulder, and rode a horse, she would guess he worked out.

Under other circumstances, and assuming she could see, he might be someone she found attractive. Not that it mattered anymore. Did the blind girl ever get the guy? Did it matter? She was hungry and tired and her skin burned from the sun. She just wanted to go home.

Except she didn't technically have a home anymore. Her quarters on the oil rig had disappeared in the explosion. When she was off work, she stayed with her sister Skye at Glory's Gate, but Skye wasn't there anymore. She'd moved in with her fiancé. And Izzy wasn't comfortable living in the family house with just her dad, mostly because she didn't think she actually belonged there.

Thoughts for another day, she told herself.

A large shape came into blurry view. She squinted, but that didn't help.

"We're back?" she asked.

"Yes. I'll help you down."

"I'm good."

She held out the water until he took it, then pressed her hands between her thighs, on the back of the horse, swung her right leg around and lowered herself to the ground. She hit a couple of inches after she'd expected to but didn't stumble.

Nick dismounted and handed the horse to someone. She tried to see who it was, but couldn't.

"This way," he said.

Dinner, she thought longingly. She would kill for a meal. Or even act nice. She couldn't remember the last time she'd been so hungry.

But the building they approached didn't look like the house. She couldn't see the details but the shape was all wrong. He opened a door, then waited, maybe for her to go first. There was no way *she* was stepping into that pit of darkness.

Seconds later he reached past her and flipped on lights. She saw a big bright room, but no details. Cautiously, she walked inside.

The ceiling was a long distance up — she couldn't say how far. The floor was hardwood. She saw shapes she didn't recognize. The place was familiar, although she couldn't say why.

"Where are we?" she asked.

"The gym. I heard you're into rock climbing. I thought we'd take a few minutes before dinner so you can practice."

She spun toward his voice. "Are you insane?"

"There have been rumors, but technically, no."

"What's wrong with you? I'm thirsty, sunburned, tired and hungry. I'm not climbing a wall just to amuse you."

"Sure you are. Besides, isn't there a part of you that wonders if you still can?"

She could accept a lot, but not that he was having fun at her expense. The bastard. She'd been right — Nick was a bully.

"I'm *blind!*" she screamed. "I can't see."

"You don't climb with your eyes. You climb with your hands and your feet. Come on, Izzy. Once to the top. Think of how it will feel."

Terrifying, she thought, angry and scared and hating life. It would feel terrifying. To be all the way up there, in darkness, or near darkness.

"I can't."

He jingled something that sounded like a harness.

"You can and you'll feel better if you do. You'll feel like there's hope."

"Are you talking? I can't really hear you. There's a lot of static."

"Ignore me if you want, but I'm right. Come on. One quick climb to the top, then we'll have dinner."

She was so weary. Exhaustion hung on her, pulling her toward the ground. She just wanted to curl up and whimper.

"Can I kick you in the balls if I make it?" she asked.

"No, but you can have dinner."

Her sisters had done this to her, she thought bitterly. Turned her over to this stranger who got his rocks off by bullying those around him. Resentment built up inside her. It burned hot and bright, until she could only think of pounding him into the ground. Of frightening him and making him whimper.

But that wasn't going to happen. Not anytime soon. She was trapped and there seemed to be only one way out.

She grabbed the harness. The shape was

familiar in her hands and she slid into it easily.

"The shoes are over here."

She pulled off her sandals, not caring that her feet were probably filthy, and slipped on the climbing shoes, then allowed him to guide her to the wall. He offered her chalk for her hands.

She rubbed her fingers together. The room was cool and quiet. She could hear herself breathing and nothing else. Her skin burned from the sun, her body ached and she was so hungry she felt hollow. But none of that mattered. Not knowing where the need came from, she suddenly knew she had to climb the wall.

She closed her eyes, because then not seeing felt like a choice. She put her hand on the smooth surface in front of her, then felt around until she found handholds. When she'd gripped them, she moved her right foot forward and up. Nick moved behind her and clipped the safety line to her harness.

She ignored him. There was only the wall in front of her and finding the next place to hang on.

Slowly, she climbed. She found her rhythm in the movements. He was right — she didn't need to see to do this and each step gave her more confidence.

About twenty minutes into the climb, she moved her foot higher, found the foothold and shifted her weight. Her foot slipped. Suddenly she was hanging in midair, with no idea of where she was or what came next. Panic surged, but she ignored it. She hung on with her hands, scrambling with her feet until she found another hold. Cautiously, she centered herself on it, easing her weight off her hands and onto her legs again.

Her heart pounded in her chest. Sweat soaked her. She kept her eyes closed. When she'd caught her breath, she began moving up again.

Nick watched Izzy's careful progress. He'd wondered if she would refuse to climb, but she hadn't. Now she worked her way steadily to the top of the wall, her body moving easily as she remembered what she was supposed to be doing.

His gaze slipped over her bare arms. Something inside him tightened when he caught sight of the curve of her breast. She was wild enough to be appealing but not so crazy that she made him wary. In other circumstances, before everything had changed, he would be interested. As it was — he could look but not touch.

She took the last few feet easily and

slapped the top of the wall.

"I made it," she yelled.

He reached for the safety rope and lowered her to the ground.

"Next time you can take it at more than a crawl," he told her.

She touched the floor and unhooked herself, then grinned at him. "Next time we'll race and I'll so kick your ass."

"In your dreams."

She laughed. "No, Nick. In yours."

By the time they returned to the main house, Izzy was hungry enough to eat a water buffalo. Or at least pretty much anything that was served for dinner. At this point, she would even consider one of her sister Lexi's über-healthy sticks and greens sandwiches on the pressed cardboard she called bread. But when they walked into the kitchen, the smells that surrounded her were rich and thick and filled with promise.

"Over here," Nick said, guiding her to the sink in the mudroom.

She found the taps, then the soap. After washing her hands, she splashed water on her face and dried herself with a towel. She turned toward the sound of footsteps.

"You're back," Aaron said happily. "I was worried. I know, I know. I shouldn't. It gives me wrinkles. So we're having pot roast for dinner. And, honey, the things Norma can do with a pot roast will make you want to weep."

Aaron linked arms with her and led her into the kitchen. "Norma, this is Izzy. Izzy, Norma, who keeps us all fed and happy."

"Hi," Izzy said, feeling a little awkward as she stared at a blurry shape that was probably Norma. Should she hold out her hand? Wave?

"You're skinny," Norma said by way of greeting. "You sit at my table, you eat food."

"Yes, ma'am," Izzy murmured. "I'm actually a big eater."

"Uh-huh. We'll see about that. Now you go sit. I don't have time for chitchat. Shoo."

Aaron guided her toward the table. She reached out her hands until she felt the chair. She could make out the shape of the table and knew there were things on top of it, but couldn't say exactly what everything was. Aaron took the chair on her right and when a man moved across from her, she assumed it was Nick.

Cozy, she thought, feeling awkward. She wasn't used to eating in front of strangers. She wished she could take a tray to her room, but had a feeling she knew what would happen if she asked.

Norma put serving bowls on the table. "Eat up," she said sternly. "I don't want to hear anything but lips smacking."

"We're not allowed to talk?" Izzy asked in a whisper.

"We can talk," Aaron told her. "She just sounds tough. Want me to serve you?"

"Okay."

"There's pot roast and potatoes and carrots. Plus biscuits. Norma, you're killing me with your biscuits. They're delicious."

"I make them because you like them." Her voice came from behind them, in the kitchen.

He dished out food as he spoke, filling her plate. "Wineglass is on your right. Tonight it's a saucy little Washington Syrah from Walla Walla. I'm in charge of the wine selection. It's a hobby of mine."

Izzy glanced across the table. She could see Nick's outline, but had no idea what he was doing. Eating? Staring? Reading the paper? He was silent, which unnerved her.

"Do you need me to tell you where the food is on your plate?" Aaron asked.

"No, thanks. I'm not that handicapped."

"You're not handicapped, you're handicapable."

His perky statement made her laugh. "Okay. If you say so."

44

"I do."

Izzy picked up her fork. Her mouth was watering before she took her first bite. She nearly swooned when she tasted Norma's perfect pot roast. Her stomach growled again, this time in appreciation.

"You'll meet Rita tomorrow," Aaron said. "She's in charge of the horses. She and her husband live a few miles away. They've been married forever." He sighed. "It's just so romantic. I want to find someone. Nick, you never introduce me to any of your friends. Why is that?"

"They're not your type."

"You don't know that."

"Yeah, I do."

There was something in his tone that made her look up. But no matter how hard she stared, she couldn't bring him into focus. Or the room. Or her plate. Her appetite disappeared, leaving her feeling sick to her stomach.

"Izzy?" Aaron sounded concerned.

"I'm fine," she whispered.

"Eat a biscuit. It'll make you feel better."

She knew he was only trying to help, but right now nothing was going to make her feel better. Nick was silent. The unfair advantage of everyone else being able to see made her want to lash out.

"You're quiet," she snapped. "Are you judging me or being critical?"

"I wasn't thinking about you at all."

She stiffened.

"Is that typical for you?" he asked. "Do you expect everything to be about you? You're only happy when you're the center of attention? No wonder you were comfortable sitting around, being taken care of. Least effort, most outcome. Being blind is probably the best thing that ever happened to you."

CHAPTER THREE

Humiliation immobilized Izzy. She wanted to bolt from the room, but couldn't figure out which way to go. The last thing she wanted was to trip or run into something.

The unfairness of Nick's words twisted inside her. If she could have been sure of her aim, she would have thrown her plate at him.

"I didn't ask for this," she said quietly. "Not the explosion or the consequences. But then it's easy to be critical of me — after all, there's nothing wrong with you, is there?"

Instead of another sarcastic reply, she heard the distinct sound of a slap.

"Hey," Nick grumbled.

"Norma hit him on the back of the head," Aaron whispered.

"Go, Norma," Izzy murmured.

"Don't be rude," the other woman said.

"Don't push me," Nick told her.

"Like I'm afraid of you."

Izzy heard footsteps retreating to the kitchen.

Aaron cleared his throat. "Nick isn't actually a horrible person."

"Really?" Izzy asked. "Could have fooled me."

"I don't need you defending me," Nick said at the same time.

"Yes, you do," Aaron snapped. "Look, Izzy, he needs to test your boundaries. Find out what kind of person you are. He sincerely wants to help."

She looked at the blur across the table. "What does he do for the people he doesn't want to help? Throw them off the side of a building?"

There was only silence.

"Izzy," Aaron said, sounding frustrated, "being sympathetic doesn't always work. But this is done with love."

"Really?" she asked, both annoyed and embarrassed. "This is love?"

"Absolutely," Aaron told her.

"Do you always talk for him?"

"Someone has to and I'm good at it."

Nick continued to keep quiet, which was seriously irritating. Didn't he get that she was at a disadvantage here? But he wouldn't care about that. Somehow he would make this all her fault.

She picked at her dinner, not eating very much and not caring that Norma would take her to task for it. But when the meal was over, the other woman didn't say anything as she cleared plates.

The second Aaron pushed back her chair, she was on her feet.

"I'll walk you to your room," he said.

"Thank you."

"I'll do it," Nick said.

"You don't have to," she told him.

"I know."

Aaron faded away. One second he was standing next to her, the next, he was gone. Izzy sucked in a breath. Just a few more minutes, she told herself. Then she would be in her room and by herself.

The blur that was Nick started walking. Izzy went after him, remembering about the step just in time to avoid tripping again. Halfway through the big living room, he stopped and turned. She assumed it was to face her.

"I'm not trying to hurt you," he said.

She pressed her lips together and didn't respond.

"Everything is different now," he continued. "Whatever you were before, whoever you were, it's all gone. This is your reality. If you won't have the surgery, then you'll have to learn to be blind."

"Neither is your problem."

"It became mine the second your sisters called me. You're here, Izzy, and you're not going anywhere. You can get through easy or you can get through hard, but you will get through."

Annoyance turned to anger. Who the hell did he think he was? "Gee, coach, when we win the big game will we all go out for ice cream sundaes?"

"Nice attitude."

"You like it? There's plenty more." She could feel him staring at her.

"What you don't seem to understand is that your way of getting by, of getting things done, is over. You're going to have to learn to be a different person. Tougher. Stronger. Whatever you were before doesn't exist. Maybe you liked yourself, maybe you didn't, it's irrelevant now."

"The psychology is interesting," she snapped, "considering the fact that you've known me all of fifteen seconds. Where do you get off with all this? You're just some guy who enjoys picking on those who are weaker. That must make you really proud."

"That's your first mistake," he said quietly. "Assuming you're weaker. As long as you're weak, you can never win."

"Oh, right. So that's the big plan? Break me so you can build me up again? That is *not* going to happen. You're not going to win and you're not going to make me grateful for the process."

"Then we have a problem."

"I'm glad you're finally figuring that out." She pushed past him and started toward what she hoped were the stairs.

"You have it all," he called after her. "You're young, healthy. You have financial resources and a family who loves you. But that's not enough."

She paused and turned toward him. "I know. I want to see, too. How ridiculous is that?"

"All that stands between you and what you want is surgery."

Surgery that could leave her permanently blind, she thought bitterly. But no one wanted to talk about that. No one wanted to deal with the risks. Because for them, there weren't any.

"Have the surgery, Izzy," she said in a sharp voice. "Just do it, Izzy. Why not? There's no downside for you or anyone but me, right? When you have something to lose, we'll talk. Until then, go to hell. I'm not playing your game. I'm not even interested in your game. I'm going upstairs to my room, that I will find on my own. You're not going to win this one, and the sooner you accept that, the easier it will be for everyone."

She turned back to the stairs and grabbed the railing. After fumbling for the first step, she got her foot on it and climbed until she reached the landing. She had no idea if Nick was watching her or if he'd already left the room, nor did she care. She was pissed and tired and sore and still thirsty. Her shoulders, arms and back burned from her time in the sun. Worse, she was completely alone. The two people she'd loved and trusted more than anyone had abandoned her and she would never forgive either of them.

She squinted, trying to bring the long hallway into focus. When that didn't work, she had a second of sweat-induced panic. How was she supposed to find her room? Then she remembered Nick telling her it was the first door on the left.

She took a step in that direction and held out her arm to help her judge the distance to the partially open door. She pushed it open as she went inside.

The sun had long since set, leaving the room in darkness. She ran her hands along the wall until she found a switch and flipped it. Lamps on either side of the bed came on.

The furniture was little more than blurry shapes. She identified them through their obvious placement in the room. The bed was easy — as was the dresser. She guessed the rectangular shape on the foot of the bed was her suitcase, packed by Lexi or Skye. No TV, which was fine. She couldn't really see it anyway and listening wasn't all that fun.

There were two other doors. One led to a closet, the other, a bathroom. She turned on the lights, then returned to the bedroom, where she fumbled with her suitcase zipper until she got it open.

She had no idea what had been packed, so there were no memories to help her figure out what clothes were there. The jeans she identified by touch. The same with the bikini panties, thongs and bras. But the T-shirts all looked similar. Was that one white or pale pink? Blue or green? In bright light she could see the difference, but two lamps on a nightstand weren't enough for that.

She carried a makeup bag into the bathroom, then clipped her hip on the dresser on her return trip. The sharp pain made her cry out, then tears filled her eyes and she just wanted to crawl into a dark hole some-where and be lost forever.

The fear returned. Fear of the darkness, of the unknown. Anger joined it. Anger that this had happened to *her*. It wasn't right, wasn't fair. She didn't deserve to suffer. Now Lexi and Skye had dumped her with a guy they didn't even know.

The sharp emotions bled away, leaving behind only despair. What was the point? She couldn't win this battle. There was no reason to try.

She pushed the suitcase onto the floor and crawled onto the bed. There weren't any tears. She'd cried herself empty for the past month. She curled up on her side, hurting on the inside from the feelings churning within her and on the outside from the sunburn. She closed her eyes, then quickly opened them to make sure the light was still there.

It was going to be a long night.

Some time later, maybe only a few min-utes, maybe an hour, she heard a knock on her bedroom door.

Great. Because Nick wasn't done being a total bastard.

"Go away," she yelled.

The door opened.

"I couldn't hear you," Aaron said. "It was

muffled, but it sounded like 'come in,' so I did."

Izzy sat up. "Did he send you? I'm serious. You can just leave."

"By he, I assume you mean Nick. No, he didn't send me. I brought some aloe vera for your sunburn. Do you always throw your clothes on the floor? Won't that make you trip later?"

His shape stiffened, then bent. She felt the weight of the suitcase on the bed.

"You're nearly unpacked," he said. "I'll just finish up so we can put your suitcase away. How does that sound?"

He was annoyingly cheerful, but for some reason she couldn't seem to snap at him. Maybe because Aaron was so obviously happy and caring. Maybe because he wasn't her enemy in all this.

"I'll put a pair of pj's on the dresser here," he said as he carried clothes across the room. "The drawer next to your panties and bras. Socks are right below. There are a few shirts to hang. Oh, this red one is nice. But you probably look best in green. It would bring out the color in your eyes. True hazel. So they can look blue or green, right? I have brown eyes. Bor-ring." He sighed. "Okay, that's everything. I'm going to zip up your suitcase and tuck it in the back of the closet."

He disappeared into darkness, then re-appeared. "That's done. Now let's take care of that sunburn. Pull off your tank top."

She sat up and looked at him. "Excuse me?"

There was a snort, followed by, "I guess I have to tell you I'm rolling my eyes. Izzy, please. You're sweet and I like you but, honey, I couldn't be less interested. I want to put on the aloe. Now take off your shirt. Oh, we'll need to pin up your hair. You have something in the bathroom?"

He disappeared again. Izzy didn't know what to think, then decided she didn't care. She pulled off her tank top.

Aaron returned. She knew because she heard him wince.

"That has *got* to hurt," he said. "Ouch. If your skin blisters, we'll need to get you to a doctor. Did you take anything? I'll get you some aspirin. But first let's get this on. I'll be as gentle as I can."

He handed her several clips. She twisted her long hair into a coil, then clipped it to her head. Aaron sat next to her on the bed.

"I'll do your back first," he said.

She turned away from him and felt the coolness of the gel, followed by the intense pain of his fingers rubbing her skin. She knew he was working carefully, but every stroke was agony.

"Arm," he said, touching her left one.

She held it out.

"I know this is hard," he said. "Being here, not knowing anyone. The thing is, Nick isn't such a bad guy. He comes off as a little gruff, but you have to look past that."

"I can't look past anything."

"Not literally. It's a figure of speech. Honestly! I'm talking here. Nick is doing some real good."

She didn't want to hear about Nick at all, but liked Aaron. Which made being rude more difficult.

"We have corporate retreats," he continued. "Management types come and explore the wilderness. We teach them how to swing from trees, start a fire with a couple of rocks. You know. Team-building stuff."

"That's hardly going to qualify your boss for sainthood."

"It pays the bills," he said as he tapped her other arm. "The real work is with kids who have been through something traumatic. A shooting. A violent crime. Parents fighting for years, then finally killing each other. They come here all shut down. It's sad. We put them on the horses, take them outside. Show them how to climb a tree. It helps. That's what he does. He helps fix them."

She didn't want to think about Nick being anything but the devil. "Which is great, but doesn't have anything to do with me."

"And it's all about you, right?" Aaron asked, sounding amused. "Honey, you've got some attitude on you."

"I know. It used to look good."

"It still could. Now face me." He rubbed the cool aloe on her chest. "You're going to be peeling like a snake in a few days. Okay. I've done all I can. You're going to have to sit like this until you dry off. Let me get the aspirin."

He disappeared for a minute or so. Izzy sat there in her bra and jeans wondering if anyone was walking by the open door and enjoying the show. Did she care?

Aaron returned. "Aspirin *and* water. Because that's just the kind of guy I am."

She took both. "Why are you here? Why Nick? Why this place?"

"I'm a Texas kind of guy."

"Uh-huh."

"I could be. I try." He hesitated. "I like it here. This is where I belong."

She knew there was more to the story, but didn't know what and she wasn't interested

58

enough to push.

"Thanks for your help."

"You're welcome. Now get some sleep." He bent down and kissed her forehead. "I just love your hair. See you in the morning."

Then he was gone.

She heard the door close, and the sense of being totally alone made her skin crawl.

She ignored it, the need to panic and every other emotion washing through her. After patting her arms to make sure the aloe had dried, she found the nightie he'd left on the dresser, slipped out of her jeans and bra, then pulled it over her head. She made her way back to bed and crawled between the sheets. She didn't bother turning off the lights. It was better if they were on all the time. Anything was better than the dark.

Nick sat in his downstairs office, staring at his computer, but he didn't see the words on the screen. Instead his attention kept shifting to the woman upstairs.

Izzy was in a bad place. All fear and attitude. Both could be channeled, used to get through. Or they could defeat her. Right now he couldn't tell which way she was going to fall.

She wasn't his usual type of client — he

didn't take on long-term care or individual cases. The corporate types came and went with forgettable ease. The kids . . . they came in groups of two or three, a weekend at a time. He'd once thought they should expand to week-long camps, but until they had the staff in place, that wasn't possible. Besides, it was always easier if he didn't get involved. If Izzy stayed, that was a risk. One he would have to control. He couldn't be emotionally responsible for her . . . or anyone.

There was also the added challenge that she wasn't a kid. She was a beautiful woman. He would have to be as blind as her not to notice that and coughing up his last breath not to be aware of the possibilities. Not that they mattered. She was off-limits.

So what happened now? Had he pushed her too hard? Would she rise to the challenge or snap in two? Sometimes the line between pushing and being a real bastard was hard to see. He tended to err on the side of being a bastard.

His phone rang.

"Hollister," he said.

"How's it going?"

"About the same," he said, pleased to hear his friend's voice. "With you?"

"Making a killing," Garth Duncan joked. "It was a good day."

Nick looked at his computer screen. "The market was down."

"Not for me. Not for you, either. At least not your shares in my company. I can't speak to what other crap you might have in your portfolio."

Nick laughed. "I wouldn't expect you to." He glanced at the clock on the wall. It was nearly ten. "Still at the office?"

"Sure. I'll head home in a few. Tomorrow I've got a charity dinner, so I'm getting things done tonight."

Garth had been born to be a tycoon. They'd met on their first day in college, when fate had thrown them together as roommates. Garth had been a charming, good-looking eighteen-year-old who made friends easily and walked with the confidence of someone who knew he was destined for greatness. Nick had been a skinny, frightened fifteen-year-old scholarship student, in theory the smartest kid on campus, but clueless when it came to real life.

Garth had taken one look at him and left the room without saying a word. Nick hadn't cared. He'd been grateful to be out of the horrors of foster care and in the relatively safe world of college. That relief had ended two weeks later when a few fraternity pledges decided that beating the shit out of him would secure their place in Greek Row history.

Garth had stopped them before they could do much more than bruise him. He'd dragged Nick back to their room and told him to stay out of trouble, then he'd left. By way of a thank-you, Nick had completed Garth's calculus homework and left him a study cheat sheet.

Eventually, they became friends, drawn together by proximity and similar backgrounds. Nick had grown up without parents, Garth had grown up without a father. In the four years it took Garth to get his bachelor's degree, Nick completed a bachelor's in petroleum engineering, a master's and most of his Ph.D. Garth taught him how to make friends and get girls. Nick got Garth through his classes with a respectable B-plus average.

That was a long time ago, Nick thought grimly. Back when everything had seemed possible.

"Your friend got here," Nick said.

"Who?"

"Isadora Titan. Izzy. The one you told me about."

Nick had taken on Izzy at Garth's request. One of Garth's former assistants had gone to work for Skye Titan and Garth had pushed her to suggest that they consult Nick. Garth had kept his name out of it, though. To hear him tell it, the Titans were his business competitors and he needed them in good shape so that they could continue to challenge him at work.

Nick knew better, though. Garth was one of the good guys — always had been. And he hated taking credit for anything nice, if only to preserve his reputation.

"So how's she doing?" Garth asked.

"She's having a tough adjustment."

"I would imagine getting used to being blind takes time. You'll work your magic. That's what you do."

"It's not magic. It's reality. She needs to get her head in the game. Otherwise she won't have the surgery that could restore her sight."

"Better you than me," Garth told him. "I don't have the patience."

"Most days I don't, either."

"Still, you're doing it. Thanks for that. I know you didn't want to do this, but it's important. Just don't let them know she's there because of me."

"Your reputation as a ruthless bastard in

business and life will stay as solid as ever," Nick joked.

"A reputation based on reality," Garth reminded him. "You see the new *Car and Driver*? What is it with those guys and BMW? As far as they're concerned, the Germans can't build a bad car."

"Not everyone has a thing for old British cars that never run."

"Not old," Garth corrected. "Classic. There's a difference."

"Sure. It's all a matter of how much money you want to sink into it. You can afford to have someone drive behind you with a tow truck. Most people can't."

"If you'd come to work for me instead of starting your own company, you could have your own tow truck driver, too," Garth pointed out.

"No, thanks. I like my truck."

"Typical Texan."

"And proud of it. Go home. It's late."

"Yeah, I will. See you next time you're in town?" Garth asked.

"Sure. I'll call."

Nick hung up and returned his attention to the computer.

So much had changed since that first meeting with Garth, he thought grimly. Too much. They'd shared a lot over the years. A lifetime. The one thing he'd never asked his friend was how well *he* slept at night. Had Garth conquered the past or did he, too, wake to the sound of the screams?

Garth Duncan replaced the receiver and turned his chair so he could see the Dallas skyline. Lights beckoned from dozens of other offices, all several stories below his own. No one else had as high an office or perfect a view. He'd made sure of that.

It had taken a long time . . . nearly twenty years . . . but he was finally ready to destroy the Titans. Everything was in place. The lines were set. It was just a matter of reeling 'em in. Even Izzy had cooperated and become a player. That damned explosion.

Who would have thought fate would be on his side?

He knew the Titan sisters believed he was behind what had happened at the oil rig. But he wasn't. His destruction of the Titan empire was subtle, untraceable. He wasn't interested in bodies, he counted his victories in dollars and bragging rights. He wanted Jed Titan broken and shunned by the society he valued. If the Titan sisters lost everything along the way, better for him.

Who had arranged the explosion? The investigation wasn't complete, but Garth was confident the authorities would find that the blast wasn't an accident. Co-incidences like that didn't just happen. Someone had done it on purpose. To put the blame on him? Or was there another Titan enemy looking to hurt Jed's family?

Either way, he would find out. And in the end, he would take everything from Jed Titan and not have a single regret.

Well, maybe one.

He hadn't wanted to use Nick. But when Izzy had turned up blind, the opportunity had been too tempting to ignore. When Nick figured out he was being played, he wouldn't be happy. Garth was counting on their years of friendship to see them through.

Besides, it was worth the risk. He had to win. Win at any price. Even the trust of the man who had once saved his life.

CHAPTER FOUR

Izzy spent a restless night. Her skin felt hot and two sizes too small. Her head ached and she was hungry. She got up while it was still dark and pulled the chair from the small desk toward the window. Eventually she saw light, then she could make out greenery and the barn in the distance. For someone who could actually see things, it was probably a great view.

She showered and got dressed, still not sure what she was going to do. While her sisters had probably thought there were no other options, Izzy refused to let them do this to her. It was her life — if she wanted to spend it doing nothing, that was up to her. They didn't understand what she was going through. They didn't know about the fear and hopelessness that haunted her. They had perfect lives, with great guys and a future that didn't include being blind.

She wanted to go home, and as she didn't

know the way, she was going to have to out-wait Nick Hollister.

Some time later, she heard footsteps in the hallway and braced herself. But a few seconds before the man entered, she realized it was Aaron and relaxed.

"Good morning, sunshine," he called from the doorway. "Are you ready to start your day? Dear God, it's a good thing you can't see yourself in the mirror. You're a lobster, girlfriend, and it's not pretty." He made a clucking sound. "You'll heal, but don't do that again. Do you need me to spell wrinkles? I don't think so. Come on. I'm taking you to the barn."

"No, thanks."

"Now, Izzy. Don't be difficult. It's not unreasonable to do a little work. We all pitch in. It's not like you can help me on the computer."

Had it been Nick, she would have told him exactly what she was thinking. But Aaron had been nothing but nice to her.

"My sisters paid Nick to kidnap me. I don't have to do work to make things even."

"Fine, but what about your karma? It seems to me you need some good vibrations in your future. Come on. It's nice out. You can meet Rita and she'll make you laugh."

His tone cajoled, which made her feel better enough to get to her feet.

"Look at you," he crowed. "Walking and everything. Who's a little trouper?"

She moved toward him. "Don't make me kill you."

Aaron laughed. "Now you sound like Nick."

"I'll have to watch that."

"He's not so bad."

"He didn't toss you over his shoulder and drag you away."

"I know." Aaron sounded sad. "My luck just isn't that good. But maybe one day."

That made her laugh.

They went outside. It was still early enough that the heat wasn't oppressive.

The barn loomed large. Izzy didn't want to go inside. All she could see was darkness. It was her nightmare come to life. Then something moved through the darkness and stepped into the morning sun. The something became a person.

"Izzy, this is Rita. Rita, Izzy. She'll be staying with us for a while."

"Nice to meet you," Rita said, sounding pleasant enough. "I've heard you're good with horses."

"I know which end kicks."

"Then you're hired. We have a dozen horses here. For now you can start with giving them a bath and making them pretty."

"I can't wash a horse. I can't see."

"So what? They're not expecting a spa treatment," Rita told her. "Just a nice bath. You'll do it by feel. Just make sure you rinse 'em good. Otherwise they'll have skin trouble. Supplies are in this cabinet out here. Your hose is coiled on the left. Faucet where it should be. Bucket and soap below. Hoof pick and file on the top shelf. They're all good horses. They'll be patient. So let's go get your first customer."

Izzy was too shocked to speak. She was expected to wash horses? She couldn't see what she was doing and Rita's perky suggestion that she do it by feel was total crap.

"Are you coming or what?" Rita asked.

Izzy trailed after her. She hesitated before stepping into the barn, then winced at the darkness that swallowed her.

The overhead lights probably provided enough light for everyone else, but not for her. It was like being in a fun house at a carnival, but a scary one, with twists and turns and unknown shapes lurking just out of sight.

"Over here," Rita called. "This is Jackson. He's a good guy. How you feeling, handsome?" She pushed a rope into Izzy's hands. "Here you go."

Izzy reached toward the large shape and touched the horse's neck. She stroked it a few times, then turned toward the rectangle of light in the distance. Jackson followed her. They walked outside.

She led him to the post by the cabinet and tied off the rope. Everything for washing him was where Rita had said it would be. But there were at least three different bottles. How was she supposed to know which one was soap and which was something else? She felt around for the brushes and hoof pick. The door swung into her arm and she dropped everything in the dirt. After fumbling around, she found the hoof pick again, but not one of the combs.

Izzy straightened and stared into the distance. Nothing was clear. No matter how she blinked or squinted, nothing came into focus. This was how it was always going to be.

She looked toward the horse, waiting patiently. She couldn't wash him. She couldn't do anything. Whatever Nick and her sisters thought, there wasn't a miracle here. There wasn't anything but frustration and defeat.

She walked over to a bench by the barn and sat down. Some time later, Rita found her.

"What are you doing?"

"Waiting until I can go home."

"You're supposed to be washing the horse."

"Not today."

Rita sighed. "I know you're upset, but you have to trust us. We know what we're doing."

"I'm not a project. I'm not looking to be healed. I want to go home."

Rita left. A few minutes later, the bell rang. Breakfast, Izzy thought, ignoring the grumbling in her stomach. She closed her eyes and imagined herself slipping into the warm water off an island somewhere. She could see the brightly colored fish, feel the whisper of the current on her skin.

Everything was beautiful. Everything was clear and colorful. All she had to do was reach out and touch whatever she wanted. She opened her eyes and stared at her blurry world. Not anymore, she thought grimly.

An hour or two later, Rita reappeared. "I don't care who you are or what you've been through," the other woman snapped. "But you left Jackson in the sun. Whatever you have going on in your life, we don't tolerate cruelty to animals here. Get him inside now."

Izzy hadn't thought about the horse. Without saying anything, she got up and made her way back to him. "Sorry, Jackson," she said and led him toward the barn.

It took her a few tries to locate his stall. He went inside. She followed him, using the walls to guide her in the darkness. After making sure he had plenty of water, she patted him in apology and then went back outside. She took her place on the bench and waited.

She had no idea of how much time had passed before Nick showed up. She sensed him before she saw his shape.

"You like to pout?" he asked.

"I want to go home."

"Not an option."

"Want to bet?"

Someone else joined him. Rita, she would guess.

"She's not doing anything," the other woman said.

"Not a surprise. She sat in front of a window all day for a month at home. Guess it's not going to be different here."

They were talking about her so that she would get angry, Izzy thought. If she showed emotion, any feelings, then they would know they were getting to her. It was the first step in her recovery. At least from their point of view.

"I don't care what you think of me," she said quietly, "I want to go home."

She stood and walked toward the house. Once inside, she managed to find the stairs, then make her way into her room. She sat in the chair by the window and remembered what life had been like before. When it got dark, she lay down on the bed and closed her eyes. In the morning, she returned to the window. She didn't eat or drink and no one came to see her. Izzy knew she would win. She no longer felt hungry or thirsty. She simply existed in an empty place where it didn't matter that she couldn't see.

"It's been two days," Aaron said as he walked into Nick's office. "She won't talk to me or say anything and you know I'm very funny."

"You're the best," Nick said, studying the proposal Aaron had put together.

"And you're not listening," Aaron told him, putting his hands on his hips. "She won't leave her room. This is day three. How long can she go without food and water?"

He saved the file on his computer and leaned back in his chair. "She has a bathroom. She can get water."

"She doesn't look good. I think she's catatonic or something."

"You watch too many movies on Lifetime. She's fine. She's pouting until she gets her way."

"I don't want anything to happen to her," Aaron told him as he took the seat across from his. "Nick, you have to do something."

"I don't know what," he admitted, angry at Izzy for being difficult and at himself for failing. "She's not a kid. She's not excited to see a horse and able to forget her problems by taking a ride. This isn't a new place for her. Barn kittens aren't going to cut it. She's angry and hurt and she needs a damn psychologist who can get inside her head."

Except she wouldn't talk to anyone. Her sisters had made that clear. She wouldn't leave her room, participate in family functions. She wanted to . . . What? Stare out a window until she died?

There was life in her. He could feel it. And strength. But she'd given up. Once a person gave up, it was over. He'd learned that the hard way. He'd known that the second he gave up, they would win. But he'd had an enemy — death. Something to defeat, something to fight. And he'd had Garth. His friend had been his responsibility. Getting them both out had driven him to

75

endure and ultimately to survive. What did Izzy have?

"If I could challenge her in some way," he said, more to himself than Aaron. But how?

"Cards are out of the question," Aaron said. "Maybe arm wrestling. Or have sex. You're a heterosexual male. You know what to do."

"It's not that simple."

Which was only half true. Izzy appealed to him. It would be that simple for him, although he doubted if she would appreciate him joining her in bed.

"Seduce her."

"That's not in the contract."

"If you do it right, she shouldn't complain."

"Any other suggestions?"

"We could drag her into the woods and then help her find her way home."

"Interesting plan," Nick said. Would that give Izzy the will to push back. Or did she need something else? Something to hate. He'd had an enemy — did she need one, too? It was worth a try.

"I like her," Aaron admitted. "I don't want her to give up."

"Me, either."

"Can I take her food?"

"You already know the answer to that."

Aaron sighed, then stood. "I always thought you could fix anyone. I hate being wrong."

"Not as much as I do."

Izzy lay on the bed. She was bored and a little light-headed from lack of water. She hadn't had anything to eat or drink in nearly seventy-two hours, but wasn't actually hungry, which was weird. Sleep was easier, as was the passage of time. Everything blurred and her sunburn no longer hurt.

She almost didn't care about not being able to see. Nothing mattered. Not even going home. She could just stay here forever.

She heard footsteps, but raising her head took more effort than was comfortable. She barely opened her eyes.

"You win."

She recognized Nick's voice. Even more interesting, she smelled something delicious. Something that made her sit up, even though the sudden movement made her head swim.

He put something on the dresser then walked over to the bed and grabbed her arm. He pulled her forward, then shoved all the pillows behind her back and let her go. She found herself propped up.

"You win," he repeated. "I give up. I'll call

Lexi and Skye in the morning and tell them to come get you. You can go back to living in Lexi's house. That's what you want, right?"

She blinked, then remembered too late that wouldn't bring him into focus. Her head felt fuzzy — almost like she was drunk.

"Why?" she asked, and was surprised that her voice sounded hoarse. Probably because she hadn't spoken in three days.

"You don't want to be here."

"I didn't want to be here before."

There was movement. If she had to guess, it was a shrug. He handed her a large glass.

"Sip slowly," he said. "It's going to taste sweet, but you need to get it down. There's water, but plenty of sugar, some herbs, electrolytes. It'll help you feel better."

She took a sip and nearly gagged on the too-sweet taste. Seconds later she felt like she was dying of thirst. Still, remembering her stroll into the wilds just outside the ranch and vomiting afterward, she continued to take small amounts.

He put a tray with stubby legs across her lap. She inhaled the mouthwatering scent of chicken and vegetables, not to mention fresh bread.

"Soup," he said. "And one of Norma's biscuits. Aaron will be by later. If you've kept all this down, he'll give you a sandwich. Go easy on the food for the next couple of days."

She wanted to dive into the soup and drink it while swimming around in the bowl. The image lightened her spirits, or maybe it was the sugar rush from the drink.

"See ya," he said and turned to leave.

"Wait." She cleared her throat. "That's it?"

He faced her again. She couldn't see his individual features, so she had to guess what he was thinking. If she had to pick an emotion, she would guess boredom.

"What do you mean?" he asked.

"This is as much as you're doing? Seriously? What kind of crap is that?"

He leaned against the door frame. "You're not interested in being helped. You've made that clear."

"Not interested? This was the best you could do? I refuse to wash a horse and you're finished? Is that what you do when those hurt kids come here? Do you even have any training for this kind of work? Are you certified? How much are my sisters paying you?"

"A lot less than they should have been."

"How did they find you? The phone book?"

"I come highly recommended."

"Oh, please. I doubt that. I'm not even a hard case. You didn't make any effort." Now that she thought about it, he'd done nothing, which really pissed her off. "One or two idiot pep talks and you're through? A three-day hunger strike and you throw in the towel? Talk about all hat and no cattle."

"What would you have wanted me to do, Izzy? Beg? I think this is all about being the center of attention. You need everyone running around, fussing over you. Then you'll be happy. You probably won't get the surgery because you like being the one everyone worries about."

"You don't know what you're talking about." She wished her throat weren't so raw so she could yell. How could he think something like that, let alone say it? "I'm not the one pretending to know what he's doing. You're nothing but a snake oil salesman. When my sisters find out about this, they're going to investigate you. You're going down."

"You think I'm all talk? What about you? You're just taking up space."

She'd never actually hated anyone before. But now the feeling burned hot inside her. "Go to hell."

"You've said that before. You need some

new material. Maybe you can take your act on the road. The pity Izzy show. Not that you'll sell many tickets. You're okay to look at but once you break the skin, there's nothing inside. To really be funny you have to be smart and have a world-view. You need to be likeable. None of those are your strengths. Still, you're a Titan. You have money. You'll survive. Maybe they'll get you a nice room with a view. Not that you'll see it."

She wanted to throw something at him. She'd nearly finished the drink so she hurled the glass in his direction. It crashed into the door.

"Plastic," he said, sounding pleased. "It didn't break. See, Izzy. You can't hurt me."

And then he was gone.

Izzy hadn't expected to sleep. She'd been so angry, so filled with rage, she'd spent the evening pacing in her room. When Aaron showed up with a sandwich, she'd eaten it because she wanted to be strong. She was going to leave this place, work out with some martial arts master, then break every bone in Nick's body.

Maybe it was the pacing that exhausted her, or the hot energy of fury or the food in her belly. But sometime in the middle of the night she fell asleep. She only knew because she could suddenly see again.

She was back on the rig, walking down the hallway. There hadn't been any warning. That's what she remembered. The absence of a whisper of what was to come. One second she was heading to the mess for breakfast, the next she was in the middle of an explosion, flying through fire.

The brightness of it battled with the sound. She couldn't think, couldn't breathe, could only be tossed around like a kite in the wind. Fire was everywhere. It licked at her skin. She felt sick and terrified and tried to scream, only she couldn't and then —

"Shh. It's all right."

The voice called her back, as did strong arms pulling her upright. She sucked in a breath, then opened her eyes.

"It was just a dream," Nick told her. "Make that a nightmare. You're safe."

Her whole body shook. She was covered in cold sweat and thought she might lose the sandwich she'd eaten earlier. No matter how she tried, she couldn't seem to catch her breath. Her heart raced around in her chest until she wondered if she was having a heart attack.

The lights were on, but she still couldn't see enough. She tried to get free, but he didn't let her go.

"I know you're scared. I know it's real. It was the explosion, right? It's a bitch to relive that. But you're safe. You're here on the ranch. I'm right here."

Words that shouldn't have comforted her, she thought, confused. Words *he* shouldn't be saying. Still, his body was warm and solid and his arms felt secure enough to keep her from falling.

Gradually her breathing slowed, as did her heart rate.

He sat on her bed, holding her against him. One of his arms wrapped around her waist, as if anchoring her in place. With his free hand, he stroked her head, the side of her face and her arm, rubbing her like a cat. The contact should have been annoying, but it wasn't. It made her feel safe.

She could feel the warmth of his chest against her cheek, the softness of his T-shirt. His heartbeat was steady and seemed to influence her own.

He drew back a little. "Lie down."

Not knowing what else to do, she rolled away from him and stretched out under the covers. He moved behind her, pressing his body against hers, her back to his front, his arm around her waist. He found her hand and took it in his.

An intimate position, she thought. It should have been uncomfortable. It should have felt awkward. But all she could think was that he would protect her, no matter what.

"The dreams never go away," he said, his voice rumbling in her ear. "They fade. You'll go months without one, but then they're back. Anything can trigger them."

"Not comforting news."

"It's a fact, Izzy. They exist. They'll always shake you. It's not how you handle what comes in the night that's important. It's what you do the next morning. And the morning after that."

"You read that somewhere?"

"I have some personal experience with nightmares."

Somehow, that didn't surprise her. "Want to talk about them?"

"No."

"Typical guy."

"That's me."

Her mouth curved into a smile. Then she remembered that he'd been a complete bastard and that she hated him so much that she was planning to learn how to beat the crap out of him. They shouldn't be getting along.

But right now, with the heat from his body

relaxing her and his arm around her like a shield, she couldn't find it in herself to be angry anymore.

"How did you know I was having the dream?" she asked quietly. "Was I screaming?"

"Nothing that dramatic. I was checking the house before going to bed. You were restless."

"You came into my room?"

"Yeah. Just like a stalker."

"What about my right to privacy?"

"What about the pain you give me in my ass?"

That startled a laugh out of her. "I bug you?"

"I can't describe how much."

"Good."

"Yeah. It's good. Now go to sleep. I'll stay right here."

"The lights are on."

"They won't bother me."

"Okay." She closed her eyes and the fear returned. "It was the explosion. I was walking down an inside hallway. There wasn't any warning. In the dream, I know it's coming and I'm still caught off guard. Then I'm flying through the air. It's so bright and loud. I can't control what's happening, I can't scream or stop it. Then I'm falling into the fire and I wake up on fire."

"No. You wake up safe. There's no fire, Izzy."

She turned toward him and stared intently at his face. Not that she could bring him into focus. "It feels like there's fire."

"I know." He brushed her hair off her forehead. "If Aaron catches us like this, we're going to have some explaining to do."

The corners of her mouth twitched. "He'll just be bitter because I got there first. He wants you."

Nick winced. "Please don't say that."

"Can't handle the pressure?"

"It's late. Aren't you getting tired? Don't you want to close your eyes and go to sleep?"

It *was* late. "You can go. I don't need you to stay." The second he left, she would sit by the window because that would feel safer.

"Me? I'm not moving. I'm too comfortable."

"Liar."

"Not me. I always tell the truth. Ask anyone."

She waited, but he didn't move. Eventually, she put her head on his shoulder. He wrapped his arms around her. She was aware of his long, hard body next to hers, but that didn't matter. Being safe was a whole lot more important than anything else.

"Go to sleep, Izzy. I'll be right here. You won't have any more bad dreams tonight."

"Promise?"

"Yeah. I promise."

Izzy woke to sunlight flooding her room. She stretched and rolled over, only to realize she was alone. Nick had left sometime in the night. Or maybe he'd waited until morning. Either way, he'd stayed with her until she'd relaxed enough to let go of the nightmare.

She got out of bed and crossed to the window. She was going home today. Back to live with Lexi, she supposed. To that window seat that had become her entire world. Back to waiting . . . for something that would never happen.

There was no miracle coming. No puff of magic that would make her see again. She either took the risk and had the surgery, or she had to learn to deal. Since getting out of the hospital, she'd been waiting for a gift from heaven.

"Get real," she told herself. Heaven was busy with people a lot worse off than her. Nick was right. She had resources, a family, a life.

She showered and made her way to the barn. She had no idea what time it was, but didn't bump into anyone else. She found the cupboard with the washing supplies and put everything on the bench next to it. She still had trouble deciding which bottle held the soap, then realized she could open them and figure it out by smell.

The barn was a little more daunting. She hit the light switch before entering, then tried to remember how far down she'd gone before.

"Jackson? Are you here, honey? Jackson?"

She heard a soft snort on her left and reached toward the sound. A horse dropped his head over the gate. She patted him.

"I have no idea who you are," she said, "but you're getting a bath. How does that sound?"

She led him outside and secured him to the post. Then she turned on the water and went to work.

Washing a horse was slow work to begin with. The animals were large and they had to be rinsed well. But doing everything by touch made the task that much longer. Izzy figured she got as much water on herself as on Jackson, but that was okay. She would get better with practice.

She'd just started rinsing the far side,

when she heard someone say, "The breakfast bell rang ten minutes ago."

She spun toward the sound and was rewarded with a yelp, followed by swearing. She turned the water off at the nozzle.

"Morning," she said, trying not to grin. "Did I get you?"

"Yes," Nick said through obviously clenched teeth. "Water's cold."

"I know. Sorry. You startled me."

"Apparently. You coming in for breakfast?"

"As soon as I finish. Um, is this Jackson?"

"Uh-huh."

She heard Nick brushing down his jeans. With luck, he was completely soaked.

"Okay. I'll just be a couple of minutes." She bit her lower lip.

Late yesterday afternoon, she'd been convinced she only wanted to go home. That there was nothing here on the ranch for her. Now she wasn't so sure.

She wanted to stay. She wanted to try to . . . something. Adjust, maybe. But her Titan pride made it impossible to ask.

She stared at the shape that was Nick, not sure how to get her point across. "Nick, I . . ."

"Yeah. It's fine. After breakfast, you can start on the other horses."

"Okay." She smiled. "Thanks."

Then she turned on the hose and heard him yelp again.

"Dammit, Izzy. You're going to make me regret having you around, aren't you?"

She turned off the water and giggled. "Now why would you think that?"

CHAPTER FIVE

Nick stood in the kitchen and watched Izzy move through the living room. She walked deliberately, touching every piece of furniture as she made a full circuit. She completed the return trip in the opposite direction, then paused. A few seconds later, she walked into the center of the room and stopped. From there, she went first to the sofa, then back to the middle. She crossed to the window and returned to the center.

She was learning the room. By the time she was finished she would know where everything was and find it easily. In a couple of days she would be able to hurry through the house like everyone else.

Even as he watched her turn and pace and count, he was distracted by her long bare legs. Her shorts barely covered her butt and her tight T-shirt outlined her full breasts. Normally he would have been able to ignore her athletic body. Normally he could appreciate the show and move on. Normally he hadn't spent a long, agonizing night lying next to a beautiful woman, her legs tangled with his, her head on his shoulder, her breasts nestling against his arm.

He told himself that the price was worth it. She'd proven her strength — not only in avoiding a crash and burn after her nightmare, but by being able to move on from their fight. He'd taunted her. She'd risen to the bait, but hadn't gotten trapped in anger. She was strong and determined — someone he could admire. Now if only he could see her naked.

Stop it, he told himself. Izzy was a client, someone he was helping. He had no business thinking about kissing every inch of her, of touching her until she begged and then losing himself in her. It was unprofessional. It was sexist. And being hard all the time was damned unpleasant.

The point of all this was she hadn't given up, which meant she was one step closer to having the surgery. There were more —

"You have some serious stalker tendencies," she said, turning to face him. "It's borderline creepy. You should go talk to someone about it."

"I've been here ten minutes. Why did it

take you so long to figure out you weren't alone?"

She continued finding her way around the room. "My bat sonar isn't fully installed just yet."

"You need to work on that."

"You need to get a life. Do you watch me in the shower?"

The image dropped into his brain and there was no way he could ignore it. "Do you want me to?"

She tilted her head slightly. Her long, dark, curly hair tumbled over her right shoulder. She walked toward him, stopping only inches away. A smile tugged at the corners of her mouth.

"You need a woman. Seriously. It's bad enough that the blind girl can figure it out. That's got to be embarrassing."

It was, but he wouldn't admit it to her. "I'm playing your game. That should make you happy."

"Maybe. I take it you don't have anyone you're seeing right now. I'm guessing it's a geographic thing. It's hard to date when your life is in the middle of nowhere."

"My work keeps my busy."

"So you're between relationships? Or are you the type who doesn't get involved?"

Why were they talking about him? "I don't

get involved." Why was he answering her questions?

Her eyes were hazel, the irises a kaleidoscope of color.

"So typical," she said. "Were you burned by love? Did someone break your heart?"

"No." No one got close enough to break anything. "What about you?" he asked. "Why aren't there a pack of guys at your beck and call?"

"I prefer one-on-one to a pack," she said. "I don't do serious, either. It's too much trouble. I like my men easy and pretty. Although I guess pretty is less important than it used to be."

It was as if a light clicked off inside her. One second she was flirty and confident, the kind of woman who made men look even when they didn't want to. The next, her shoulders slumped, her chin dropped and her energy faded.

She turned away, obviously lost in defeat.

He grabbed her arm. "Don't," he told her. "Don't give in. You have to stay strong. It's worth it."

"You don't know what you're talking about."

"Yeah, I do." He wanted to shake her until she figured out there was a process and she had to keep moving forward.

"Were you really going to let me go home?" she asked.

"You *could* have gone home."

"You were a bastard on purpose. I suppose I should thank you."

He would like it better if she were yelling or throwing things. Anger had power behind it. This acceptance would kill her . . . or at least keep her from getting well.

"Don't thank me," he said, frustrated. "Get pissed off. Yell at me. Hate me."

"Why? You haven't done anything wrong."

"Sure I have." He was a guy — there had to be something he'd done. "I think you're an idiot for wasting the opportunities you've been given."

"Like I'm buying that." She pulled free and turned to leave.

"You've wasted your life. You're a Titan. You could have done something with all that money, but you haven't. You're useless. Being blind just makes it obvious to everyone else. Because you've always known the truth."

She turned back to him, her expression more annoyed than angry, but at least it was better than defeat.

"You have some serious psychological problems," she told him. "I don't think your geography has anything to do with why

95

you're not in a relationship. I think it's you."

"What's your excuse for being alone? Since when are relationships too much trouble for a woman? It's what you all live for."

"You are seriously grasping here."

"Whatever works."

"What's your end game?" she asked.

"For you not to give up."

"And then what? Do I get a cookie?"

"You get your life back, Izzy. That has to be worth something."

"According to you, it isn't. I'm useless."

"So be mad at me. Have something to prove."

"You know, you need a strategy," she told him. "Right now you're just bouncing around from point to point. There's no cohesive argument here."

"I'm thinking on my feet."

She smiled. "Not your greatest strength, huh?"

He relaxed a little. "I do okay."

"The people who say that are your employees, aren't they? You have to pay them a lot of money to get them on your side."

"You're saying I don't inspire loyalty?"

"I'm saying you have issues."

"So do you."

"One or two."

"Like not having the surgery."

She poked him in the chest. "We are so not having that conversation."

The fire was back. Good. As long as she stayed strong, she would make it.

"We have to have it sometime."

"Not today."

She looked at him. If he didn't know better, he would swear she could see everything. Her eyes were so damn beautiful . . . just like the rest of her. Without thinking, he reached toward her and cupped the side of her face. Her skin was smooth and soft.

"You can't hide from me forever," Aaron said as he walked into the kitchen. "You can run but you can't hide. I've always loved that saying. I have proposals that need your approval and a lot of other details you keep avoiding."

Nick dropped his hand and Izzy took a step back. Aaron rounded the corner, then came to a stop.

"Oh, my," he said, glancing between them. "You could cut the tension in this room with a knife. What have you two been up to? It's bad. I can tell. I'm just going to back out and we can pretend I was never here."

"You don't have to do that," Nick said. "I'm leaving."

"But you're the one I have to talk to."

97

Izzy heard footsteps retreating. Based on the sound and cadence, she knew Nick was the one who had left.

"What did I miss?" Aaron asked, sounding intrigued. "You both looked guilty. There's something going on between you two."

"Not that much," she said, thinking that last night had been about comfort. He'd kept her sane through a rocky couple of hours. But what had today been about?

"Honey, I know sexual tension when I see it and it was filling this room. Come have a seat and tell Uncle Aaron everything. Start at the beginning and talk slow. My love life sucks so I'll have to live vicariously through yours."

He took her hand and led her to the sofa. When they were seated, the cushion moved as if he were getting more comfortable or angling toward her.

"Tell me everything."

"There's nothing to tell. We were arguing." Sort of. "Nick wants to make sure I don't give up. Sometimes he's a jerk about it."

Aaron sighed. "Don't you love it when he gets all manly. I know it makes *my* heart beat faster."

She laughed. "I find him annoying."

"I don't think so. The way he was looking at you."

"Really?"

"Uh-huh. Like he hasn't eaten in three days and you're the buffet."

Something deep inside her belly quivered to life. "Nick is nice," she said cautiously, aware she was at a serious disadvantage. She couldn't tell what Nick was thinking by looking at him.

"Nice? He's a lot more than that. Have you seen those muscles. Oh. Right. Probably not. Well, they're there and they're fabulous."

She'd felt them when he'd dragged her out of Lexi's house and again last night. He'd been strong and safe and, well, kind. Not exactly a word she would have expected to use where he was concerned.

"You're not seeing anyone, are you?" Aaron asked. "I don't want Nick hurt."

"What? You should be worried about me. I can't wear makeup or fuss with my hair. I have to shave my legs by feel, which is probably not pretty."

"You're beautiful and sexy and something tells me you've been fighting off the boys since you were thirteen. It's not about makeup, Izzy, it's about you. Nick is drool-worthy. Believe me, I know. But he keeps to himself. No one gets in, because he makes sure they don't."

The compliments made her feel good, but she was more interested in what Aaron *hadn't* said.

"Why doesn't he get involved?"

Aaron was silent.

She sighed. "If you're making a face, I can't see it."

"Oh. Right. Sorry. He has a past. Most of it, I don't know either. Some I've figured out. Some he's told me. He was raised in foster care. I don't know what happened to his parents. He's smart. Scary smart. Went to college on a full scholarship when he was fifteen or sixteen. It's never good to be the smartest kid in the room. Then he grew up and . . ." Aaron paused. "The next few years aren't clear to me. Anyway, he ended up here with this ranch and his business."

Talk about a lot of gaps, she thought, wondering how many were because Aaron really didn't know and how many were because he didn't want to tell her.

"Did he buy the ranch or was it in his family?" she asked.

"He bought it and fixed it up."

"Specially for the corporate retreats?"

"Specifically for the kids. The corporate stuff happens to pay the bills." The sofa shifted as Aaron stood. "Like I said, don't hurt him."

"As if I could. I'm not here to get the guy. I'm here to get better."

Aaron said something and left, but she wasn't paying attention. Until that second, she hadn't been willing to admit the truth to herself. But there it was, at last. Her admission of something she'd been avoiding since she'd first found out she'd lost nearly all her sight. She wanted to get better. To heal. She didn't know if that meant having the surgery or adjusting to what she had, but at least there was a goal.

It had been a long time since she wanted something. It felt good to have a purpose and maybe, just maybe, get it right.

"You've done this a thousand times," Rita said calmly, as Izzy wrestled with getting the pad in the right spot.

"Jackson's going to hate me pretty soon," Izzy muttered, smoothing the pad in place. "Does this look right?"

"Don't ask me," Rita told her. "You're the one saddling the horse."

"You can be very frustrating," Izzy told her, as she made a couple of adjustments. "Okay — that should be good." She bent over to grab the saddle.

"I would appreciate a little cooperation," she told the horse. "Just don't step on me."

"Jackson is too much a gentleman for that," Rita said.

"I hope you're right."

She raised the saddle to what she hoped was the correct height and lowered it onto his back. When it was in place, she made sure the right stirrup was still hooked out of the way, then walked around him and checked the saddle placement by touch.

"This seems good," she said quietly, patting Jackson as she went. She secured the saddle in place, grabbed it with both hands to make sure it was tight, then fumbled for the stirrup. "Now for the real test."

She swung herself up into place. Except for the fact that she felt too far off the ground and dangerously vulnerable in a blurry world, it was good.

"I did it," she said, oddly proud of herself.

"Yes, you did. Next time you'll do it faster."

"Why do I have visions of you holding a stopwatch?"

"I have no idea. I'm not the stopwatch type."

Izzy removed the saddle and pad, putting both away before returning to Jackson's side and offering him a piece of apple. "You were very good for me and I appreciate that."

"Next we'll get you exercising the horses," Rita told her.

Izzy wasn't too sure about that, but she would deal with that fight when it was time. For now she was getting through each day, making progress, albeit slowly. She was learning how to function. Sometimes she was pleased with her progress, other times she still wanted to scream at the heavens, complaining this shouldn't have happened to her.

At least the nightmares hadn't returned. Not since that night Nick had shown up and comforted her.

"Tell me about Nick," she said.

"What do you want to know?"

"Has he been married?"

"Not that I know of. He keeps to himself, which is a shame. Every good man needs a wife."

Izzy grinned. "So speaks someone who has been married a long time."

"Why should I be the only one? Besides, my husband would be happy to tell you that I'm the best thing that ever happened to him."

"I'm sure he would."

"Nick is . . . complicated. I don't know very much about his past and I'm not sure how much he'd tell you if you asked. He has secrets. I know he spent at least a year traveling the world, learning survival training. He's studied with monks to learn to control his body — his breathing and heart rate. He is a surprising combination of dangerous and spiritual. Why do you ask? Interested?"

"What? No." Afraid she was blushing, something she never did, Izzy turned away. "He runs this place. I've never met anyone who does what he does."

"Uh-huh. You need a better story. No one's going to believe that one."

"I'm not interested. Not romantically or anything."

"Are you saying you'd tell Nick no if he crawled in your bed?"

Actually he already had, although it hadn't been for sex. Which now that she thought about it, was kind of sad. "He's a friend," she began.

Rita laughed. "Words every man longs to hear. If you decide to turn him away, send him over to me."

"You're happily married."

"I know, but I'm still allowed to have fantasies. I doubt there's a woman alive who would tell him no."

Izzy suddenly had a burning need to know

what he looked like. She had a sense of his height and shape. She knew he was strong and she could pick out his scent in the dark. But what about the rest of him? Did he smile much? What color were his eyes?

As for telling him no, she thought about their earlier conversation. How close they'd been standing. The way he'd touched her cheek. She'd liked the feel of his fingers on her skin and for a second, she'd thought he might kiss her.

An unexpected sense of loss made her chest hurt. She couldn't shake the feeling of having missed out on something important. Which was insane. She was here because she had to be here. When she could get along in the real world, she would leave. Nick wasn't any part of her life.

"Okay, go grab me a dandy brush from the storeroom," Rita said. "Then it should be time for lunch."

Izzy turned toward the barn. "I don't like the storeroom. It's too dark."

"So?"

"It scares me." Even with the lights on, she couldn't see anything in the storeroom. "Like a creepy cave."

"Life is full of creepy caves. Take them one at a time."

Rita's dismissal annoyed her. Everyone

was so free with their advice. "I agree that I have to work through things, but not all in one day. Give me a break. I'm making progress. Isn't that enough? Let me guess. It's not. Because everyone here has an opinion about my life. You don't know what it's like to be blind."

"Neither do you. You have thirty percent of your sight."

"Big whoop."

"It would be to someone who was totally blind. To them you'd have everything."

"Right. Because I always have to remember there are people worse off than me."

"Not worse off. Just dealing with more. And you're wrong about me. I do know what it's like to be blind because I am. Completely. Have been since birth."

She kept talking, but Izzy couldn't hear the words.

Rita, blind? But she ran the stable. She fed and exercised all the horses, knew where they were, took care of them. She told Izzy what to do, explained how and then corrected her if she was wrong. She moved easily, never stumbling.

"I don't understand," Izzy breathed.

"What's to understand? It's a pretty straightforward condition. My parents put me on a horse when I was four and I never wanted to get off. I've always been around them. They seem to know I can't see because I've never been stepped on or even pushed down. Nick had to pay a lot of money to get me away from my last job. But I was interested in a change and he sweet-talked me the rest of the way."

Blind. Izzy couldn't believe it. "I never would have guessed."

"No offense, but you're not tough to fool. It's not like you see 20/20." Rita patted her on the shoulder. "It's only the dark, kid. Just because you can't see what's there doesn't mean you should be afraid. It's only the dark."

It was a whole lot more than that, but Izzy wasn't going to argue. Especially not with Rita, who obviously had no trouble getting along in the world. There was a lesson there, Izzy thought. One about courage and determination. One she apparently needed to learn.

Two days later Izzy stood in the shade, grooming Jackson. She and the horse had come to terms with each other. At least that's what she told herself. One of these days she was going to get on him and ride, just like she used to. The fact that she couldn't really see where she was going was an issue to be dealt with another time.

She heard footsteps, but didn't bother turning around. Based on the speed and sound, she knew exactly who it was.

"Hi, Aaron."

"You're getting spooky. I won't ask how you knew it was me. I have a surprise for you."

She might not have been at Nick's ranch all that long, but she knew enough to guess not every surprise was one she would enjoy. "A good surprise or a bad surprise?"

"A good one. At least I think so. Your sisters are here. Norma said they could stay to lunch and she won't do that for just anyone. So she likes you." He paused. "Should I pause for a dramatic reaction to the news?"

"That Norma likes me?"

"Oh, please. To your sisters being here."

Izzy patted Jackson's neck. She didn't know what to think. When she'd first arrived, she'd been so angry at them for abandoning her. She'd seen their actions as a betrayal. Now . . . she wasn't so sure. While she was starting to see their point, she wasn't ready to completely forgive them. Although if they groveled enough, she was willing to be persuaded.

She unhooked Jackson and led him toward

108

the stable. "Tell them I'll be in shortly."

"That's it?"

"Disappointed?"

"Yes. I thought you might scream or something. I adore drama."

She grinned. "Then stick around for the reunion. There might be a shriek or two."

"You're just saying that to make me feel better." He followed her into the barn. "Your sisters are very beautiful, but they don't look alike."

"Different mothers," she said. When Jackson was safely back in his stall, she turned back to the door. "Skye and I share a mother. Lexi's mom was Jed's first wife."

"How very Dallas." Aaron linked arms with her. "So who's Dana? She's here, too."

"A mutual friend."

"She so doesn't do the girly thing. She could be pretty if she put a little effort into it. And what's with the chip on her shoulder? I swear, she has to work out. Otherwise, she wouldn't have the strength to walk straight. That chip would make her lean."

She squeezed his arm. "You're rapidly becoming one of my favorite people ever."

"I know. Everyone adores me."

Izzy laughed. "Dana's a deputy."

"I can totally see her in uniform and not in a happy way. She needs a man more than

I do and that's saying a lot."

They reached the back of the house.

"I put them in the living room," Aaron said, holding open the door. "Go say hi. I'll bring in refreshments. That will give you time to do the family greeting thing before they get to know the new light of your life. That would be me, of course."

"Of course," she said, chuckling as she walked. It was only when she'd nearly reached the living room that her humor faded. She paused in the hallway. She could hear low murmurs of conversation. Skye sounded nervous, which made Izzy feel better. She stepped into the room.

"Hi," she said.

There were a couple of gasps, then blurry shapes rushed toward her. Lexi got there first and hugged her.

"How are you? Are you okay? You look good."

Skye pushed Lexi aside and wrapped her arms around Izzy. "I'm sorry," she said. "I know it was the right thing to do, but I'm sorry."

"You can't have it both ways," Izzy told her. "You can't tell me it was right to have me kidnapped and apologize at the same time."

"Of course I can," Skye told her. "I'm a Titan."

"She can be so annoying," a third voice said.

Izzy turned as Dana hugged her, as well.

"You smell like horse," her friend said. "And I had nothing to do with the kidnapping."

Izzy laughed. "I know. You're not the one who's in trouble."

"Am I in trouble?" Skye asked, sounding upset.

"Trouble?" Aaron walked into the room. "My favorite. Is someone going to be punished?"

Izzy introduced him to her sisters. He passed out drinks, then got everyone seated. Izzy noticed that Aaron stayed beside her and led her to the sofa, so she wouldn't have to guess where everything was. Despite the time she'd spent memorizing the room, having four other people around made it impossible to remember what was where.

"So, you probably have a lot of questions for me," Aaron said when they were seated. "I *am* the most important person in Izzy's life. She depends on me for everything."

Izzy laughed. "You are the air that I breathe."

Aaron sighed heavily. "It's a massive

responsibility. Oh. Norma's waving frantically from the kitchen. I think she wants me to leave you girls alone. Normally I would ignore her but she makes these amazing biscuits and I am a slave to my senses. Ladies, it's been lovely. I'll see you at lunch."

Izzy felt him get up and heard him walk out of the room.

"Who's that?" Dana asked. "He doesn't seem your type."

"He's Nick's assistant. He pretty much manages everything."

"You seem to be doing well," Skye said. "This was a hard decision for us, Izzy. You weren't leaving your room, let alone the house."

"I know."

"Even if you decide not to have the surgery, which we still don't understand, you have to do something with your life."

"I know."

"Losing part of your sight isn't the worst . . . What?"

"I said I know. I might not agree with what you did, but I understand why you thought it was important. I don't mind being here. Which is not the same as forgiving you. Just so we're clear."

"Why am I not surprised?" Lexi asked, sounding more relieved and happy than frustrated.

"You shouldn't be. Okay, enough about me," Izzy said. "What's been going on with you two? What have I missed? Erin's getting ready to start school soon, isn't she? Third grade. I can't believe how fast she's growing up."

She'd been there when Skye's daughter had been born. While birth was a lot more messy than she'd expected, it had still been something amazing. Erin was . . .

She realized that no one was talking.

"What?" she asked.

"Nothing." Skye sounded shocked. "It's just you said 'enough about me.' I've never heard you say that before."

"What are you talking about?"

"Just that you're usually . . . You enjoy . . ."

"Stop trying to be so damned delicate," Dana grumbled. "She's trying not to say you usually like it when we talk about you."

Izzy frowned. "That's not true. I joke about it, but I'm not totally self-centered."

There was more silence, and this time it was less comfortable.

"I'm not," she insisted.

"Of course not," Skye murmured soothingly.

Izzy had a feeling they were all exchanging looks she couldn't see. Ones that said they shouldn't upset her.

Did her sisters really think she was self-ish? That she didn't care about them? Or anyone? Hadn't she been the one to try to protect Skye from lying, slimy T.J. Boone earlier that summer? Not that Skye had appreciated her effort.

She shifted on the sofa and did her best to keep her confusion from showing on her face.

"How are things going with Garth?" she asked, to change the subject.

"He's been quiet," Lexi said. "Which makes me nervous. Jed is still being investigated for the arms shipment. So far he hasn't been officially charged with treason, although the threats are there. Garth hasn't attacked my business lately."

"Mine, either," Skye said. "I suppose we should be grateful, but not having him do anything is nearly as stressful as having him coming at me. I keep waiting for the next shoe to drop. It's impossible to relax."

"Maybe that's part of his plan," Dana told her. "I swear to you, I'm going to get him. I'm talking to a couple of guys at the Dallas PD, and they've hooked me up with a Texas Ranger. These are guys who know how to investigate. We're doing our best to build a case. Garth Duncan isn't going to get away with any of this."

She sounded fierce, which made sense, given their history with Garth.

A couple of years ago Lexi's banker had offered her a loan to expand her day spa. The terms were good enough to be seriously tempting and the investor didn't even want a piece of the action. Just principal and interest. The only catch had been that the note was callable without warning. The past spring, the note had been called and Lexi had scrambled to find a way to repay the mystery lender in less than a month. She'd nearly lost everything.

Then she'd been sued by a former client, several of their father's race horses had tested positive for performance-enhancing drugs and someone had leaked damning but false information to the district attorney about Skye's not-for-profit foundation. Only Izzy had been spared, probably because she didn't have anything worth taking.

The sisters had struggled to figure out what was going on. Their investigation had led them to an impossible truth — their businesses were being targeted by a half brother they didn't know about. Garth Duncan was Jed's oldest child — one he'd never acknowledged. For reasons they didn't understand, Garth was after them, with a vengeance.

Dana, a Titanville deputy, was doing all she could to protect her friends.

"Garth has always come at you in ways you didn't expect," she said now. "From our perspective, his attacks seem random, but I don't think they are. I think he has a master plan. I just want to throw his ass in jail. Very little else would make me happy. We need to —"

Dana stopped talking.

"What?" Lexi asked, but Izzy had already heard the footsteps approaching.

"It's Nick," she said, recognizing the sound.

"Ladies," he said as he entered the room.

She heard Lexi and Skye stand.

"We can't thank you enough," Skye began.

"You don't have to thank him at all," Izzy grumbled. "I'm the one doing the work. He's just part of the background."

"What draws me most to your sister is her charm," Nick said dryly.

But she knew he was smiling as he spoke. She could hear it in his voice.

"How is she doing?" Lexi asked. "Really?"

Izzy rolled her eyes. "Do you care that I'm in the room?"

"No."

"She's doing well. You can see that for

yourself."

"And?" Skye prompted.

"And I don't discuss my guests with anyone. If you want to know that information, ask Izzy herself."

"Nice," Dana said. "A man with principles. I approve."

"You sound surprised," Nick said.

"I am."

"You don't think much of my gender?" he asked.

"Not really."

"Fair enough. Ladies, enjoy your visit."

He left.

Lexi and Skye sat back down. Izzy grinned. "I love that he won't tell you anything."

"I'm sure you do," Lexi said. "I find it annoying, but I'll get over it. I didn't realize he was so hot."

"Excuse me?" Izzy said.

"Oh, yeah," Skye said. "Not that I don't love Mitch, but I didn't notice it before."

Nick hot? Aaron had said the same, which only made Izzy want to see him more. Being blind really sucked.

"You were probably too upset about betraying me," she said, not really meaning it in a bad way. "Hot, how?"

"Interesting," Dana said slowly. "Why

would you care?"

"I spend a lot of time with the guy. Good-looking is nice, even if I can't see it."

"Beautiful eyes," Skye said.

"Body to die for," Lexi told her.

"Love the butt," Dana said.

Interesting comments, but no details. And if she pushed the point, her sisters would remind her that, in theory, having the surgery would allow her to see for herself.

"Do you think he heard us talking about Garth?" she asked.

"I hope not," Dana said. "This isn't information we want getting out."

"I'm sure it's fine," Skye murmured. "We weren't talking that loudly."

"I guess it doesn't matter," Izzy said. "It's not like Nick and Garth know each other."

Nick drove directly to Dallas. It took nearly two hours, but this wasn't a conversation he wanted to have on the phone. He was immediately waved in by Garth's assistant and stalked into his friend's office.

Garth finished up a call and then stood. "I didn't know you were coming into town. Want to grab some dinner?"

Nick looked at the man who'd been like a brother to him and the only family that had ever mattered. The man he'd nearly died with. The one he trusted with his life.

"What's going on with you and the Titans?" he asked.

CHAPTER SIX

Nick watched closely, paying attention to Garth's breathing and his pupils. Things the average person didn't notice often gave away the truth. His friend barely blinked.

"Odd question," Garth said. "What do you want to know?"

"Izzy Titan is at my ranch because of you," Nick said, walking toward one of the leather chairs in front of the desk and taking a seat. "According to her sisters, you're responsible for their business troubles and they're investigating you."

Garth shrugged. "It's not what you think."

"You don't know what I think."

The other man smiled. "I know *you.*"

Nick was willing to give his friend the benefit of the doubt. In the twenty years they'd been friends, Garth had never lied to him or let him down in any way.

Garth looked at Nick. "Jed Titan is my father."

An unexpected piece of information. "You never told me." Garth had mentioned not knowing his father before, saying the man was alive but that he didn't have a relationship with him. A mystery father was very different than Jed Titan.

"I never told anyone," Garth said. "He was rich, my mother wasn't and when she turned up pregnant, he ended things. To give the old bastard his due, he paid her off. She never told me who my father was and I eventually stopped asking. I found out by accident. Then, when I was thirteen, she started getting headaches."

Nick had only met Garth's mother once. Kathy Duncan was a pretty woman with an easy laugh and a slow way of talking. It was obvious there was something different about her. Something not quite right. He'd never asked what had happened.

"She went from doctor to doctor," Garth continued. "They did tests and found a tumor. There was surgery, rehabilitation, more surgery. Did you know that most insurance policies have a lifetime limit? She didn't, but we both learned about it fast enough. When the insurance ran out, there was the money Jed had given her, then that was gone, too. By then I was fourteen and the tumor was back."

Garth stood and walked to the window. He stood with his back to Nick. "We found a doctor who understood her condition. He was willing to operate. A last-chance effort to save her life. But there wasn't any money left. I went to Jed Titan."

Nick had never met Izzy's father, but he'd read about him enough to guess what had happened.

"He refused."

Garth faced him, his expression hard. "He had me thrown out. Eventually the doctor agreed to perform the surgery for nothing and I found a charity to help cover the hospital costs, but it was too late. You've met her — you've seen it. She has irreparable brain damage. She lived but she will never be the same."

There was no anger in his friend's voice, barely any emotion. But Nick knew him well and could see past the game face. "You want revenge."

"I want Jed Titan to lose everything. Piece by piece."

Then Jed was in trouble, Nick thought, suspecting that if he'd ever known his mother or been in a position to care about her, he would do the same thing.

"What does that have to do with his daughters? They're not a part of this." He meant Izzy, but he wouldn't say that.

"I'm using them to get Jed's attention." He held out his hands, palms up. "I haven't hurt them." He shrugged. "Okay, I've messed with them a little, but no permanent damage was done. It's all part of the game."

"Why send Izzy to me?"

"So you can keep an eye on her. Something happened on that rig and I want to find out what."

Nick was on his feet. "You think the explosion was deliberate?"

"I don't know. I have people checking it out. But there are more players in this game than just me. Besides, she's my sister and she needs help. You're the best."

Nick understood he wasn't getting the whole story. He had the sense that Garth was using him, but wasn't sure for what. Had it been anyone else, he would have insisted on the truth. If that wasn't enough, he would have taken things to the next level.

But this was Garth. The one man on the planet he trusted with his life and his secrets. Garth had never blamed him, never thrown his mistake back in his face. Until this second, he would have risked his life on the fact that Garth was the best man he knew.

"How's she doing?" Garth asked.

"Better. She's stronger than I thought. Determined."

"Will she have the surgery?"

"I don't know. Something's holding her back. Until I know what it is, I can't help her." Now it was his turn to shrug. "There's time."

"And you're a patient man. Are you going to tell her about knowing me?"

Nick hesitated.

"If she knows you know me, she'll leave," Garth said.

"I figured that out myself."

"Your call."

There were missing pieces to the puzzle. Until he had them, he would take the road that led to Izzy's healing. "I won't tell her for now," he said.

Later, on the drive back to the ranch, Nick wondered if he was making the right decision. Or would it come back to bite him in the ass? But this was Garth. They'd spent months together in a jungle prison being tortured. Months of sitting in the stifling heat, of being eaten alive by bugs, of being blindfolded and living in the dark. Of not knowing when their captors were going to strike next. There had never been any warning, just the burning slice of a knife on an arm or a leg. The sharp blade separating flesh, followed by the screams. His screams . . . or Garth's.

Nick had been willing to give up. To surrender to death — to stop trying. Garth had kept him alive and in the end, he'd hung on long enough to carry Garth from their jungle prison.

They'd been friends before that, but their months of hell had made them brothers.

Garth had never lied to him, but Nick couldn't shake the sense that there was more to the story than Garth let on. But for now, he would do as his friend asked. Because he owed him. Because they both carried the scars. Because neither of them ever slept in the dark.

Izzy stared at the blurry shape that was Aaron and did her best to keep her mouth from hanging open. "Are you serious? They attacked you?"

Nick had disappeared in the afternoon and hadn't returned for dinner. Norma had decided two people weren't worth cooking for and had gone home, leaving them to find food in the packed refrigerator.

Aaron moved around the kitchen, dumping things into bowls and sticking them in the microwave.

"I'm from New York, I'm obviously gay, I

was in a cowboy bar in a tough part of Dallas. It happens."

Not in her world. People didn't just get beat up for being different. "I hope you pressed charges."

Aaron patted her shoulder as he walked past her. "You're surprisingly naive, but sweet, which is why I like you. I wasn't worried about anything but getting out of there alive. If Nick hadn't come to my rescue, I'd be dead now." He sighed. "He was magnificent. He seriously kicked some straight-boy ass. In the movies he would have realized he'd been playing for the wrong team all along and fallen passionately in love with me."

Izzy hid a smile. "Maybe next time."

"Don't tease me. Anyway, he brought me here to heal. Norma fed me until I begged for mercy. And that's the story of how Nick and I met."

"What was he doing in a cowboy bar?"

"An interesting question. You'll have to ask him."

"What were you doing there?"

From the change in his voice, she knew he was grinning. "I saw the hats. I thought it was a *gay* cowboy bar. My bad." He got plates down from the cupboard. "Make yourself useful and put these out, please."

She grabbed the plates.

"I was tired of New York," he continued. "The same guys, the same work."

"What did you do there?"

"I was a party planner. It was fun and I made a lot of money, but it just wasn't me. One day instead of looking through the singles ads in the paper, I found myself looking at used cars. I bought one and then I ended up here. I like Texas. Now if I could just find a cute boy."

"Me, too."

"You have Nick."

If only.

Izzy stood by the table, turning the thought over in her head. If only? As in she *wanted* Nick? As in sex? Did blind girls have sex? Stupid question. Of course they did, but did she? If she couldn't see his face, how could she know what he was thinking? Or know that he really wanted her?

"Izzy, I'm talking," Aaron told her. "At least pretend to pay attention."

"Oh. Sorry. I was just . . ."

"Thinking about Nick."

"Maybe."

"Uh-huh."

She smiled. "Back to you."

"Finally."

"You bought a car and drove to Texas,

where Nick saved you."

"From certain death." He sighed dramatically. "While I was recovering, I found out about his business. Or what he called a business. He doesn't really have the right personality to schmooze with the corporate types, so he wasn't getting as many bookings as he wanted. I took over as soon as I could hold a phone. We doubled our income in six months. Now we have a reputation, I'm adored by millions. It works."

"Don't you love it when the universe gets it right?"

"I do. It's really the perfect relationship. Nick focuses on his kids and I run everything else."

She'd heard about the kids before. "What kids? How does he find them? Why here?"

"Because he's good and it's free. If you ask me, he has a dark, dangerous secret from his past he doesn't want to talk about. I can tell. He's a man who carries guilt, and does it look good on him. Anyway, he's atoning."

"For what?"

There was silence.

"Are you giving me a look?" she asked.

"Oh, yeah. Sorry. I don't know. You can ask him if you want. God knows I've tried."

He went on to talk about the last corporate

retreat and what had happened. Izzy only half listened. She kept glancing out the window, not that she could see anything. Not only was there the whole lack-of-sight thing, it was already dark. Where was Nick and when was he coming back? And why did his being away bother her so much?

After dinner Aaron wanted to watch *Project Runway,* but Izzy was too restless. She tried listening to a book on tape, but it wasn't enough of a distraction, so she went upstairs and changed into shorts and a T-shirt, then returned to the living room.

"I'm going to work out," she said.

"Sweat?" Aaron asked, sounding horrified. "On purpose?"

She rolled her eyes. "Call it a quirk."

"I call it smelly, but you go have fun. I'm sorry you can't see the show. Tim Gunn is such a hottie."

Izzy waved and walked to the back door, then opened it and stepped into the darkness.

She realized her mistake at once. While there were lights around the property and she knew the general location of the gym, she couldn't see it. There was no big, looming shape to guide her.

"One creepy cave at a time," she told

herself, remembering Rita's words of encouragement.

Closing her eyes, more out of habit than need, she imagined the location of the various buildings on the property. The barn was directly ahead, the gym to the right. If she missed the gym, she would run into the fence, so she didn't have to worry about getting lost. Unfortunately she'd never counted the steps to the gym. Something she would do in the morning.

But for now, she simply had to go on faith. She opened her eyes — not that she could see all that much — and struck out in what she hoped was the right direction. A minute or so later, she saw the door to the gym, illuminated in the darkness. As she stepped inside and hit the light switch, she realized it had never occurred to her to go back into the house and ask Aaron to take her.

"Progress," she told herself.

The gym had every piece of equipment imaginable. Izzy considered the elliptical, then found herself wandering over to the rock-climbing wall. She'd done it once before. It had been hard and terrifying, but satisfying. Could she do it again?

She found the ropes and harness. Climbing alone wasn't smart, but she was experienced enough to handle it. And if she fell, she would pick herself up again. Or not. Either way, she wouldn't be afraid.

She climbed slowly, carefully, feeling her way up the wall. Sweat poured down her back and her arms trembled but she was determined to reach the top. With each step, each movement higher, she felt stronger and more herself. This was what she liked to do, she thought. Test herself. Experience the rush.

Because thinking about the wall meant she didn't have to think about anything else.

Izzy stopped in midreach and frowned. Was that true? Was she addicted to the adrenaline rush because it was, in a way most people couldn't understand, safe? It was a distraction, she knew that.

She grabbed the next hold. Was the hunt for sensation so much of a distraction that it allowed her to forget? Like everyone else, she had issues she didn't want to deal with. Some people drank, some gambled. She swam with sharks. Because while she was putting her life on the line, she didn't have to think about the fact that neither of her parents had given a damn about her.

"Seriously?" she asked aloud and stopped again.

Izzy didn't usually allow time for intro-spection. She didn't like it, but here, sweating, in the silent gym facing a wall that didn't care if she could see or not, everything came into focus.

Pru, her mother, hadn't seemed to notice she had a second daughter. Izzy always had the sense Pru was looking right through her. As for Jed, his daughters were a means to an end, nothing more. She'd spent much of her life trying to be the son he'd never had. It hadn't helped, so she'd lost herself in a world of death-defying sports.

"Insight," she murmured. "Who knew?"

Now that she was dealing with the insights, she found they weren't half bad. Okay, she wasn't ready to take up meditation or start a dream journal, but this was good. Knowing why she'd started risking her life was important. But it didn't mean she had to stop. There were —

"What the hell do you think you're doing?"

The voice came out of nowhere and caused her to jump. Not a good thing when she was halfway up a rock-climbing wall. Her fingers slipped, her feet lost their hold and then she was falling toward the ground.

She only had a second to tell herself to relax. If she tensed she would hurt herself more. She took a deep breath and —

Strong arms caught her. She recognized

Nick at once and opened her eyes.

He was a blurry mess of features she couldn't quite see and a body she couldn't bring into focus. She scrambled to her feet and pointed her finger at him.

"Are you stupid on purpose?" she demanded. "You came out of nowhere and yelled at me. I could have been killed."

"While we're on the subject of stupid, what were you doing climbing alone?" he asked, his voice just as loud as hers. "It's dangerous. It's irresponsible. Do you know what could have happened?"

"Nothing. I was fine until you decided it would be fun to startle me."

"You could have broken your neck and slowly asphyxiated. Not the way anyone would choose to go."

It wasn't a visual that made her comfortable, Izzy thought, involuntarily rubbing her throat. "You're ignoring the fact that you waltzed in here and scared me. I was perfectly safe until then. Just because I can't see everything doesn't mean I'm not capable."

"You think I don't know that? I'm the one teaching the class."

She could hear the frustration in his voice, and the temper he was trying to control. She had the thought it would be interesting to see what he was like when he lost it.

"Don't put the blame on me," she snapped. "You screwed up."

"You were climbing alone."

"You keep saying that. Take responsibility for messing up and I'll do the same."

"What are we? Five?"

"You're acting like *you* are."

He growled low in his throat and reached for her. She couldn't really see the movement, but she wasn't surprised when he grabbed her by her upper arms and pulled her against him.

"You make me crazy," he muttered.

"Then my work here is complete."

He gave a short laugh, swore, and pressed his mouth to hers.

The kiss was as hot as it was unexpected. His lips seemed to burn hers, but in the best way possible. His fingers held her tight, not that she was interested in going anywhere.

He didn't move much at first. There was just his mouth on hers, as if he were surprised to find himself in this position. Then he shifted slightly, exploring, discovering. Everywhere his lips brushed hers, she felt heat and sparks. Desire turned liquid and poured through her. She could hear her own heartbeat thundering in her ears.

She broke free of his hold so she could

wrap her arms around his neck and leaned into him. He grabbed her around the waist. They touched from shoulder to thigh, body against body. He was strong and big and getting harder by the second.

He parted his lips slightly, she did the same and he moved his tongue against hers. She accepted him with a quick stroke, then they were kissing deeply, exploring and feeling.

She lost herself in him, in the sensation of passion and wanting. When he nipped on her lower lip, her insides clenched. He kissed his way along her jaw, then down her neck. She began to tremble in anticipation. He drew his hands across her waist and up her rib cage before cupping her breasts.

Even through her T-shirt and bra, she felt the warmth of his fingers as he caressed her. He brushed his thumbs across her nipples, sending jolts of pleasure all through her. Her breath caught. Need exploded. She angled her head and claimed his mouth, kissing him with all the fiery passion that surged inside her.

He met her stroke for stroke. His arousal flexed against her. She dropped her hands to his chest and explored his hard, sculpted muscles even as he continued to tease her breasts. Their arms bumped and brushed, their breath merged. Between her legs, female flesh grew swollen in anticipation.

And then he was gone.

One second Nick was kissing her back, taking as much as he gave, making her ache, the next he'd released her. She heard footsteps. A door opened and she was alone.

CHAPTER SEVEN

The night was endless. Nick knew better than to try to sleep right away. He escaped to his office, where he did his damnedest to get lost in spreadsheets and numbers. It rarely worked, but he never stopped trying. This time was even more difficult, with his blood still pumping and his dick rock-hard.

He swore silently, cursing himself more than Izzy. He knew better. She was a guest here, a client of sorts. Someone he was trying to help. He shouldn't have kissed her, shouldn't have *kept* kissing her. Shouldn't have touched her.

He'd studied with the best — he knew how to get control. He could slow his heart rate to a dozen beats a minute. He could cut off the sensation of pain, send blood to part of his body to promote healing. He was so fucking one with the world, he was practically a tree. But here he sat with a hard-on he couldn't make go away and hands that still carried the feel of Izzy's breasts.

He was beyond stupid, he thought grimly. He liked her. The wanting was easy. Eventually he would figure out how to make it go away. But the liking was a complication he hadn't expected. Worse, now Garth was in the mix, involved in ways he wouldn't explain.

The simplest solution would be to send Izzy back home. She was better than she had been. She would be fine with her sisters. Only fine was different than healed and he wasn't one to walk away before the job was finished. He wouldn't ask her to go. The problem was his and he would find a way to fix it.

Sometime around two he felt himself getting sleepy. He made his way to his bed and collapsed on top of the covers. He closed his eyes, knowing he probably wouldn't sleep. Only he was wrong. Sleep claimed him instantly, but it was cruel that night, sending him directly into the dream.

No matter what he did, however many spiritual techniques he practiced, he hadn't ever conquered the dream. It came without warning, always starting the same way. In silence.

He was in the jungle. He knew because he

could smell the musty combination of life and rotting leaves. He could feel the dampness as the thick, humid air clung to him. It should have been dark because he'd always been blindfolded, but in his dream he could see everything. The trees, the birds, the sunlight filtering through the rain forest. What he couldn't see was the knives.

They came without warning, invisible. There was the cool sensation of steel cutting through flesh. In the heartbeat of disbelief, as he watched the blood run down his arm, there wasn't pain. That came a second later, the searing burn as healing scars were cut open again.

He clenched his teeth against the agony only to have the knives strike again and again. His chest, his legs, his belly. He wouldn't scream, he told himself, sweat dripping nearly as fast as the blood. Wouldn't let them win. But the sound was pulled from him, the agony winning yet again.

He came awake as suddenly as he'd fallen asleep. Every light was on, but the darkness still pressed down on him. His scars burned, as they always did. Phantom sensations that faded with the dawn.

He saw Aaron standing in the doorway. They stared at each other.

Nick's throat was dry, his breathing harsh. Still he managed to say, "I'm okay."

"You don't look it."

Nick shrugged.

"You need to talk to someone about this," Aaron told him.

"No."

"And here I thought you were more than a pretty face." Aaron continued to study him. "The dreams aren't going away."

"I know."

"That can't be good for you."

"I'm fine."

"I can't decide if you're just stubborn or genuinely stupid."

"Let me know what you come up with."

"Don't act tough with me," Aaron told him. "Don't forget I've heard you scream."

He left. Nick lay back down, knowing he wouldn't sleep again until dawn. He would get up in a few minutes, when the shaking had stopped, and catch his breath.

Aaron was only trying to help. The problem was, Nick didn't believe there was a solution. The dreams were part of the price of what he had done. As he couldn't find forgiveness, he would settle on making payments. Tonight had been little more than another installment.

■ ■ ■ ■

Izzy stood in front of the storeroom, wishing someone other than her was in charge of feeding the horses. Or that someone else was responsible for getting the oats. But no. Feeding the horses was her job and she'd run out of oats two horses shy of finishing.

"Would you guys accept a couple of carrots instead?" she yelled into the barn. "Or an apple? How about a cookie?"

She sensed someone behind her seconds before she heard footsteps or words.

"Who are you talking to?" Nick asked, coming up behind her.

"No one you know."

She hadn't seen him all the previous day. Aaron said he'd gone into town to run errands, but she thought maybe he'd been staying away from her because of the kiss. And if he was, did his disappearance mean something good or something bad?

This was when not being able to see was really annoying, she thought. Normally she could take one look at a guy and know if he wanted her. Or if he'd enjoyed himself. Now she couldn't tell and she sure wasn't going to ask.

What worried her most wasn't the lack of

information, it was that sex had always been a game for her. One she enjoyed and played well. But now she didn't understand the rules. She couldn't read the other player, which put her at a serious disadvantage. There was also the teeny, tiny fact that she hadn't been playing when he'd kissed her. She'd felt the passion, the need and had wanted more.

"You need something in the storeroom?" he asked.

"Well, duh."

"You think that kind of attitude is going to make me want to help you?"

She folded her arms across her chest and stared at him. "So you're a conditional sort of person. You want to get before you give."

"You're the one who insisted we both take the blame for you falling the other night."

"You scared me."

"You were climbing alone."

She sighed. "You need a new topic of conversation."

"Get the surgery. Once you can see, you won't be afraid of going into the storeroom."

Not exactly the topic she'd been hoping for. "No, thanks."

"Why not?"

"I don't want to. Get off me."

He moved closer. "Dammit, Izzy, talk to

me. You need the surgery. You can't live like this, afraid of a storeroom because it's dark. Don't you want more?"

She turned to leave. "I don't need this."

He grabbed her. "Yes, you do."

She pulled free. "Stop it."

"Then tell me why?"

"Fine." She dropped her hands to her hips and glared at him. Or at least in his general direction. "I was just a kid when my mom died." She shook her head. "Died. We always say that like it was cancer or she was hit by a car. She killed herself. My mother committed suicide and planned it so my sister, her nine-year-old daughter, would find the body when she got home from school."

There was only silence. Izzy wished she could see his face to know what he was thinking.

"I'm sorry," he said at last.

"Yeah? Me, too. Skye freaked, which makes sense. I didn't know what was going on, but I got scared, too. So scared that I ran and hid in the closet under the main staircase. Only the door got stuck and I couldn't get out. It was dark in there." She shivered at the memory and dropped her arms to her side.

Not just dark. Dark and cold and full of

scary shapes. She could taste the terror in the memory but refused to give in to it.

"I called and screamed until I made myself sick, but no one heard me. I don't even know if they were gone. It took nearly twenty-four hours until they found me. By then I was so hysterical, I had to be taken to the hospital and sedated. I never went to my mother's funeral. I hate the dark. I hate it. So don't tell me to just have the surgery. Not when the alternative is being in the dark forever."

"Okay," he said at last.

"Okay what?"

"I understand why you're scared of the surgery."

She waited. "That's it?"

"Yes."

"You don't want to tell me that I need to talk to a professional?"

"I'm the last guy to say that. You've probably seen a dozen."

"One or two," she admitted. "Back when I was a kid and someone could make me. Now I climb mountains and go cave diving."

"Which is in the dark."

"I always bring an extra flashlight."

"Not going to solve your problem now."

She couldn't believe it. "Are we back to

the surgery again? How many times do I have to tell you that's not going to happen?"

"I don't believe you," he said quietly. "You're too tough. Too determined. You're not going to settle on this half life forever. I guess the trick is to figure out how to survive being permanently in the dark so you don't have to be afraid anymore."

"Your ability to reduce my problems to the obvious is pretty amazing," she snapped. "It's the equivalent of telling someone with a fear of heights to simply jump off a tall building and she'll be cured."

"The difference is the fall won't kill you."

"You don't know that."

"I do and you know it, too. You've never walked away from anything, Izzy. Why this?"

Because it was a nightmare he couldn't begin to understand. Because he had no idea what it was like to be so terrified that breath was impossible and death seemed much easier than living with the fear.

"Go away," she told him.

"I'm not giving up."

"Yay, you."

"Fine," he said. "You win. For now. What do you need in the storeroom?"

She thought about telling him she would get it herself, then she looked into the darkness. "Oats," she said at last.

He disappeared, then reappeared with a large container on a wheelbarrow. "Anything else?"

"I'm good."

"Yes, you are," he told her. "If only you'd believe it."

"Normally I require people to take notes at my meetings," Aaron said from his side of the kitchen table. "But in your case, I'll make an exception."

Izzy laughed. "Lucky me. I could take notes, if you insisted, but it would be messy."

"It's far more important you take me seriously."

"Of course I do. I know who's in charge." Plus she was intrigued by the planning process for a corporate retreat. The first one for her was in a few days. From what Aaron had said, she was expected to help. She was both excited and nervous at the thought. Part of her wanted to run and hide, but most of her was more interested in how long it would take everyone to figure out she couldn't see.

"The company we're hosting is in aerospace," Aaron told her. "They manufacture airplane parts. That means lots of engineers." He sighed. "I don't know. Do you think I could find true love with an engi-neer?"

"Maybe."

"At this point, I'd settle for a night. Anyway, we're doing the usual format. They have their boring little meetings in the morning, then we do the group activities in the afternoon. This time there are a lot of team-building activities. Bor-ring. But we'll be up in the trees later."

Up in the . . . "As in climbing trees?"

"Uh-huh. Using ropes. And walking a rope bridge between trees. Very flashy. It can be a problem for people who have a thing with heights."

"Or are blind," she mumbled.

"You're late," Aaron said.

"Take it out of my paycheck," Nick said, pulling out a chair next to Izzy and sitting down. "What did I miss?"

She'd been so caught up in the thought of dangling from a rope bridge, fifty feet in the air, that she hadn't sensed or heard his ap-proach.

As he leaned forward, his arm brushed hers, making her hyperaware of him. She could feel the heat from his body, inhale the scent of him. Her skin got all prickly and she felt her toes curl inside her boots.

"We're talking about the upcoming retreat," Aaron said. "Nick, your attitude isn't helping. You never take these events seriously."

"You can handle it. You're way better at this than me."

"Oh, please." There was a pause, then Aaron said, "I'm rolling my eyes, Izzy. Just so you know."

She grinned. "Thanks for the update. Does Nick look appropriately chastised?"

"Not really."

She nudged Nick's arm. "Don't mess with him. We all know he's the one who's really in charge."

"So he keeps telling me."

"Isn't it true?"

"Maybe."

Aaron cleared his throat. "If I could have the class's attention," he muttered. "Honestly. This is serious. In three days we have thirty businesspeople showing up for a weekend retreat. They're going to expect us to act professionally. Now, for the details. The menus have been approved. I have to say I love Texans. I never get a string of impossible dietary demands here like I did in New York. No lactose-intolerant vegans who can only eat based on the cycle of the moon. Anyway, we have our usual catering and housekeeping staff ready. The rooms are clean in the guest cottages."

Izzy turned to Nick. "Did I know about cottages?"

"Not a clue."

"You have cottages?"

"Six cottages," Aaron told her. "And a building with another dozen rooms. That has the main dining room, along with the meeting space."

"That's a lot of real estate," she said.

"It's a big ranch."

"But you only do retreats every few weeks. What happens the rest of the time? Does everything just stand empty?"

"Except when we have a few kids through," Aaron said. "We have some scheduled in a couple of weeks."

She'd heard about the kids. They'd been abused or injured in some way and came here for a few days of healing. The horses were a main part of their therapy.

"What about the other days?" she asked. "You have facilities and beds. Why not do something with that? Get a manager in for a B and B. If you already own the buildings and the land, the marginal expense would be minimal. If nothing else, keep the rooms in use. Studies show an empty house actually breaks down faster than one used. You'd be protecting your investment while bringing in income."

There was silence. She glanced between the two men but couldn't see enough to know what they were thinking.

"What?" she asked.

"I guess you really are a Titan," Nick said slowly.

"Like I was lying about my last name?" What did that have to do with anything?

"He means you have business sense in your blood," Aaron told her. "You rattled all that off without thinking about it. Do you have a degree in business or something?"

"No. I've never been to college. It's not a big deal. Everyone knows this kind of stuff. It's common sense."

"Not as common as you'd think," Aaron told her. "Interesting."

But Nick was quiet and Izzy wished she knew what he was thinking.

"Okay, enough about what Nick should do with the ranch," Aaron said. "Everyone focus on me. Nick, you've worked out what you'll be doing for the team-building?"

"Uh-huh. Same as the last two."

"Good. Izzy will assist you. I'll be in charge of standing around looking good."

Izzy laughed. "I'm sure you'll excel."

"I always do."

She turned to Nick. "How will I be helping?"

"I'm going to send you up the ropes first," he said. "And across the bridge. When the guys see a girl doing it, they'll be forced to participate."

"Okay. Sure." While she appreciated the psychology behind his plan, she was a little worried about the actual execution of the plan. "Will I, um, get to practice ahead of time?"

"If you want."

"It's probably for the best. So I know what I'm doing."

"You two work this out among yourselves," Aaron said, as he pushed back his chair. "I have calls to make."

He left the room. Izzy turned to Nick. "What else happens at the retreats?"

"Nothing that interesting. The company human resource departments always have their own ideas about different activities. Holding hands and singing. That kind of crap."

She chuckled. "Stop holding back. Tell me what you really think."

"Yeah, I know. I'm sure it works fine for them. The rest of it is easy. Climb the tree. Cross the rope bridge. A little rappelling. Nothing too challenging. Every now and then someone wants a fire walk."

She straightened. "Seriously? Walking on hot coals? Can we do that?"

"It's not a big deal."

"I've never done it. I've heard it's actually pretty easy. I'd love to try."

"Don't get out the barbecue set. You need special coals and some training by someone who knows what he's doing. Maybe next time."

"I'm going to tell Aaron to book a retreat with a fire walk," she said, wondering if not being able to see the coals would make it more or less scary.

"Just my luck. He'll probably listen."

"I hope so. And don't sound so disgruntled. Aaron is an important part of your business."

"I see he's been talking about himself. His favorite topic."

"Aaron is great and you know it."

"Maybe."

"You'd be lost without him."

"Don't make it more than it is."

She heard the affection in his voice. "He says he's responsible for growing your business to where it is today."

"Of course he does."

"How did you meet?"

She wasn't sure why she asked the question. Aaron had told her the story, but she suddenly wanted to hear it from Nick's point of view.

He hesitated. "In Dallas. He was in a bar."

"You two went to the same bar? The same *kind* of bar? Gee, Nick, is there something you want to tell me?"

"It wasn't a gay bar," he growled. "It was a regular kind of place. I was with a friend."

"Girl or guy."

"Not the point."

She couldn't see for sure, but she would guess he'd clenched his teeth. Nick was amazingly easy to mess with. Which probably should have made her guilty for pushing his buttons, but it didn't.

He sighed. "I went into the bar with a friend and Aaron was . . ." He hesitated again. "He stood out. I could see there was going to be trouble, so I got him out of there."

Izzy frowned. "And then what?"

"We talked and he seemed like someone who knew what he was doing, so I invited him here to see what he could do with the business."

The story was light-years away from what Aaron had told her. What about the part where he'd been beat up and Nick had saved his life? Someone wasn't telling the truth.

She was about to say that, when another possibility occurred to her. Maybe Nick didn't want to admit what had happened. Because he was embarrassed? No, that didn't make sense. Guys loved to brag about how they saved the world. Or at least their little piece of it. Then what? Why wouldn't he want her to know he'd been incredibly heroic? Was it just his style?

Once again not being able to see frustrated her because she had a feeling Nick's eyes would give her plenty of hints. That she would be able to read the truth on his face. The disadvantage annoyed her. It was like the kiss. How was she supposed to know what he'd been thinking? Had he enjoyed himself or had it just been a mercy kiss?

"Izzy?"

It was her second impulsive act in five minutes, only this one wasn't about speaking. She put one hand on the side of his face to guide her, the other on his shoulder, then leaned in and kissed him.

He wasn't expecting the contact. She felt his surprise in the tension in his body. For a second he didn't react, but she held her ground, moving her mouth against his. Teasing. Promising.

One heartbeat. Two.

He grabbed her arms with both hands and held on tight. At the same time his tongue pushed into her mouth, plunging and exploring with enough heat to set Texas on fire. She was instantly lost in erotic sensations as she strained to get closer, kiss deeper. To feel everything.

His mouth was hungry, giving and taking. She met him stroke for stroke. Every part of her body yelled for attention. Her breasts ached, her legs trembled and that place between her thighs clenched tightly.

Nick pulled back and stood. "What the hell is wrong with you?"

Izzy drew in a slow breath and smiled. Oh, yeah. That was good. There was no mercy kissing going on in this world. Nick wanted her as much as she wanted him. Maybe more.

She rose to her feet and felt like a cat in the sun. All languid and content. If she knew how to purr, she would have.

"Just checking," she said. The confidence she'd been missing since the explosion all rushed back. "You're good-looking, right? My sisters said you were hot, but they might have been saying that to be nice. Because of what you're doing for me."

"What?" He sounded both confused and

outraged. "Your sisters?"

"I'm asking because I generally date good-looking guys. I know it's shallow of me, but it's a standard. Part of my charm, I guess."

"We're not dating."

She held in a laugh. There it was. The clench-teeth voice she was growing to adore. If only she could see the look on his face. She would bet his eyes glowed with annoyed fire and that he had tightened his fists in frustration. It was good to be her.

"I know." She reached up and patted his cheek. "I mean, we're already living together. But we're involved and I do have my reputation to think of. Don't worry about it. I'll ask Aaron. He'll tell me the truth. Hmm, now that I think about it, Aaron's always going on about how yummy you are, so never mind. I have my answer."

"We are *not* involved."

She tilted her head. "Silly man. You can't kiss me like that and think there aren't going to be consequences."

He muttered something she couldn't hear.

"Vowing never to kiss me again?" she asked with a smile. "We both know that's not going to happen." She moved closer, until they were touching everywhere and she could feel his arousal. "Want to test the theory?"

She expected him to cut and run. Instead he ran his fingers down the side of her face, then rubbed his thumb across her mouth.

"This is a mistake," he said in a low voice that made her shiver. "All of it. I don't get involved. Ever."

Her mouth went dry. She had to clear her throat before she could speak. "Are you challenging me? I love a good challenge."

"I'll bet you do."

He wrapped his arms around her and kissed her with a hungry passion that made her ache with longing. He claimed her with his mouth, even as his hands moved up and down her back.

She wanted to get closer to him, to crawl inside him. She wanted them both naked. She wanted to touch every inch of him, and have him touch her in return. She wanted breathless cries of surrender. She wanted him filling her, taking her, making her scream.

He pulled back. "I can't do this."

She stared at him, wishing she could see his face as more than blurry features she couldn't make clear. "Why?"

"Because I can't be what you need."

"Cryptic guy statements never do it for me. Let's talk about something else. Like how much you want me."

"Wanting you isn't the problem," he said and abruptly left.

He was good at leaving, she thought. Too good. Which meant he did it a lot. Fine by her — she wasn't looking for anything permanent. She wanted Nick and she would get him. In her bed . . . or his.

She laughed as she headed for the barn. For the first time since the explosion, she felt fully like herself again. Izzy was back and Nick had better watch out.

CHAPTER EIGHT

Garth parked his car and reached for the grande latte from Starbucks. Extra foam, two sugars, just the way Kathy liked it. He tried to get over to Titanville every few days, but didn't always make it. Sometimes he got busy, sometimes he couldn't face Kathy's happy smile and trusting expression.

He told himself she was fine. That she didn't remember much about what she'd been like before. He told himself that she loved the pet store and that he should be relieved he was able to take care of her. Sometimes he nearly believed it. Most of the time he didn't.

He'd bought the pet store for her about twelve years ago. He had a manager in place and plenty of employees. Kathy didn't have any specific responsibilities. She mostly took care of the animals and decided which ones got adopted by whom. He'd heard she had a gift for matching the right person with the right pet. Not that he gave a damn. As long as she enjoyed her day, the rest of the world could go to hell.

He walked into the brightly lit store and nodded at the teenager behind the counter.

"Hi, Mr. Duncan," she said.

"Morning, Luanne. How are things?"

Code for "How is Kathy today?"

"Good. She's good."

He tried to remember when his mother had changed to "Kathy." Because that was how he thought of her now. He had for years. She didn't mind. To her, their relationship was in the past tense, as if it were a story someone had told her. She used to have a son. He didn't know what he was to her now or how she thought of him. She was always happy to see him, but she was happy to see everyone. It wasn't personal.

He heard voices in the back of the store and walked toward them. He would guess that Kathy was interviewing someone to discover if they were worthy of a bird or a kitten. But when he stepped around a large display of cat litter, he saw a tall woman in a familiar uniform. She looked up at him, raised an eyebrow, then returned her attention to Kathy.

"You have a visitor," Dana Birch, Titan-

160

ville deputy, said.

Kathy turned toward him. Her whole face lit up as she smiled broadly. "You came to see me."

She always sounded surprised, as if each visit were a treat.

"Hi, Kathy," he said as he approached. He kissed her cheek, then handed her the coffee. "Just how you like it."

Kathy took the container in both hands and sighed. "He always brings me coffee. Isn't Garth nice?"

Dana eyed him with all the affection one would give a colony of ants at a picnic. "He's just swell." She nodded. "Garth."

"Dana."

She tapped the name tag on her dark blue shirt. "Deputy Birch."

"But we're so close now."

He didn't like that she was here. The need to protect his own made him want to lash out. He held back because this wasn't the time.

While he and Dana had never been officially introduced, he knew who she was. She was more than one of the deputies in town, she was close friends with the Titan sisters. She knew all about his plan to take down the family and was determined to stop him. Objectively he knew that her perseverance and loyalty were a testament to her good character. But if she got in his way, he would crush her just like he planned to crush Jed Titan and his daughters.

"Dana is my friend," Kathy said between sips of her latte.

"Yes, I am," Dana said. "But now that Garth's here, you'll want to talk to him, so I'm going to go. I'll see you in a few days."

Garth touched Kathy's hand. "I'll walk Dana to her car. Be right back."

Kathy nodded happily.

Garth followed Dana out of the pet store.

"How unexpected," she said cheerfully, when the door had closed behind them. "I never thought of you as the gentleman type."

He grabbed her elbow hard enough to bruise and stepped in front of her. "What the hell are you doing?"

She put her hand on his wrist and pressed with two fingers. Pain shot through his arm. "You'll let me go right now or I'll change you from a stallion to a gelding with a single shot and swear on a stack of Bibles that it was an accidental discharge."

Her brown eyes flashed with temper and a promise to follow through. He knew she would happily take him on. Not just because of her position as a deputy but because she was loyal to the Titan sisters. They were her friends and she protected what was hers.

Something they had in common, he thought, noting the shape of her mouth was surprisingly sensual for a woman who wore no makeup and obviously thought acting girly meant being weak.

"You think you can take me?" he asked, releasing her.

She did the same, letting up the pressure on his arm. Whatever nerve she'd irritated continued to tingle. He ignored it.

"I'm more than confident," she told him.

"Confidence is good," he said. "But don't get cocky. I always get what I want."

"All you're going to have in the end is some guy chasing your ass all around your prison cell. You won't like being Bubba's bitch, but you will have earned it."

He chuckled. "Very visual. I'm impressed."

She poked him in the chest. "You don't get it. I *will* take you down. I don't care about money or mind games. All I know is you're hurting people I care about. They're my family, as much as Kathy is yours. I can't wait for the day I get to drag your sorry self to jail. And I'll be the one, Garth. I don't care how many favors I have to call in. I'll be the one."

"I'm counting the minutes," he told her,

meaning the words. Dana was a formidable adversary. He could respect that. And her. Which didn't change his mind about what he was doing.

He thought about warning her away from Kathy, then realized he didn't have to. Dana would never hurt her, never use her to get to him. She had principles and character.

"It wasn't me," he said. "The explosion. It wasn't me."

She rolled her eyes. "Right. And I suppose you're not responsible for everything else that's been happening?"

"I'm not talking about that. Dana, it wasn't me, which means whoever did it is still out there. I don't know who or what he was after. I have some ideas, not that you're interested in them."

She shook her head. "You're right, I'm not. I'm done listening to you and your lies. Say what you want. I'll have you in jail before long."

He wasn't surprised she didn't believe him. But he'd tried. That was as far as he was willing to go.

"You keep promising," he said, mostly to annoy her. "Yet night after night I wait and nothing happens. I'm starting to think you're all talk."

She made a noise that was as much growl

as a threat, then she walked to her marked sedan.

He watched her. She was strong and frustrated and desperate to hurt him, but constrained by the law and the oath she'd taken when she put on the badge. What would she be like when she let loose?

Not that he would ever find out. But it was certainly something to think about.

Nick waited until the vice president of human resources signed the last of the paperwork.

"None of this is going to happen, right?" he asked.

Nick grinned. "We've never had a problem at a retreat. Just making sure we're protected if one of your people breaks the rules."

The HR guy didn't look convinced, but nodded anyway.

Nick pointed to the door. "Aaron will show you to your room."

"Okay. Thanks."

He left the small office Nick used during corporate retreats. It was in back of the meeting rooms, giving him easy access to his clients. Not that he spent a lot of time here. The corporate functions were an unwelcome reality. They provided him with a steady income, and gave him credibility. It meant he could offer his facility to kids who needed it. He could make a difference, try to atone for the past.

He turned off his computer and walked down the hall. He could hear Aaron directing people to their rooms, handing out keys to the cottages and pointing out the posted schedule. He'd gotten lucky when he'd found Aaron and seeing as Aaron wasn't dead, his friend had gotten lucky when he'd been found.

The central gathering area of the big house had a half dozen or so sofas, small tables scattered around, and overstuffed chairs. Aaron had overseen the decorating, picking warm reds and golds for the furniture and a few woven throw rugs for the hardwood floor. It was a comfortable space. There was a large media room in back, with theater-style seating and a movie-size screen. The corporate types used it for presentations during the day and movies at night.

He looked at the mostly male group. They were still in button-down shirts and ties. Corporate types, he thought, remembering how he'd been one of them. Briefly. It had ended in disaster, with him and Garth held prisoner in the South American jungle.

"I have T-shirts," Izzy said, walking into

the room with a stack of folded shirts in her arms. "I don't know what it is with you guys and your matching outfits. If you don't like them, don't complain to me."

She wore a tank top tucked into a short skirt. Her hair was a wild mass of curls, her smile easy and welcoming. The men swarmed around her. Nick couldn't blame them. She was a walking, breathing male fantasy. Well, not for Aaron, but for anybody else.

He didn't like the way they crowded her, but he didn't intervene. Izzy could handle herself and it wasn't his business. She was there for a specific purpose and him getting laid wasn't it.

Of course he wanted her. It wasn't just how she made him feel when they kissed, although that had been hot and arousing and made him burn to take her every way he knew how. It was more than that. It was her laugh, her voice and her strength. It was how she pushed back and didn't play games. It was everything about her.

Which meant he couldn't get involved. He wasn't allowed — not just because he had a responsibility to get her ready for her surgery, but because of what had happened before. Because of what he'd done and who he was. If she knew . . .

Aaron rushed up to him and grabbed his arm. "Did you see him?"

"See who?"

"That really cute guy. Over by the staircase."

Nick turned to look.

"Don't stare!" Aaron hissed. "Don't be obvious. He's gorgeous. If we could have babies together. He's being very friendly, but I'm not sure. Do you think he likes me? Could you ask him? Isn't he adorable?"

Nick pulled free of Aaron's grasp. "I'm not the one you should be talking to. Go talk to Izzy."

"I would because she's much better at the bondy thing than you are, but she can't see him. So how can we talk about how cute he is?"

"She'll figure it out. Seriously? She's a much better choice."

Aaron sighed. "Fine. Be that way. But I'll remember this and when you're in a world of hurt about something I'm just going to laugh at you."

"No, you won't."

"No, I won't because I'm a better person than you. Oh, he's looking. That's good, right? It's been so long since I had a boyfriend. What if he's the one? Wouldn't that be fabulous? Aren't you excited?"

"I can barely speak for the thrill of it," Nick said dryly.

Aaron slapped his arm. "You're not getting into the spirit of this."

"I'm doing my best."

"Then you need to work on your people skills."

"I'm having a little trouble finding my table," a low, male voice said. "Can you help me?"

Izzy turned toward the man. She couldn't see him very well, but she could tell he was only a few inches taller than her and she thought he might have blond hair. The light was bright, but it was hard to be sure.

Under normal circumstances, she would have been in her element. The corporate types were mostly guys and several of them were very into her. It was flattering and kind of funny, she thought. So far no one had figured out she was blind. She wanted to see how long it took them to notice.

"What's your table number?" she asked, staring directly at his face so he wouldn't hand her the paper with the information.

"Eight."

Aaron had explained the seating chart so she knew the layout of the dining room.

"Third row, far right," she said, pointing

in the general direction. "There's a sign on each table with the number."

"Want to show me personally?" he asked, putting his hand on the small of her back.

She sidestepped him easily. "I think you can find it all on your own."

"I'm Jeff," he said.

"Izzy."

"A beautiful name for a beautiful woman."

"Oh, please. Is that the best you can come up with?" Aaron joined them. "Straight guys have the worst pickup lines. Now leave Izzy alone and go get your dinner. Go on. Shoo."

The guy left.

Izzy grinned. "You crushed him."

"He deserved it. Tell me you weren't falling for that horrible line."

"I wasn't, but it's nice to be flattered."

"I'm sure it is. Now, I have important news. I've met someone. His name is Steve, he's single and too cute for words. We're meeting for a drink in the main house's living room after dinner, so when you're done here, go straight to your room. I don't want you lurking and spoiling the mood."

She laughed. "Aaron, you've got to stop being shy. If you want to tell me something, then just say it. Don't hide behind polite euphemisms."

"Am I being too blunt? I'm sorry. You

know how I adore you, but it's been a long time between boys. This is different. At least I hope it is. I think I really like him."

"Then you should go for it. I will go directly to my room. I promise. And in the morning, you can tell me everything."

"Believe me, I will. Oh, Norma needs you to open the wine."

An easy task, Izzy thought. One she could do completely by touch. "Sure. Point me in the right direction."

He turned her to the left. "There's a table against the wall. Wine bottles on the right, corkscrew on the left. We have red and white. The red is a saucy merlot with a yummy finish and the white is crisp and dry. The buffet has opened so they'll all rush to the food. The servers will deliver the wine to the table. Oooh, Steve's smiling at me. I'm all quivery. See you later."

"Young love," Izzy murmured as she made her way to the table.

The bottles were set up as Aaron had described. She carefully used the foil cutter, then went to work removing corks.

"Hi."

She pulled out a cork, then turned toward the guy standing next to her. "Hi."

"I'm Byron."

"Izzy."

"This is a great place. You must really like working here."

It was a better line than "beautiful name for a beautiful woman," she thought with a smile.

"Yes, it is."

"Can I have a bottle of red, please?"

"The servers will bring bottles to the table."

"I know, but if I waited for that, I wouldn't get to talk to you."

She laughed. "Don't you have girls back where you live?"

"Plenty, but there's something about you."

She handed him a bottle. "Here."

"Thanks. Would you — Oh. This is white." He handed it back to her.

She passed him another one. "Sorry. I had a fifty-fifty chance of getting it right."

"Why wouldn't you know the difference? Are you color-blind?"

"No. Just regular blind."

The guy was silent.

"It's okay," she added, not sure why it was her job to make him feel better. She was the one who couldn't see. "Go back to your table, Byron."

"Right. Yeah. I, ah . . . See ya."

Izzy watched him walk away. She paused to see if she would be upset by his dismissal, then realized she didn't care. If he couldn't handle her lack of vision, then that was his problem.

The realization was kind of freeing, she thought happily. Which was strange, but true.

A few minutes later a couple of guys came up to the table.

"Hi," one said loudly.

So word had spread, she thought, turning to them.

"Blind, not deaf," she said.

"Oh, right. Sorry. So you're Izzy?" As he spoke he raised his hand in front of her face.

She grabbed his arm. "Partially blind," she said. "Not totally. Don't be a jerk."

"He can't help it. He's also really ugly," the other guy said. "I'm much better-looking."

She leaned against the table and glanced between them. "Why should I take your word on that?"

"I'm telling the truth. Ask anyone."

They were flirting, she thought, not the least bit interested, but pleased that she felt comfortable in the situation. To think of all the time she'd wasted hiding out in Lexi's guest room.

Someone else approached. Someone she recognized immediately.

"Is there a problem?" Nick asked.

She saw the other guys take a step back.

"No," the first one said. "Not at all."

Nick ignored him. "Izzy?"

"I'm fine, but these two seem like they need help finding their seats."

"I'll take care of that."

She wasn't exactly sure what he did but suddenly she was alone at the table.

Aaron sidled up. "That was very macho."

"I know. Impressive."

"I'm sure it was. Now let's dish. Steve is the director of finance. That's good, right? I mean he's successful?"

"You're not just in it for his pretty face?" she teased.

"That, too. I'm so excited. I hope this works out. I'm ready for a real relationship. Oh, and you should head up to the house. The guys are really putting away the wine. They're going to get rowdy pretty soon and you don't want to be here when that happens."

"Are you worried about me? That's so sweet."

"I know. I'm an incredible human being. Be sure to tell Steve if he asks."

"I will," she promised. "Have fun tonight."

"It's what I do best."

■ ■ ■ ■

Izzy took a long bath. As she soaked in the large tub, she listened to music and hummed along with the songs.

This was good, she thought. She was adjusting. Happy, even, which she wouldn't have thought was possible just a couple of weeks ago.

She got out of the tub and used her favorite scented lotion, then pulled on bikini panties and an oversize Dallas Cowboys T-shirt to sleep in. She'd just walked into the bedroom when the door to the hall opened.

Her first thought was that Nick had finally come calling. Anticipation flooded her body, making her thighs a little shaky.

"Don't you knock?" she asked, smiling as she spoke. Then she turned and caught sight of the man standing just inside her room.

It wasn't Nick. The shape was all wrong, as was the way he moved. She figured it had to be one of the guys from the retreat, but didn't know which one.

Irritation replaced eagerness.

"You have the wrong room," she snapped. "Turn around and go back where you belong."

"Hey, baby." The man's voice slurred slightly. "I thought I'd come say good-night personally. You're with the staff, right? This is a full-service kind of place." He moved toward her. "And in the morning, you won't even know it was me."

"Jackass," she muttered, moving away from him. "I'll break your nose. That will make you easy to identify."

She wasn't afraid. Not really. She was more annoyed than anything else. He was drunk. Guys did stupid things when they were drunk.

He reached for her. She sidestepped him, but bumped into the dresser. For a second she was off balance and he grabbed her arm.

She yelped as she kicked out at him. Her bare foot caught the chair instead of the man. It hurt a lot, but she kicked again and this time landed a direct hit on his thigh.

He swore and grabbed her hair. "Bitch."

"Tell me about it," she said, letting him pull her against him.

When she was close enough to do serious damage, she jabbed him with her elbow, using as much force as she could. He grunted and released her. She jabbed again and spun to face him. Then she was grabbed from behind and lifted out of the way. Someone else joined the fight.

Izzy stood on the far side of her bed, trying to catch her breath, watching Nick pummel her attacker. She couldn't tell exactly what was happening. There were a few thuds, several groans, then silence as a body hit the floor.

She rubbed her arm where the guy had bruised her.

"I'm really hoping you won," she said.

Nick moved to her side. "I did. You okay?"

She stared into his face and wished she could see his eyes.

"Fine."

He brushed her shoulders, then down her arms. He paused on her left one. She thought he might be examining the growing bruise. He swore.

"Anything else?"

"No."

"You sure?"

"Yes. He didn't have time."

Nick turned away. There was another thud followed by a crunching sound.

"What did you do?" she asked anxiously.

"Broke his nose."

"I threatened to do that."

"Good. I hope he thinks you did."

She stared at the shape on the floor. The fear for herself was gone. "Are you going to get in trouble for that? You can't go around beating up people."

"I can when they walk into your room and attack you. Besides, they all sign a release. Short of hanging them, I can do whatever I want."

He cupped her face in his hands. His fingers were warm and strong as he stroked her skin.

"I'm sorry," he told her. "I'll make sure all the doors are locked. No one else will get in."

"I know. It's okay."

"It's not. You're in my house. You're my responsibility."

She cared a whole lot less about that than the feel of his skin against hers.

"What are you going to do to him?" she asked, trying to distract herself.

"Dump him in the barn and let him sleep it off. I'll take all his clothes. He'll wake up feeling like shit and naked. That should teach him."

"I don't think you should be too hard on him. I mean, hey, it was me. I'm fairly irresistible."

He chuckled. "The Izzy defense?"

"It works in a court of law."

"Because you're a wild temptress?"

"Think you can resist me?"

"I'm doing my best."

"Maybe you should stop working at it. Sometimes giving in is a good thing."

The fingers stroking her skin stilled. "Izzy . . ."

"You talk too much," she whispered, then raised herself up on tiptoe and pressed her mouth to his.

He kissed her lightly, then stepped back.

"You should have the surgery."

The unexpected statement stunned her. "What?"

"You heard me. Have the surgery. You're ready. What's stopping you?"

She was offering him sex and he wanted to tell her to go ahead with an operation that could leave her totally blind?

She didn't know which made her more mad — his dismissal of her invitation or his butting into her personal business.

"Get out," she said. "Get out and take the jerk with you."

"Why are you mad? It's time. You know it's time."

"Get out!"

He grabbed the body and dragged it out into the hall. She slammed the door behind him and threw herself on the bed.

"Jerk," she muttered, not sure which of the two men she meant.

■ ■ ■ ■

The next morning Izzy debated not helping with the retreat. She was supposed to demonstrate the rope bridge, but wasn't sure Nick deserved that. Let him deal with the corporate clients on his own.

But instead of staying in bed, she found herself showering, then dressing. While the thought of letting Nick down helped her battered ego, she still liked Aaron. And she was intrigued by the thought of the rope bridge. She would just ignore Nick.

Aaron was waiting for her downstairs. "He's thirty-three and came out ten years ago after a disastrous six-month marriage to a woman. Why do they even bother to try? Anyway, he works in finance. He likes the same movies as me, we both love to cook and he's totally yummy."

She followed him outside to the Jeep they would take to the event area.

"Good kisser?" she asked, thinking Nick was an amazing kisser. Wait. No. He wasn't. She was mad at him and wanted nothing to do with him.

"Excellent." He drew out the word to seven or eight syllables. "I really like him. I don't want to get too excited, though. That road always leads to heartache. I just . . ." He started the Jeep. "I really like him."

She smiled. "Then you should enjoy yourself."

"But? Aren't you going to warn me to be careful? To not trust too easily? To avoid handing over my bank account numbers or house keys until I'm sure?"

She turned toward him. "It sounds like you already know everything you should be doing. I'm the girl who just goes for it, consequences be damned."

"Does that work for you?"

"It did until the explosion."

Which was the wrong thing to say. Now she was thinking about the surgery again — surgery she didn't want to have. Being in the dark forever. Could she do that? The thought of it terrified her.

Aaron patted her hand. "You're a brave little soldier."

"Not really." A brave little soldier would have scheduled the surgery.

Fortunately, they'd arrived at the site before she could depress herself.

She climbed out of the Jeep and sensed someone at her side.

"Nick," she said calmly.

"I didn't think you'd show."

"Why wouldn't she show?" Aaron asked.

"What happened? Are you two keeping secrets? Did you fight?"

"Some guy got into my room last night," she said, telling only part of the truth. "He was drunk. Nick took care of him."

"Who was it?" Aaron demanded. "What bastard did that? Can you hold him so I can hit him? Or get someone bigger than me to hit him?"

"I broke his nose," Nick told him.

"That's not the part that should be broken," Aaron muttered. "Are you okay?"

Izzy assumed Aaron was talking to her. "I'm fine. He was a jerk and I suspect he's learned a lesson."

There was a long silence. She didn't know if Aaron and Nick were exchanging looks or secret codes and she didn't care.

"Where's the bridge?" she asked. "I'm ready to intimidate the hell out of these guys."

Nick put his hand on the small of her back. "Straight ahead, toward that big tree."

She saw vague shapes and started walking, doing her best to ignore the feel of his palm and the heat from his skin. She was still annoyed with him and wouldn't give him the satisfaction of responding.

Someone stepped in front of her.

"Hey, Izzy," the man said. "I'm Jeff. We

met last night. I heard about what happened and wanted to tell you I'm sorry. We all are. We're not like that."

"One of you is."

"You're right. When he gets out of the hospital, he'll be fired. I know it's not much, but it's the best we can do."

"Hospital?" she asked, feigning surprise. "For what?"

Jeff chuckled. "He fell or something. Broke his nose. Woke up naked in the barn."

"Oh. How horrible. I hope he's okay."

"I don't know and I don't care. I just wanted you to know we're all sorry."

"Thanks."

He stepped out of her way. She continued walking.

"He was nice," she said. "I wonder if he's single. We could go out. Get married. Have a couple of kids."

Nick didn't say anything. Izzy glanced back at him.

"No comment?"

"I hope you'll be very happy together."

The wrong thing to say, she thought, annoyed all over again.

They stopped in front of a tall tree.

"Rope ladder up about twenty feet," Nick said as he helped her step into a harness. "The rope bridge swings a little. If you feel yourself starting to lose your balance, drop into a crouch. Lower your center of gravity. Ethan, a mountain-climbing buddy of mine, is in the other tree. He'll talk you in."

"Is he cute?"

"Adorable." Nick seemed to be speaking between clenched teeth. "Maybe you could take them both on at once."

"Because *you're* not interested."

"Dammit, Izzy, would you just climb the tree?"

She wanted to tell him no. She wanted to stalk away. But there were a group of guys watching her. They all knew what had happened the night before and it was up to her to show them what strength of character meant. It was up to her to demonstrate what a girl could do and challenge them to be men enough to follow.

She started up the tree. The rope ladder made it easy and she climbed until Nick yelled at her that she was there. Then she felt her way onto the rope ladder.

"Who's next?" she yelled down.

No one answered.

She laughed. "Come on, guys. This is team building at its best. Face death with the person in the next cubicle. Are you really prepared to be shown up by a girl?"

"I'll go," someone muttered. "It can't be

that hard."

"Hey, Izzy."

The voice came from in front of her. "You must be Ethan."

"I am. Come on. I'll talk you in. It's about twenty feet. The bridge sways the most in the middle. Keep a steady pace."

She couldn't really make out the details of the rope bridge, but she did have a sense of the ground being way down below.

"Is there a net?" she asked.

"Yes."

"That's no fun."

Ethan laughed. "If we kill them, they tend not to rebook."

"Oh. Good point."

She stepped out onto the rope bridge. She had to feel for the thick bands and place her foot there. It was slow work, but she moved fairly quickly. Before she expected it, Ethan was telling her she was only a couple of feet from him. Then strong hands pulled her onto a platform.

"Like a pro," he said. "Good job. Are you really blind?"

"Enough that they won't let me drive."

"Impressive."

"Thanks," she said, heading down and wondering why Nick couldn't be more like him. Supportive and complimentary. But, no. Nick was only interested in pushing too hard.

Once she reached the ground, Aaron took her back to the barn. She climbed out of the Jeep and headed toward the entrance while Aaron drove back to the retreat. She'd barely stepped into the shadows of the doorway, when she heard a familiar voice say, "Hello, Izzy."

CHAPTER NINE

Izzy took a step back, so she was in daylight. It seemed safer. "Dad."

Jed Titan stood up from the bench by the door. "How are you doing?"

"Fine."

"Still blind?"

She shook her head. "I suppose the real miracle of this is you asked how I was first. No. I haven't had the surgery."

"What are you waiting for?" he demanded. "You're no good to me as you are. You're nothing but a liability. At least if you could see, you'd be worth something."

"I'm sorry to hear my stock is down," she said, determined not to let him upset her. She would see the ridiculousness of the situation, nothing more. She wouldn't think about how he hadn't bothered to visit her in the hospital. That she was nothing to him but a possible means to an end. She wasn't anyone he cared about. Certainly not a daughter he had ever loved.

"Are you getting the surgery or not?" he asked, sounding annoyed. "If you don't, you're an idiot. At least if you can see, you can marry well. You weren't ever going to inherit the family business, but you could have done something."

The words weren't a surprise, but they still hurt. Her mother hadn't left her anything, either. Apparently she was quite the disappointing child.

"You're only interested in what I can do for you," she said.

"What you *could* have done for me. You're stubborn and difficult and now you're blind. What a waste. That's all you are. A waste."

"Then you shouldn't be standing here, talking to me," she told him. "Get out, Jed. I don't have time for this."

"Right. Too busy learning Braille. All three of my daughters are a disaster. Don't bother moving back to Glory's Gate. You're not welcome there."

Glory's Gate had been the Titan family home for generations. Izzy had grown up there with her sisters. She hadn't been back since Skye had moved out after Jed had threatened to have her declared an unfit mother and lock her away. Izzy had no plans to go back now.

But knowing it was no longer her choice bothered her more than she wanted to admit. Rather than listen to any more of Jed's vicious words, she retreated into the barn, thinking that for the first time since she'd arrived at Nick's ranch, the shadowy space felt like a sanctuary.

Jed didn't follow her. She hoped he left, but refused to find out. Instead she led Jackson out of his stall and quickly saddled him. Then she walked him outside, swung onto his back and let him pick his way.

She didn't know where they were going and she didn't care. As long as it was away from here. Away from her father and Nick and the jackass who'd attacked her the previous night. Men were becoming a serious problem in her life.

Jackson rode toward the sun. He started to run. She could feel the heat on her face and the rush of the wind. Riding felt good. She wouldn't think about anything or worry. She just hung on for the ride.

When he finally slowed, she brushed her face with her hand and refused to admit the moisture there came from tears. She didn't cry. She was stronger than that. Stronger than anyone knew.

But not strong enough to risk the surgery. The truth hung on her shoulders, heavy, like a thick, damp cape. She wanted to be different, wanted to face the darkness bravely, but she couldn't.

She turned Jackson back the way they'd come. "Time to go home, boy," she told him.

A few minutes later, she heard the sound of hoof beats racing toward her. She reined in Jackson and waited until the rider approached.

"What the hell do you think you're doing?" Nick demanded. "You took off without telling anyone where you were going."

"I didn't know where I was going," she snapped, too exhausted by one emotional upheaval after another to deal with Nick and his tantrums. "I can't see, remember? I just went for a ride and now I'm coming back. What's your problem?"

"What's yours? You just admitted you can't see, but you took off on a ride by yourself?"

Oh. Good point. "I was upset," she admitted. "I needed to get away and think."

"Can't you go sulk in your room like everyone else?"

"I'm not sulking. There are things in my life I have to deal with."

"You could have been thrown. It might have taken days to find you. Resources would have been wasted because you needed to think."

She ignored him and urged Jackson forward. "Because that's all that matters," she muttered. "Resources. How you'd be put out. Tell you what. Next time I go riding, don't bother coming to look for me. I wouldn't want you wasting your time."

"I'm not going to leave you out here to die."

"Why not? I'm not good for anything. I'm useless. Taking up space, right?"

Jackson came to a sudden halt. Izzy wasn't sure why, but she had a feeling that Nick had grabbed his bridle.

"What happened?"

His tone was soft, curious. The anger was gone.

"Nothing. Let me go."

Jackson began to move again. Nick moved next to her.

"What happened?" he asked again.

"My father came to see me."

"And?"

She sighed. "What do you know about Jed Titan?"

"He's a successful businessman with a reputation for being ruthless."

"That's a good start. He's determined, egotistical and only interested in how the

191

world serves him. And that's on a good day."

"So he didn't stop by to see how you're doing?"

"No. He came by to see if I was still blind. Because if I am, I'm no good to him. I can't even marry well. Not that he was going to leave me any of his considerable fortune."

"I'm sorry."

"I'm not. I never wanted the money. None of us did. We wanted a father. Pretty dumb, huh?"

Nick didn't say anything. Izzy drew in a breath.

"You've met my sisters. Lexi is the oldest. She's a brilliant businesswoman. After college, she went to work for Jed, where she was pretty successful. But she quickly realized she would never have her own identity at his company, so she left and started her own day spa. Skye went to finishing school, if you can believe it. When she came home, she married the man Jed picked for her, had a perfect daughter, then used her inheritance to start a foundation that feeds hungry children."

"Good for her."

"Yeah. Good for her. I, on the other hand, barely graduated from high school. I've held a series of jobs that require minimal skill. The only thing they had in common was that they were dangerous. I knew I wasn't the son my father wanted. Maybe going fast or higher is my way of getting his attention. Not that it ever worked. I guess I hoped I would be enough for him."

But she wasn't. She never had been. Lexi and Skye weren't enough either, but somehow knowing that didn't help.

"I was nine when my mother died. Prudence Lightly."

"The actress?"

"That's her. She left everything to Skye. I wasn't mentioned in her will. And I'll never know if she did that on purpose or if she just never got around to making the change. It's not like I was six months old and she was busy, right? I mean eight-plus years is a long time."

"Izzy, there could be a lot of reasons she didn't change the will."

"List five that don't include me not registering on her radar."

"Is that what you think?"

She stared at the blurry horizon. "What would you think?"

"I don't remember my mother. She dumped me in foster care when I was four."

She turned to him. "I'm sorry."

"Don't be. I got over it."

Had he? Did any child get over being

rejected?

"What happened?" she asked.

"I grew up. I got lucky. I was in my first home nearly five years, so I had some stability. Joan, my foster mother, realized I was pretty smart and encouraged me in school. I skipped a couple of grades. Then she got sick and I was moved somewhere else."

Losing his family all over again, she thought sadly. It put her pain in perspective.

"After that I moved around a lot," Nick said. "It's never easy being the smartest kid in the class. I buried myself in books, graduated at fifteen and got a full ride to Texas A&M."

"At fifteen?"

"I was nearly sixteen by then."

"Still."

"It was better than foster care. I became an emancipated minor, so I was out of the system."

Easy words, she thought. But a much harder life. Was his past the reason he kept everyone else at a distance? Was it the reason no one got close enough to touch any part of him? Or was she just looking for a way to mitigate the fact that he didn't want to sleep with her?

"What happened after college?" she asked.

"I went to work for an oil exploration company a friend of mine owned."

"So you raped and pillaged our natural environment?" she asked, teasing.

"I did my best not to. I had some ideas about drilling that were different. We tried them out."

He paused for a long time. There was something about his voice, she thought, not sure what it was. Staring at his face didn't help, either. She couldn't really see any details.

"How did you get from oil exploration to here?"

"By car, mostly."

"Very funny. You know what I mean."

"I had some second thoughts about my career choice."

She remembered Aaron telling her that Nick had a mysterious past. "Someone told me you traveled the world or something."

"For a while."

"What were you looking for?"

"Peace."

"Did you find it?"

"No."

"Before the explosion I would have told you I'd found what I was looking for," she said.

"You would have been lying."

"What? That's not true."

"You chase the thrill for a reason. What are you hiding from?"

"Nothing I'm going to discuss with you. Besides, I'm not hiding."

"Look at what you do with your life. Your extreme sports. What you do for a living."

"I was a welder. That's not dangerous."

"An underwater welder."

"Okay, sure, but it's not all that different. And it's not like I drowned. The explosion wasn't my fault. I'll admit it's not a completely normal job, but it's not totally crazy, either. As to the explosion . . ." She hesitated, not sure what to say. "I think it was deliberate."

"What are you talking about? Someone trying to get the oil company?"

"Not exactly." She drew in a breath. "It seems that Jed had an affair before he married Lexi's mom. He had a child — a boy — with the woman. While he set her up with a lot of money, he wouldn't marry her. It's an old story. Flash forward thirty-plus years, the boy in question grows up and he's pissed. Something happened to his mother. She had an accident or got sick. We don't know, but she's no longer completely normal. She's sweet and lovely, but different. My sisters and I wonder if Jed's responsible for that. We're not sure. So maybe it's that, maybe he was just born mad, but our half brother, Garth Duncan, is doing his best to ruin the entire family."

Nick didn't say anything. She couldn't tell what he was thinking.

She frowned. "Is this boring?"

"No. Sorry. I was listening. What do you mean he's trying to ruin the family?"

"You name it, he's done it. He tried to take Lexi's business, legally, but it was pretty ruthless. We think he's responsible for doping Jed's race horses, for sending a false tip to the district attorney that Skye's foundation was a front for money laundering. He also planted a software program into the books at Skye's foundation making it look like executives were paid bonuses and that Skye was taking money. It's nasty stuff. Skye doesn't even take a salary. So money that could have gone to feeding hungry kids had to go to legal counsel. He's planted illegal arms in some of Jed's international shipments, so now Jed's being investigated for treason, and we're guessing he's behind the rumors of mad cow on the Titan ranches. I have to say, Garth isn't my favorite person."

"That's a long list."

"He's a pretty bad guy. There's been

more. He's come after everyone in the family, except for my niece and she's only eight. Hopefully he isn't going to do anything bad to a little girl. Two months ago I would have been a lot more sure, but then there was the explosion on the rig. And here I thought I didn't have anything to lose."

Nick heard the words and didn't want to believe them. Not Garth. Garth was his friend. He'd said he was playing a game, that he wasn't out to get anyone but Jed. He was just using the sisters to get their father's attention. But what Izzy described was completely different. A dangerous vendetta that might have killed her.

Nick had met the Titan sisters. Lexi was pregnant. What was Garth going to do to her? Skye had a daughter. Who else was at risk? He swore silently. Had Garth really been responsible for the explosion that had nearly blinded Izzy? That could have killed her and anyone else on the rig at the time.

He wanted to say no. He wanted to say "not his friend." Garth had always been one of the good guys. Like family. But how could he be sure nothing had changed? He and Garth had faced death together, but years had passed since then. Years of Garth channeling his anger, apparently toward the annihilation of the Titan family — innocent bystanders be damned.

"We know he has a plan," Izzy was saying. "But we don't know what it is. It started earlier this year." She shook her head. "I can't believe it was only a few months ago. This started in spring, it's now late summer. By Christmas he could crush us all."

"You don't mean that," he said sharply. "You're not the type to be beaten."

"I know. I'm being dramatic. We'll be fine. It's just we don't have a good counterattack. Jed won't talk to us about any of it. He's doing his own thing. Sometimes it seems as if he's almost proud of Garth. Like father, like son." She sounded bitter. "So my sisters and I are on our own. Well, Cruz and Mitch help. Cruz is Lexi's fiancé and Mitch is Skye's."

Jed wasn't helping his daughters? Nick told himself not to be surprised. Based on the little he knew about Jed Titan, he only cared about himself. Everyone else simply got in the way.

"I never thought he'd come after me," she said softly, looking sad. "When Lexi, Skye and I met to talk about Garth, I didn't ever worry about myself. They thought I was safe, too. I guess we were mistaken."

Anger burned inside him. Izzy had worked too hard to recover from what had happened to her to slide back now. He had to find out what was really going on. He had to know the truth.

But first he had to get Izzy back to the ranch.

He urged his horse to go faster. Jackson kept up easily and Izzy didn't seem to notice the increased speed. As soon as he could see the barn, he turned to her.

"I have a meeting in town," he said. "You going to be okay?"

"I'm more than capable. I have to get the horses ready for the guys who want to go riding, anyway."

"Okay. See you later."

He raced to the barn and handed his mount over to Rita, then got in his SUV and headed for Dallas. During the drive, he debated phoning Garth, then decided he didn't want to talk to his friend. Not until he could see his face.

What was the truth? he wondered. Which Garth was the man in charge? The friend who had kept him alive during their captivity? The friend who never blamed him for what had happened? Or the ruthless stranger who might have caused Izzy's death?

He drove faster than he should have and made it to Garth's high-rise building in less than two hours. The doorman knew him and let him in.

"Evening, Nick," he said with a smile as Nick crossed to the elevators that would take him to Garth's penthouse condo.

"Evening, George. How's it going?"

"Better now that football season is about to start. I think the Cowboys will go all the way this year."

"I hope you're right."

The elevator arrived. "Have a good night," he called before the doors closed.

The ride up seemed to take forever. Nick knew that George would have phoned ahead to let Garth know he had company so Nick wasn't surprised when he saw the front door standing open. He stepped inside and pushed it shut behind him.

"I just got home," Garth called from the kitchen. "I picked up takeout from the Chinese place. There's plenty. Want some?"

Nick ignored the question and stalked into the kitchen. "You said it wasn't about the sisters. You said you only wanted to get Jed Titan. You implied they wouldn't be hurt and you lied. You lied to me, Garth. What the hell is going on?"

Garth turned and the overhead light cast shadows on his face. His eyes were unreadable, his mouth a thin line.

"What are you talking about?" he asked, sounding unconcerned.

"You went after all of them. Lexi and her spa. Skye and her foundation. Now Izzy."

"I never touched Izzy. She doesn't have a business I can fuck with. Which is kind of a shame, I admit."

"You blew up the oil rig. You could have killed her and everyone else there."

Garth walked out of the kitchen. Nick followed him into the large living room with its floor-to-ceiling windows. Garth crossed to a cabinet on the wall and pulled out a bottle of scotch. He poured a generous serving into two glasses and picked up one.

"I didn't have anything to do with the explosion on the rig," he told Nick, then took a sip. "I'm interested in taking down the Titans — all of them. But not by putting anyone's life at risk. Yes, I did my best to trip up Lexi and I might have set the D.A. and the press on Skye and her foundation. I took advantage where I could. I've used people — exploiting their weaknesses. Especially Jed's. But blowing up an oil rig? Not my style."

"Why should I believe you?" Nick demanded, still furious.

"To me the more interesting question is why should you care, but we won't go there.

You should believe me because you know me. You've always known me. Come on, Nick. We're family. I didn't blow up the oil rig. I had nothing to do with it. But, according to my sources, it was deliberate, which means someone else is involved. Maybe to set me up. Either way, I'm going to find out who's responsible."

Nick didn't know what to think. He'd never been in a position not to believe his friend before.

"What's your end game?" he asked at last. "How much destruction will make you happy?"

"I haven't decided."

Another lie, Nick thought grimly. Because Garth always had a plan. So was his friend using him? Or had Nick simply been caught in the cross fire?

"You lied to me," Nick said.

"I didn't tell you everything. There's a difference."

Semantics. Misrepresentation. Lies. They were the same. "You used me."

"I asked you to look after Izzy. Aren't you helping her? Isn't she getting better?"

"Yes, but that's not why you asked me to do it."

"Does it matter why, if she gets better in the end?"

The expected answer was yes. Did the road matter if Izzy got where she needed to go? If she had the surgery and got on with her life, wasn't that enough?

He didn't want this to be Garth. He didn't want to have to doubt his friend. He didn't want to have the questions. But they had been planted and taken root. Now he didn't know how to make them go away.

"It's been a lot of years," Garth said, holding out the second glass of scotch. "We've been through more than most. I trust you with my life and I'd like to think you'd say the same about me. Don't let this come between us."

Nick ignored the glass. "I'm not the one who made the decision to put our friendship on the line."

Garth returned the glass to the cabinet. His expression was still unreadable, but tension crackled in the air.

"You're either with me or against me," Garth told him.

Nick smiled. "What a cliché." His smile faded. "Don't make me choose. You may not like the outcome."

"You'd pick a woman you barely know over me? Over all we've been through? Have you forgotten I'm the one who helped you survive college? I'm the one who taught you how to get the girl?"

It was true, Nick thought, sad that he and Garth had to have this conversation at all. His friend had saved him countless times. Nick had been a geeky, innocent kid. He'd been picked on unmercifully until Garth had stepped in to protect him. Nick might have all the smarts, but Garth knew about getting along in the world.

Later Nick had tried to repay him by figuring out how to exploit one of the largest untapped oil reserves in South America. An expedition that had nearly killed them both. To this day, the majority of Nick's wealth was tied up in Garth's collection of companies.

"I haven't forgotten anything," Nick told him. "This isn't about choosing you over her. It's about what you're doing and what that says about you as a person. When did you change?"

Garth's lip curled. "Maybe it was when I rotted in a South American prison, getting tortured day after day."

Nick knew he deserved that. "Blame me if you need to. Just know that I'm not someone you want as an enemy."

"You don't scare me," Garth told him.

Nick walked toward the front door, before pausing. "Then I guess you don't know me any better than I know you."

The ranch was quiet after the corporate types left. Izzy was still busy, working in the stable, but she hadn't realized how isolated she'd become until everyone was gone. She didn't go anywhere, talk to anyone other than Nick, Aaron, Norma or Rita. Occasionally her sisters called, but they were busy and didn't have time to chat very long.

Maybe she should speak to Nick about going somewhere. The problem was she didn't have a destination.

She couldn't drive, there wasn't bus service, even if she could figure out how to use it. The ranch was isolated — she didn't even know the neighbors, so a drop-in visit wasn't going to happen. What on earth was she going to do with the rest of her life?

Unable to answer the question, she went into the house after dinner and made her way upstairs to Aaron's room. He was busy getting ready for his date with Steve, but she wanted to talk to someone and for the past couple of days Nick had kept to himself. Every time she was around him, she had the feeling she'd done something wrong. But she couldn't figure out what.

Sighing heavily, she walked down the hallway and knocked on Aaron's door.

"It's me," she called.

"Come in. I'm nearly ready. You can tell me how fabulous I look."

Izzy laughed as she pushed open the door. "Hardly. I can't see anything. You know that." She stepped into the room. "But I am confident you are beyond fabulous."

"But you don't know for sure, do you?" Aaron snapped. "We both know it's time for you to get the surgery so you can get on with your life. Have a little courage, Izzy. It's so exhausting having to deal with your world of self-pity."

CHAPTER TEN

Aaron's words were an actual slap. Izzy felt the heat on her cheek, as if he'd hit her. She stood frozen for a moment as they echoed inside her, then she turned and ran.

She took the stairs two at a time, then paused at the bottom, not sure where to go or what to do. Tears — hateful, weak tears — filled her eyes. They made it even harder to see in the dim light of a few lamps. She wanted to scream that this wasn't her fault, that she was doing the best she could. But she didn't. Wouldn't that simply be more self-pity?

Every part of her hurt. Shame made her skin burn. She'd been so happy. She thought she was fitting in. Had it all been a joke to everyone else? Had Nick mocked her feeble attempts to seduce him? Had those really been pity kisses?

She covered her face with her hands, then dropped them back to her sides when she heard footsteps upstairs. She didn't want to run into Aaron, she thought grimly. She raced toward the front door and stepped out into the night.

It might be early September, but it was still warm after dark. Humidity hung in the air, a wet blanket of moisture. Crickets called to each other. Other bugs chatted and sang. This was their time. Still, Izzy felt cold and she hugged herself as she eased toward the benches she knew lined the porch.

The darkness seemed a good place to hide, she thought as she sank down and pulled her knees to her chest. Aaron would go out through the rear of the house. She didn't have to worry about running into him here. She could gather her strength and figure out what she was going to say the next time they crossed paths.

He hadn't tried to be mean, she told herself. Not really. He was just being Aaron. He'd been good to her and he was very much a friend. But with affection and connection came the ability to wound.

She heard footsteps and turned toward the sound. It was dark, so she couldn't see anything, couldn't find a way to escape.

"Izzy?"

Relief allowed her to breathe again. "Nick."

"What are you doing out here?" he asked.

"Hiding," she admitted. "Aaron and I had a fight."

"How is that possible? He loves you."

"He thinks I should get the surgery so I can tell him how great he looks."

"It's as good a reason as any."

She dropped her feet to the floor. "Very funny. Look, this is my body and my decision. You both need to lay off about the surgery. It's not for you to say."

"I'll agree, but only for tonight."

"Great. I'll take what I can get. Where have you been for the past couple of days?"

"Here."

"Okay, yes. You've physically been on the ranch, but you've been hiding out. What's going on?"

"Nothing I want to talk about. Want to go for a run?"

"What? Now? It's dark."

"It's barely dark and there's a full moon coming up. Come for a run with me. You'll be exhausted and you'll sleep better."

"I don't have any trouble sleeping," she grumbled, but she stood as she spoke and followed him down the two stairs to the front of the house. "Where are we going?"

"To the main road and back. It's barely three miles. You up to it?"

"I have no idea. I've never been much of a runner."

"I'll go easy on you."

"Like I'll believe that."

She didn't like that it was dark. There might be a moon but it wasn't like the sun as far as illuminating the world around her. Everything was blurry and menacing. But then she remembered Rita's words about taking life one scary dark place at a time and moved next to Nick.

He jogged silently at first, setting a pace that challenged her without being impossible. They were in the center of the paved road that passed as a driveway. It was wide and relatively flat.

"Is Aaron already gone?" she asked. "I'm not in the mood to get run over by a man eager to be on his date."

"He left a while ago."

She nodded.

He'd left without trying to find her. Without saying he was sorry. She told herself their fight wasn't important, but was the larger message that she wasn't significant to anyone here?

"Focus on your breathing," Nick said. "Feel it moving in and out of your body. Steady breaths. Match it with the sound of your feet and the way your body feels with each step. The energy flows through you. Every beat of your heart makes you stronger. Can you see the moonlight at all?"

She squinted at the sky. "Maybe. A little."

"The glow is there, even if you can't see it. The moon moves, goes through its cycle, regardless of what we do here on Earth."

"Why are you talking like this?" she asked.

"Because it's what you need to hear."

"I gotta tell you, this is a little Zen for me. I'm not especially spiritual."

"Maybe that's the problem."

"Do you want me to hit you? Because I can. I've been working out. I can hit you really, really hard."

"If you can catch me."

Who *was* this guy?

"Did you fall and hit your head?" she asked. "Do you need to see a doctor?"

"I'm showing you there's another side of life. There's a pattern to all that happens. You're a single part of a greater whole. At the same time, you are the greater whole all on your own."

She slowed, then stopped. "Now you're freaking me out."

He stopped in front of her. "What are you most afraid of in the world?"

That was easy. "The dark."

"There's no moon tonight, Izzy. Even you

would be able to see it. It's completely dark and yet you weren't afraid."

She shoved him as hard as she could. It was like trying to push down a house. "What? You lied to me? That's really nice. Because I wasn't already having a bad enough day?"

"You have it within you to be anything you want. You have the power. You always have. You're not afraid of the dark. It's not a wild animal that can hurt you. What you're really afraid of is how you'll deal with being in the dark. What you fear is yourself."

She glared at his blurry shape, then pushed past him and headed back toward the house. "I liked you a lot better when you were just a guy."

He followed her, staying behind her, but always close enough for her to hear his steps. Probably a deliberate act, she thought, furious with him for misleading her and herself for falling for it.

She wanted to scream at him that she was tired of the games. She just wanted to go home. Except where was home? Not Glory's Gate. Even if she wanted to go back there, which she didn't, Jed wouldn't let her. So what was left? Living with Lexi and Cruz? Talk about three's a crowd. She could get her own apartment. Except how would she get around? How would she buy groceries and find a job and support herself?

Maybe Skye would change the trust she'd created for Izzy out of her inheritance, allowing Izzy access to the money now. Only then what? She would be a semi-wealthy blind woman living in an apartment she couldn't leave? What was she going to do with her life?

Suddenly it wasn't the dark she wanted to escape, it was the uncertainty. She started to run again, only faster this time. She ran and ran until she saw the house in front of her. She dashed inside and took the stairs as quickly as she could. She raced into her bedroom and shut the door. Then she carefully turned on all the lights.

Between her last conversation with Aaron and with Nick, Izzy didn't know what to do with herself. She seriously debated getting the address of the ranch from Norma and calling a cab for a ride to Dallas. The only thing that stopped her was what she would do when she got there.

She sat at the breakfast table, sipping on coffee, staring out into the bright light of the morning. She could almost convince herself last night hadn't happened. But what was the point in that? She might not appreciate Nick's tactics, but she understood the purpose behind the message.

Someone entered the kitchen. She recognized Aaron's footsteps.

"I'm sorry," he said as he approached the table. "I was bitchy because I was nervous about my date. I just want you to be able to see, if only to be able to compliment me on my tasteful ensembles."

"Thanks," she said. "It's okay."

"I don't think so. You look pouty. And puffy. Were you crying last night?" He sank down next to her and took her hand. "Did I make you cry? Say that I didn't. I couldn't stand it if I did. Izzy?"

She managed a smile. "I don't believe in crying, but if I did, it wasn't so much about you. I had a fight with Nick, too."

"Oh, well, that makes sense. You two are circling each other like dogs in heat. Oh, wait. I don't like that visual at all. You're circling each other like . . ." He sighed. "I can't think of anything, but you know what I mean."

"I think so, only you're wrong. Nick isn't interested in me."

"Oh, honey, you haven't seen him looking at you. Trust me, the wanting is so there."

She wanted to believe him, but didn't dare risk it. After finally feeling more like herself it was icky to feel vulnerable again. Icky and uncomfortable.

"Maybe," she said, not really believing him. "So tell me about your date with Steve."

"You don't have to ask me twice. It was fabulous. He made me laugh, he was charming. We talked about everything. Our past relationships, what we're looking for in a man, the future. The time flew by. He's very good-looking."

"So are you."

"Well, thank you. Although, and don't take this wrong, a compliment from a blind woman isn't as thrilling as you'd think."

She grinned. "Really? Color me shocked."

"Oh, good. Your attitude is back. Okay, let me tell you more. Steve likes his job, but he doesn't love it. He's into cooking and wine. We're both from somewhere else — he's from L.A. — but we both love Texas. We love the same wines, we both enjoy travel." He sighed. "It was perfect. I'm so happy and completely terrified."

"Because you're afraid it's not going to work out?"

"Of course. Love isn't easy. Every time I get burned, it's that much more difficult to take another chance. But he's too yummy for me not to try."

"Because the reward is worth the risk."

"I just said that."

"Right. Sorry. I was actually talking about myself."

"But we already talked about you. It's my turn."

True, and Aaron loved taking his turn. Still, his words connected with her on another level. They could be talking about her situation.

She leaned toward him. "Will you take me into Dallas?"

"Of course. Do you want to see your sisters?"

"No. I want to see my doctor and I can't ask them."

"Why not? They'd take you."

"I don't want to get their hopes up."

He was silent for a minute. "You want to talk about the surgery."

"Maybe. I don't know. Don't tell anyone. I need to call." She gave a nervous laugh. "Actually I need you to call. Dialing is a bit of a challenge for me."

"Do you think he'll see you today? Ooh, this is very exciting. I feel like a spy. Should I disguise my voice when I call?"

"I don't think that's necessary."

"Let me know if you want me to. I can do a British accent. Hello, this is Nigel Barker and I'm verry, verry handsome."

"Anything?" the doctor asked.

Izzy stared at the screen in front of her and shook her head. "It's all blurry. At first I kept thinking if I blinked enough, everything would clear."

"Sorry, that's not going to happen." Dr. Greenspoon moved in closer, a handheld light/lens thing held up to his own eye. "Look to your left."

Izzy did as he requested. She'd had her eyes dilated, stared into what felt like the sun, had her eyes numbed, filled with drops, stained and now stared at.

"You're holding your own," he said as he straightened. "That's a positive sign. Sometimes there's deterioration. Your best option is still the surgery. There's a better than ninety percent chance your sight will be restored to normal."

Her stomach lurched. "But a ten percent chance I'll be permanently blind."

"I've never had it happen, but, yes, that's a possibility. Izzy, if it would make you feel better, we can do one eye at a time. See how it goes."

She shook her head. "If it went badly, I'd never do the other eye. It's all or nothing."

"That works for me. After the surgery,

you'll be in bandages for a week, then we take them off and witness the miracle."

"You're optimistic," she grumbled.

"I'm a surgeon — it's one part confidence, two parts ego. I need a couple of days to schedule it. I'm off next week on vacation but anytime after that."

"Okay," she said, oddly grateful that she couldn't do it today, even if she wanted to. There was time. Time to think, time to assess the risk. "If the surgery fails, there's no going back, right?"

Dr. Greenspoon hesitated. "There are always innovations," he began.

"But I'd be dependent on a miracle."

"Yes."

She stood. "Okay, thanks for seeing me."

He rose and squeezed her arm. "You're a beautiful young woman. You have an excellent chance of fully restored sight. I know you're afraid, but I do think your best option is to take a chance on the surgery."

"I know." Everyone was so free with advice. Of course no one else had to live with the consequences if things went wrong. "I'll call the office when you get back and let you know what I've decided."

"Take care, Izzy."

Aaron was sitting in the waiting room when she walked up front. "And?" he asked.

"Nothing's changed. I can have the surgery anytime after next week. There's a good chance my sight would go back to normal."

"So what are you waiting for? Why not go for it?"

"Because the alternative is being permanently blind forever. I can't handle that."

"You can handle anything." Aaron put his arm around her. "You're full of attitude. You'd manage. Look at Rita."

"Rita's a better person than I am."

"It's not about being a good person. It's about not giving up. I would have thought you were the kind to move forward, no matter what."

They walked outside. The sun was bright, but Izzy didn't have to squint or put on sunglasses. It barely bothered her at all. What would it be like to be normal again? Was that possible? And if it wasn't, could she live with the darkness?

"You face scary stuff all the time," Aaron continued. "Didn't you tell me you went swimming with sharks?"

"That's different."

"How?"

"I got to pick the time and place. It didn't just happen. And the consequences weren't nearly this scary."

"You mean losing an arm or a head is less frightening than being blind?"

"Something like that."

"You're a very weird person. You know that, don't you?"

"So I've been told."

Izzy couldn't sleep. No matter how many times she stretched out on her bed, she couldn't relax. She got desperate enough to turn out the lights, but the total blackness wasn't comfortable, either, so she clicked them back on.

Possible scenarios flashed through her mind. What would happen if she had the surgery and couldn't see? How would she survive? She knew that taking the chance would ease things with her sisters and maybe with herself. She wouldn't have held back out of fear anymore, which was great for family relations but left her with a much bigger problem.

There were services, she told herself. Places where she could go to learn Braille and other skills. People had satisfying lives while still dealing with all kinds of handicaps. Maybe she could go to college and get a degree in something. Probably nothing in the fine arts department or, say, nursing, but something. She would get an apartment, maybe a guide dog. She would go shopping with Lexi and be a stylishly dressed blind person. Not that she'd ever been especially stylish before, but a girl could dream.

She stood and crossed to the window. As it was probably close to midnight, she couldn't see anything, but she could pretend.

Of course if the surgery were a success, she would have her life back. She would be able to see and then do anything she wanted. Which posed nearly as big a question. What *did* she want? Her old life of thrill-seeking had lost a little of its charm. So then what? Did she still go to college and try to find something useful to do? And if she planned to live on her own and go to college either way, then did having the surgery really make that much difference?

To test her theory, she turned out the lights again. The instant darkness made her throat tighten. Terror flooded her, making her want to throw up. She was a kid again, trapped under the stairs, screaming and screaming, only no one heard. No one bothered looking for her. No one let her out.

The walls closed in. She couldn't breathe. There was only the fear and the knowledge that she was completely alone.

Sucking in a breath, she flipped on the lights and leaned against the wall as she tried to calm down. So much for a restful night's sleep.

She left her room and made her way downstairs. Maybe if she walked around outside, she'd be able to relax.

Halfway across the living room, she heard an odd sound. It was almost a yell. She paused and frowned, trying to get her bearings in the house. If the living room was in front of her and the kitchen to her right, then behind her was the hallway that led to Nick's office and his bedroom. She turned in that direction, listening.

The sound came again. Muffled, but definitely human. Was it Nick? Was he in trouble?

Her first thought was that he could more than take care of himself. Her second was that she had to make sure. It was a compulsion, or maybe just a female thing.

She walked down the hall, feeling her way along the walls. She passed the door to what she knew was his study, then saw light spilling out from the end of the hall.

She pushed open that door and stepped into what seemed like a bedroom. She could make out a bed and several large pieces of furniture against the walls. There was a fireplace and drapes pulled shut over large windows. But what stopped her was light.

It glowed everywhere. There were lamps on nightstands, an overhead light, floor lamps in the corners. It was as bright as midday.

There was another sound from the bed, but whatever worry Izzy had brought into the room quickly dissipated. She crossed to the bed and shook Nick by the shoulder.

"What do you think you're doing?" she said to him, not sure if he was awake or not but figuring he would be soon. "All that stupid Zen talk you're giving me. Telling me to get used to the dark. That I have to deal. And Rita with her one-scary-cave-at-a-time bull. Does she know about this? Those who can do and those who can't teach? You expect me to risk the little sight I have left, but you sleep with the lights on?"

Nick came awake at Izzy's first touch. He sat up as her words poured out, still caught up in the nightmare, not sure what was real and what wasn't.

She was beyond pissed. She glared at him as if she wished her eyes were laser beams that could burn him to dust.

"Don't think you can make this right with me." Her voice rose. "What's going on? Just tell me that. What's going on?"

He saw movement out in the hall and watched as Aaron stepped into the room, saw Izzy and quickly left. Nick wished he could escape so easily, but that wasn't going to happen.

"Stop yelling," he told her.

"You're really getting on my nerves."

"I got that."

He stood and crossed to the door, carefully closing it before he faced her.

She wore a long T-shirt that came to midthigh. She probably had on panties underneath, but he didn't want to think about that or her body or how good she looked glaring at him.

"You have issues," she said, practically frothing with rage. "You have your own damn issues, but, hey, go ahead and tell me what to do with *my* life."

He didn't know what to say. The truth? Was that possible? There was a part of him that didn't want her to know. Maybe because it made him feel damaged. Maybe because if he told her part of it, he would have to tell her all of it and he wouldn't sound very good.

The mistake had been his, but Garth had shared in the punishment. It was only one more thing to feel guilty about.

"You have to say something," she told him. "Just say that you fell asleep with the lights on. I might even believe you."

He crossed to her and pulled off his T-shirt. Then he picked up her hand and placed it on his chest, over one of the thicker scars.

"I sleep with the lights on," he said quietly. "You're right. I have issues. A few years ago I was working in South America. A friend and I were captured and held prisoner. We were blindfolded and tortured. They kept us chained, in the open, exposed to the elements. But that wasn't the worst of it. It wasn't the bugs or the rain or the snakes, either. It was the knives. They came without warning. There would be nothing, then the feel of a knife slicing through flesh and the only sound was my screams."

CHAPTER ELEVEN

Izzy sank down on the bed and clutched her stomach. She felt seconds away from throwing up. "I should have stayed in my room," she murmured.

Nick sank down next to her and put his hand on her back. "Sorry. I shouldn't have said that."

He'd used very few words to paint an incredibly vivid image, she thought grimly, swallowing and trying to get control. "No, it's okay. I went off on you." She thought about the sounds she'd heard. "Were you having a nightmare?"

"Yeah. I get them a couple of times a week."

That often? She sucked in a breath. "Tell me what happened."

"You don't want to know."

"I already do. All I'm missing is the details. What happened?"

"You should go to bed."

She angled toward him. "I should do a lot of things. Have you noticed I'm stubborn and used to getting my way?"

"You? I don't believe it."

She managed a slight smile, then let it fade as she reached out and touched his bare shoulder.

He didn't move as she worked her way down his chest. The scars crisscrossed his flesh, some deeper than others, some just thin lines.

"Are they on your back, too?" she asked.

"They're everywhere."

The nausea was back, but she ignored it. "What happened?" she repeated.

He took her hand in his. She wanted to think it was for comfort, but she had a feeling it was more about keeping her from finding additional scars.

"It was about ten years ago. I was working for an oil company. Some of the work I'd done in graduate school was about imaging. It's technical, but basically there are ways to look below the earth's surface to find potential oil deposits. There was a big one in South America. We knew about it for a while but there were complications with getting it out of the ground."

She pulled her hand free. His gentle touch was more of a distraction than she needed.

"I know what extraction is. I'm Jed Titan's daughter. I practically have oil in my blood."

"Right. As part of my work with the imaging, I discovered a new way to extract the oil. It avoided most of the geographical problems, so a couple of guys and I flew down to check out the area ourselves."

"And?"

"It was perfect. Using my new techniques we could get to all the oil and do minimal damage to the environment." He shifted on the bed. "The land was owned by a few dozen families. I met Francisco, who sort of ran things. I convinced him and he convinced the others. The beauty of the plan was they still had access to nearly all their acreage. They could farm and live their lives while raking in the money from us."

"So where's the bad?" she asked, knowing she wasn't going to like how this was going to end.

"I thought I was smarter than everyone who said it couldn't be done," he said. "I ignored the warnings, both scientific and spiritual."

"There were spiritual warnings?"

"Local legends not to take from below the ground. Anyone who did would be cursed by the gods."

"Creepy," she said as she rubbed her

hands up and down her arms. "What happened?"

"In the early stages of drilling, we hit a lot of gas. I didn't think anything of it. We were testing the local air and there wasn't any hint of a problem. Three months later, the people started getting sick. We figured out right away we'd poisoned the water, but by then it was too late. Three people died."

Izzy stared at him, not sure what to say. "I don't understand. Why didn't you know there was a risk before you started?"

"It was an impossible chemical reaction. Unpredictable. Nothing like this had ever happened before. If we'd used traditional drilling methods, we might have caught it. But we didn't." He sounded disgusted with himself. "We managed to save the rest of the village, but it was too late. Two of the dead were from Francisco's own family. Everyone blamed him and he blamed me."

She didn't know what to say. She knew firsthand the dangers of drilling miles deep into the earth. People could die — but not the innocents. Not those who hadn't signed up for the risk.

"It was my fault," Nick said hoarsely. "I did it. In my arrogance, I was so sure. I went to Francisco to apologize. He took me prisoner and he took a friend captive, as well. The men in the village held us for months, torturing us with knives. They fed us just enough to keep us alive, but never enough that we weren't starving. They broke my friend's legs and he nearly died from an infection. I don't know how many times I faced death. If I'd been by myself, I would have given up, but I couldn't. My friend wouldn't let me. We kept each other alive."

Nick drew in a breath. "He never blamed me. Not then, not now. Most people would. I screwed it all up and he never said a word."

"You made a mistake. There's a difference."

"Tell that to the people who died."

"Nick, you can't blame yourself."

"Sure I can. Eventually I realized I had to get us out. He was close to dying and I couldn't hang on much longer."

Now she grabbed his hand. Maybe to try to offer comfort, maybe to anchor herself in the middle of a particular level of hell.

"It was my fault," Nick continued, his voice thick with pain and remorse. "All of it. I killed them. I live with that every minute of every day. I was arrogant. I thought I knew better. I deserved to die. But my friend didn't deserve what was happening. One day I managed to pull the chains loose. I got us free and I walked us out of the jungle."

He squeezed her fingers. "When we finally made it back to the States, I went to the police and told them what I'd done. No one could help."

"What do you mean help?" she asked, suspecting the answer. "You mean no one would throw you in jail?"

"Yeah. I went to the state department. They sent out a team, but by then Francisco and his family were gone. There was nothing but the drilling site and the damn oil flowing like water. The treaty between the two countries meant I couldn't be prosecuted there — not for what everyone claimed was an honest mistake. I spent months trying to find Francisco. Maybe to say I'm sorry, maybe to let him finish the job. I don't know."

She turned to Nick and grabbed his face in her hands. "You have to let it go."

"Why? I was stupid. I thought I knew better, but I didn't."

"Doesn't that define a mistake? You were wrong. You didn't mean to be. Yes, it's terrible that people died. Yes, you have responsibility in that, but you can't spend the rest of your life paying for it."

"Why not?" he asked bitterly. "When is it enough? When is it okay?"

"It's okay now."

"No, it's not. After I couldn't find him, I traveled around the world, looking for something. Maybe peace. Maybe a reason it all happened. Then I came back here. I didn't know what to do. Ironically, all that oil made me rich. I gave every penny away, but I still had shares in a few companies from before. I bought this place and started hosting a few kids here and there. That's the point of the place. Aaron thinks the corporations pay the bills, but I use them to make us more legitimate."

"You offer free weekends to kids who have been victims of violence. That's wonderful."

"It's not enough."

"Then make it more," she said. "Do it full-time."

"I can't."

"Why not? Get a staff. If you need money, find a grant. Or ask around. I wouldn't know where to begin but Skye could help you."

"I can't risk it. What if I screw up again? What if this time I kill a kid?"

And then she understood it all. Nick wasn't just tortured by the people he'd inadvertently killed, but by the possibility of doing it again. Of making a mistake. He was immobilized by terror. In his mind, he was a walking time bomb, so while he wanted to help, he was afraid of doing the opposite.

Her situation might be different but she knew the quicksand that was indecision. She understood the sense of being trapped by circumstances and fear.

"So instead of taking a chance, you let kids suffer because you're scared?" she asked, pulling away. "I don't accept that. You have to face the fear and move on with your life."

"You're not."

"Oh, sure. Throw the surgery in my face. Nice."

He stood and crossed to the wall, where he pulled open drapes and she guessed stared out the window.

"You don't understand," he told her.

She crossed to him. "You're right. I don't understand. I didn't live through what you did. If I had, I couldn't have made it. Francisco got his pound of flesh out of you."

"I killed his family."

"And he tortured you. He knew you'd made a mistake — that you hadn't hurt anyone on purpose. You're making a difference. That matters."

"Not to the people who are dead. Nothing will bring those three back."

"Neither will cutting you over and over again."

"He had his reasons."

She wished she could shake him. "So that's it? There's no forgiveness? I believe our entire Judeo-Christian way of life is based on forgiveness and atonement. Is that for everyone but you? Don't you forgive either?"

"It's not the same."

He was haunted in a way she couldn't understand. Haunted and in pain. If this was what he lived with day after day, no wonder he lived such a solitary life. How could he bear anything else?

She didn't know who his friend was, the one who'd been with him through the torture, but she was grateful to him. She believed down to her bones that if Nick had been alone, he would have surrendered to the torture, thinking it was his due.

"I'm sorry," she whispered.

"Don't be. I got what I deserved."

"No, you didn't."

Yes, Nick had been young and stupid and three people had paid the ultimate price. But she refused to accept there was no place of forgiveness. No moment of being allowed to go on living. Not forgetting and wanting to make amends was very different than a lifetime of self-punishment.

"What about what you learned from the experience?" she asked. "What about the lives you touch now? Doesn't that count for something?"

"Not enough."

There was raw pain in his voice. And resignation. As if this would never end.

Without thinking she reached out to him. Her fingers found his shoulders. She turned him toward her, then raised herself on tiptoe and kissed him. She wasn't sure what she meant by the action, but she knew she had to touch him, try to heal him in some way.

He resisted her at first. He remained straight and unmoving. His arms hung at his sides. She kept her hands on his shoulders and continued to press her mouth against his. Somehow she had to get through to him.

Finally he grabbed her and pushed her away from him.

"Don't," he said, his voice thick with what sounded like pain. "I don't deserve this."

Meaning what? He wouldn't allow himself to be with a woman? That he couldn't risk any pleasure at all?

She stared at his face, wishing she could see into his eyes. Wishing she could see *him.*

"Maybe I do," she told him. "Maybe this

is all about me."

He brushed her cheek with the back of his knuckles. "Liar."

She shook off his hold and stepped close. Once again she found his mouth without hesitation. As if being guided by an inner sight that knew everything about Nick. Because now she did. Now she knew the best and worst about the man. She knew why he avoided the dark and because she had her own demons, she could accept his.

He was still for a second, before angling his head and kissing her with an intensity that stole her breath. He hauled her against him, as if he would never let her go.

She wrapped her arms around him, wanting to feel all of him. His strength and even his scars. He was tall and muscled and made her feel protected. She who had never needed protection from anyone.

Their lips clung, pressing until she parted unasked and he swept his tongue inside her mouth. It was electric and thrilling. His kiss aroused her, teased her, made her want to give back more than he was giving her. His hands were everywhere — up and down her arms, stroking her back, before moving lower, to her hips.

She leaned into him and felt the thick hardness of his erection. He wanted her.

The last of her doubts faded. The last of her fears melted until she was practically giddy and giggling. He wanted her. Those kisses hadn't been about pity. They'd been the kisses of a man who wanted her.

She moved her hands to his back, then stilled when she encountered more scars. There were so many, she thought, feeling sick again. Dozens of thick raised lines where Francisco and his friends had cut through living flesh.

Nick must have sensed her distraction. He pulled back. "We should stop."

Because he didn't deserve to make love or because he thought she couldn't handle what had been done to him?

She stood in his room and stared at the blurry shape of him. While the details were impossible to see, she could sense his pride at work. He wouldn't take what wasn't offered. Wouldn't beg. He would do without because that's what he believed he deserved.

What did she want? This man? Nick? Or was this just a fun way to pass the night?

The answer was clear. It was what it had always been. There had been plenty of men in her life, but none she respected as much. None who understood the best and worst about *her*.

She pulled off her oversize T-shirt and

tossed it away, then slipped out of her thong. She moved closer, took his hands and placed them on her breasts.

"We're not stopping," she told him. "At least I'm not."

How was he supposed to resist her? Nick stared at the beautiful, naked woman in front of him. The aching, pulsing desire wasn't about getting laid. That would be easy. Instead it was about Izzy — about wanting *her* in his arms, in his bed, under him. He wanted her wet and moaning and begging. He wanted to fill her until she screamed, then lose himself in her, surrendering all he had.

The power of his hunger nearly drove him to his knees. But he couldn't move, not with her small hands holding his against her bare breasts.

He was aware of every inch he touched. The full curves, the smooth skin, the pebbled texture of the skin around her nipples. Unable to help himself, he moved his fingers against her right nipple. Her mouth parted as she sucked in a breath. His gaze dropped to the dark curls between her legs. If he touched her there, would she be swollen and wet already?

He had to find out.

He moved his hands to her waist and

pulled her close, then lowered his head and kissed her.

"Finally," Izzy murmured against his mouth. She wrapped her arms around his neck and hung on as if she would never let go.

He kissed her deeply, wanting to take all of her. When he touched her back again, this time there was warm, bare skin. The hard bone of her spine, the soft curve of her waist.

She wiggled closer still, until he felt the heat of her against his hard-on. Then she dropped her hands to his ass and squeezed.

It was a playful touch. But he went from hungry to desperate in a tenth of a second.

Without considering what he was doing, he swept her up in his arms, crossed the room and lowered her onto the bed. He paused to push off his sweatpants and briefs before joining her in a tangle of arms and legs.

He touched her everywhere. Her breasts, her belly, her thighs. He swept his fingers between her legs and nearly lost it when he felt the sweet, damp, swollen flesh. But he didn't linger. There was more to touch.

The back of her knee, the arch of her foot, the tiny dimple on her cheek when she smiled. He kissed her again, then moved his hand lazily over her breasts. The full curve more than filled his palm. He brushed her nipple again and again, enjoying the catch in her breathing. When he bent down and took her nipple in his mouth, she groaned.

She tasted sweet and tempting. He circled the tight tip, then sucked. She grabbed his head, as if she didn't want him to stop, which was good with him. He could do this forever. He moved between her breasts, first one, then the other, matching the movements of his tongue with his fingers. She held on, her breathing faster now, her hips moving slightly.

His erection thickened to the point of aching. Pressure built at the base. It would take so little, he thought grimly. A few strokes. But he held back, refused to think about what it would be like to be inside her. Eventually it would be his turn.

He shifted on the bed so he could kiss his way down her belly. Moving his hands to her sides, he slid along her body, tracing curves. He used his tongue to tease her belly button and make her squirm. She laughed, then gasped as he nipped the skin just to the side.

"You're killing me," she whispered. "You know that, right?"

It was his plan. He wanted her complete

surrender. He wanted her so far lost in passion that she would have trouble finding her way back.

He continued to kiss and lick and nibble his way down. Over her hip bone, across her thigh, to her knee where he discovered she was ticklish. He crossed to the other leg and worked back up, pausing just shy of her curls. Then he waited.

Izzy tossed her head back and forth. She pumped her hips, as if urging him to finish what he'd started. Slowly, oh-so-slowly, he moved a single finger through her curls to her waiting center.

She moaned.

She was beyond ready. He rubbed lightly, as if he was only passing through, then moved away. She gasped.

"Are you doing this on purpose?" she asked, breathlessly.

"Uh-huh."

She swore, then reached between her legs and parted herself for him. "Just touch something. Anything!"

The room was bright and he could see every perfect detail. He took her at her word, leaned in and pressed the very tip of his tongue to her engorged center. She sighed. He moved slowly, learning all of her with his tongue before returning his attention to the place that made her writhe.

He kissed her intimately, finding a rhythm that caused her to tense and shudder. He could feel her thigh muscles tighten. Up and down, a little faster, a little more pressure, listening to her breathing, feeling the tension build inside her.

When he was sure she was on the road to her release, he stopped and kissed the inside of her leg.

"You hate me," she whispered. "I see that now. I don't know what I did, but you hate me."

He chuckled, then lightly bit down on the sensitive skin of her inner thigh.

"I don't hate you," he said as he slid a finger inside her. "Don't think that."

She was tight and hot. Slick. Feeling her tighten around him made him want to thrust into her and push and pump until he came. And he would. Just not yet.

He pulled out his finger, then slid in two. She gasped and pushed down. Her muscles clamped onto him. He went in deeper and circled his fingers toward her belly, stroking her from the inside. She cried out.

He lowered his head and licked her most sensitive spot, at the same time rubbing his fingers around and around. Every now and then, he withdrew them only to fill her again. Her breathing quickened until she was panting. He could feel her muscles getting tighter and tighter. He kept his rhythm as steady as possible, driving her to the edge, forcing her over. More and more and more . . .

She cried out. At that exact moment, the convulsions began. He felt the rapid contractions against his fingers. He continued to lick her center, drawing out every part of her orgasm. She drew her knees back, exposing herself more, taking it all.

His own need was nearly unmanageable. His whole cock ached as his body desperately sought a way to find release. He ignored the pressure, the pain, the frantic desire until the last of her contractions had stilled. Then he sat up, shifted onto his knees and moved between her thighs.

Izzy opened her eyes and smiled at him. "Amazing," she breathed. "You can't top it, but give it your best shot." She reached between them, taking him in her hands. "Oh, and for the record? I like it hard and fast."

Magical words, Nick thought, doing his best not to lose it. Her fingers were slick and sure as they guided him inside. He braced himself for what it was going to be like, then had to call on every ounce of control he had left when he felt her slick heat. Worse, as he pushed inside, she gave a little shudder, as if starting to come again.

He would never survive that, he thought, clenching his teeth.

He withdrew, only to push in again. She shuddered again.

"More," she whispered, raising her arms and grabbing hold of the pillow. "I'm right there. Just go for it."

He bent over her and braced his hands by her shoulders. Her eyes were closed, her face flushed. He could see her tight nipples straining toward him. As he moved in her, they moved, bouncing slightly. It was the most erotic thing he'd ever seen, he thought, unable to stop staring at her. Then she raised her legs to wrap them around his hips and hold him inside her. The action was clear — she was ready.

He told himself he was good with direction. He pulled out and thrust in hard and fast, just going for it. By the third thrust, she was holding on to his upper arms and breathing hard. By the fifth, he was barely able to hold back and she was pumping her hips as hard as he was.

One more push and she was coming. He felt the contractions drawing him in. The inevitable began, the pulsing promise, the pressure that built until it had no choice but to explode.

Izzy stretched out on the bed. Nick had pulled up the sheet and lay next to her. She could feel his body pressed against hers as his strong arms held her close.

"Impressive," she murmured, still dealing with mini aftershocks. "Nice technique, an attention to detail. You've been trained by some very smart women."

He chuckled. "How do you know it's not innate ability?"

"Oh, please. No man is born knowing how to do *that*."

"And the thought of other women doesn't bother you?"

"I don't want them in bed with us, but I can still appreciate their efforts. Was it in college?"

"Yeah. My roommate helped transform me from a complete geek into a guy who could get the girl. At first I didn't know what to do with them once I got them, but I'm a fast learner."

"Yay, you." She snuggled closer. "Can you sleep with me here?" Normally she didn't like to spend the night. Hers was more of a get-to-the-good-part-and-leave attitude. But Nick had exhausted her and his bed was so comfortable. As was the man.

He kissed her nose. "There will be hell to pay if Aaron finds out you were here."

"Because you picked me rather than him? He has a shiny new boyfriend." She closed her eyes. "I'll leave before he gets up."

He rolled onto his back. She slipped her leg onto his and in the process, bumped into something very hard and manly.

Her eyes popped open. "Seriously?"

"Ignore it. It'll go away."

She reached down and felt his erection. Immediately her insides did a little shimmy of appreciation. It would take her all of thirty seconds to be ready again. There was something about Nick that worked for her in a big way.

"You know," she said, sliding on top of him and lightly kissing him. "I was raised not to be wasteful."

His hands found her breasts and teased her nipples. "Our own private brand of recycling?"

She slid back and pushed herself onto his arousal. "Just close your eyes and think of the environment."

"I'd rather think of you."

"Good answer."

Izzy felt like a princess in a cartoon musical. She felt so good, she half expected little woodland creatures to show up and dress her the next morning after she crept back to her own room.

Her whole body hummed with satisfaction. She was achy and sore, in the best way possible. She and Nick had made love all night. It might be a couple of days before she was healed enough to go horseback riding, but that was a small price to pay for hours of incredible pleasure.

It wasn't just the sex, she thought as she stepped into the shower. It was how he joked with her and got her sense of humor. Not everyone did. He was gentle and forceful, caring and stubborn. And the man had a mouth that could make her give up state secrets, assuming she had any.

She hummed her way through the morning, happily working with the horses and avoiding Aaron. She had a feeling he would take one look at her silly grin and know exactly what had happened. Not that she was keeping secrets, exactly. It was more that she wanted to hug the information close for a little while.

A little after ten, she heard familiar voices and went outside to find her sisters walking toward the barn.

"What's up?" she called, not sure why

they'd stopped by without calling first. "Is everything all right?"

The hesitation before either of them spoke burst her happy bubble. "What?"

"Jed's being named in a prostitution ring," Lexi said. "He's going to be charged with importing underage girls and holding them as sex slaves."

Izzy sank onto the bench by the door and cupped her head in her hands. "I don't believe it."

"It's true," Skye said. "The never-ending nightmare. Between this and the potential treason charges, Jed is going to lose everything. We're talking to Dana later. She's going to give us the names of a few attorneys."

Izzy dropped her hands and straightened. "Why? Has he come after you again?"

"No, but we need to start protecting ourselves. We're tired of reacting. We need to go after him."

"We've talked about this," Lexi added. "We're taking the fight to him."

"Not a good idea," Izzy told them. "You're out of your league." She heard more footsteps and recognized them. "It's Nick."

"Then we'll talk later," Skye said.

"We can talk now. He knows most of what's going on."

"You told him?" Lexi sounded surprised.

"Jed was by a few days ago. He wanted to confirm I was still blind and make sure I understood how inconvenient that was for him. Sweet guy, our father. If he can't use me, I don't exist. Oh, and he made it clear I was never in the will. Which is hardly a surprise."

Even she heard the bitterness in her voice, but before she could figure out what to say so her sisters didn't worry, Nick had joined them.

"Ladies."

"We're talking about Garth," Izzy said bluntly and told him the latest news. "It's not that Jed is my favorite person, but these days I'm liking Garth even less. Do you have any ideas of what we could do?"

"Do you know what he wants?" Nick asked.

Izzy frowned. There was something strange about his voice. She couldn't figure out what, but it was there. As if . . . But she couldn't pin it down.

"Revenge," Lexi said. "Obviously. But maybe there's more. Maybe he wants the family annihilated. Maybe he wants everything. The business, the land, the house."

"The house is available," Skye said. "Dad's moved out. He's mostly staying in his condo in Dallas. I'm with Mitch, Lexi's with Cruz and you're here."

Temporarily, Izzy thought. When she left the ranch, she didn't know where she was going to go. A worry for another time, she reminded herself.

"If he hadn't gone after Izzy, I would have considered letting him just take it all," Lexi grumbled. "But he crossed the line when he hurt you."

Izzy smiled at her. "Thanks for the support." She turned toward Nick. "No brilliant ideas?"

"Not right now. I'll get back to you."

Something was wrong, she thought, still not sure what Nick was thinking. Was he upset that they were dragging him into their family business? Or was it something else? The next time they were alone, she was going to have to remember to ask.

CHAPTER TWELVE

Nick paced the length of Garth's office. He'd stopped by to see his friend because he didn't know what else to do.

"You have to stop this," he said forcefully, turning back to stare at the one person he'd considered his family. The one person he trusted above all.

"Going after the Titans?" Garth leaned back in his chair and slowly shook his head. "Nick, don't get involved in this. You're helping Izzy. Make that enough."

"You're going after her family. A prostitution ring? What the fuck?"

Garth smiled. "Come on. You have to admire the inventiveness of it. That on top of the treason charges should keep Jed Titan in jail for a long time."

"Did he do any of it?"

Garth shrugged. "Does it matter?"

"Yeah, it does. When did you become the asshole who did the wrong thing?"

Garth's easy smile faded. "When I was fourteen and Jed threw me out onto the street. When I watched my mother nearly die and then lose herself because we didn't have the money to get the surgery done in time."

"Jed's a bastard. I get it. But his daughters didn't know about you. Why are you taking this out on them?"

"Because I can. Because anything that hurts the old man makes it a good day."

Nick walked to the front of the desk and braced his hands against the hard surface. "It doesn't hurt him. He doesn't care about his daughters. I doubt he ever has. He came to see Izzy last week. He told her that because she was still blind, she was no use to him. That's not even human. I understand he turned his back on you. I understand he has to pay, but the Titan women are innocent."

"They've got you snowed."

Nick read the truth in his eyes. He'd been avoiding it because he wanted his friend to be someone different. He didn't know when Garth had changed — when he'd decided the end justified the means — but he had. Everything was different now.

Nick understood that he'd been living an illusion a long time. The friendship he'd counted on, that had shaped his life, was over.

He straightened. "I'm out of the company. I'll be selling my shares over the next few weeks." He pulled a letter out of his back pocket and dropped it on the blotter. "I'm resigning from the board of directors."

Garth ignored the letter. "You're going to choose a piece of ass over a guy you've known nearly twenty years?"

Nick moved like the wind. One second he was on the other side of the desk, the next he was spinning Garth's chair toward him and wrapping his hand around the other man's neck.

The skills were there, along with the strength. He'd learned how to protect himself with nothing but his body to use as a weapon and he'd learned every trick.

He stared into Garth's dark eyes. "I won't squeeze because of our shared past. Because until today, you were all the family I had. But don't cross me. Don't test me and don't come after the Titan sisters again. Hang Jed Titan if you want. He's yours, but they are not."

He stepped back.

Garth stood. "So this is it?" he asked. "They matter more than what we've been through?" He pulled open his shirt, exposing the scars that matched Nick's. "This never happened?"

"It happened," Nick said slowly. "My regret for what you had to endure goes to the bone. But that doesn't make what you're doing here right. The Titan women aren't up for grabs. Cross them and you cross me."

Garth slowly rebuttoned his shirt. "Izzy doesn't know, does she? That you know me. That we've been friends for years."

"Let me guess. You're going to tell her." Nick didn't know how to stop him. The truth — would she understand? Or would she blame him and walk away from all the progress she'd made just to punish him?

"Are you?" Garth asked.

"After she has the surgery." He wanted to put it off as long as possible. He wanted to get her well first.

Which sounded good, but there was another truth. He didn't want to lose her. Somehow she'd become important to him. He could trust her and that was hard for him to admit. There might be something more, but he wasn't willing to go there. Not now, probably not ever.

"You'll want to make sure she hears it from you," Garth said, the threat obvious. "If it comes from someone else, it could break her heart. Or worse."

"Don't threaten me," Nick told him, then started for the door.

Garth called him back. "You're going to regret this. We're like brothers, Nick. We always have been. Don't give that up because of a woman."

"Izzy isn't a part of this, but you can't understand that. And that's why I'm walking away."

Izzy fully expected to confront Nick after her sisters left, but he disappeared and being nearly blind meant a serious handicap on her part when trying to search a large open area, like a ranch. Then at dinner, Aaron upset her whole day by telling her that three kids were coming to visit for the Labor Day weekend.

"It's Labor Day already?" she asked, then shook her head. "Never mind. What kind of kids? What if they don't like me? What if I mess up?"

"Did you count the number of I's in that sentence, young lady?" Aaron asked. "Who should this conversation be about?"

"The kids. I know, the kids. What was I thinking?"

But she wasn't thinking. She found herself oddly nervous at the thought of dealing with kids who had issues.

"What kind of issues?" she asked. "Like physical handicaps?"

"Not usually. We don't have any special facilities for wheelchairs or kids on crutches. Mostly we get kids who have been through something really tough." He sounded uncharacteristically subdued.

"Like?"

"Like we're not supposed to know. We get a general outline of the issues so we don't schedule fireworks for a child who's lived through a gunfight, but nothing specific. Two of the kids have been here before, though, so I know their story. Their mom shot their dad and then killed herself. They were in the room when it happened. The old man had been beating them for years, but still."

Izzy pushed away her plate as her stomach got queasy. Where was Nick? Hearing this would be slightly easier if he was around.

"What are we supposed to do for them?" she asked.

"Let them get away from their regular lives. They ride horses, walk the rope bridge. They get to play and run without anyone pointing."

"I could point, I just wouldn't know the right direction," Izzy murmured. "What if I mess up?"

"You won't. You're a nice person." He sounded way too cheerful as he spoke.

"What does that mean? What aren't you telling me?"

Aaron sighed. "We're getting a difficult case. Her name is Heidi. She's twelve. Two years ago, her uncle raped her and then set her on fire, trying to kill her so she wouldn't tell on him."

Izzy's dinner did a slow, uncomfortable turn in her belly. "I read about that in the paper. The uncle was arrested then killed in prison."

"Sometimes the criminal justice system works," Aaron told her. "Anyway, Heidi has been through a dozen or so reconstructive surgeries. She's sarcastic, unfriendly and hates the world. Nick and I thought you'd be great with her."

"What?"

"We're not saying you're like that, but you have some attitude on you. I think you're young enough for her to relate to without being too young."

Izzy held up both hands. "I don't think this is going to work. Shouldn't we have a professional dealing with her?"

"She has plenty of those. We're talking a long weekend, girlfriend. You can suck it up for that long. At the end of the day, she's still burned and you get to be pretty. So manage."

"Ouch," Izzy murmured. "That hurt."

"I'm sorry. Heidi needs help. You need to try. I'm just saying."

"Okay." She felt stupid and small, but understood his point.

"You'll like it," he said, his voice softening. "Trust me. These kids can break your heart, but in a good way."

"So why not have them here for more than a long weekend at a time?"

Aaron was quiet for so long, she wondered if he'd left the room.

"I don't know," he said at last. "I've tried to talk to Nick about it, but he won't listen. He says it would be too complicated. We'd need a full-time staff of health care professionals."

"Is it a money thing?"

"Have you seen Nick's bank account balance?"

"No."

"Oh, right. It's not a money thing."

"Then what?" she asked before she could stop herself. She knew the reason. It was fear. Fear that he would do more damage than good. Fear that he could destroy even more. Because he hadn't forgiven himself. He probably never would.

"You'll have to ask him yourself," Aaron told her.

"Sure," she said, knowing she didn't have to.

Izzy paced nervously outside the barn. She and Rita had discussed the best choices for horses for the kids. The two who had been on the ranch before had some experience, but as far as Izzy could tell, Heidi had never been on a horse. Izzy felt that Flower was the right mount. An even-tempered mare with a maternal streak, Flower was patient and gentle with the most skittish of riders, but she had plenty of speed for a good, long ride.

"They're here," Rita said, seconds before Izzy heard the SUV approaching.

"You're good," Izzy murmured and wiped her hands on her jeans. Everything would be fine, she told herself. This wasn't a big deal. Kids loved horses. Her fears that she would say or do something so wrong as to damage Heidi was an inflation of her importance in the girl's life. Which sounded good but didn't take away the knot in her stomach.

She turned toward the sound of running feet and saw two blurry shapes hurrying toward them. Rita hugged both kids and introduced Izzy.

"Are we going riding soon?" the girl, Emily, asked.

"Very soon," Rita promised.

"Where's Heidi?" Izzy asked.

"She's scared," Ned, Emily's brother, said. "She looked like she was going to cry the whole way here."

"New places can be confusing," Izzy said as she walked toward the SUV. She could see Nick unloading luggage. As she approached, a tall girl climbed out of the car.

"You must be Heidi," Izzy said cheerfully. "Hi. Nice to meet you. Do you want to get settled or would you like to come meet your horse for the weekend? Flower is very excited about all the riding we're going to do."

There was something odd about the girl's posture. She was bent over, as if . . .

The burns, Izzy thought, mentally slapping herself. She was hiding her face.

"I'd rather go to my room," Heidi whispered.

"Okay. I'll show you the way." She pointed at the suitcases. "Which one is yours?"

"The green one."

Which was less helpful, Izzy thought as she stared at the dark-colored luggage. Nick handed her one. She smiled at him.

"Thanks."

Izzy took the suitcase and led the way inside. As there were only three guests, all the kids were sleeping in the main house. She went up the stairs and walked into the bright, cheery bedroom Norma and Aaron had prepared.

"Here you go," Izzy told Heidi. "You have your own bathroom, which is pretty cool. I hate sharing a bathroom. Even with my sisters. I should probably get over that, I know, but here it's not an issue. Now do you want to unpack first or come meet Flower?"

"I don't want to meet a stupid horse. I'm only here because my doctor said I had to come. I'm going to stay in my room and read until it's time to go home. You can go now."

Izzy dropped the suitcase and put her hands on her hips. "Oh, really. Because you think you're in charge?"

"No. Not really." Heidi took a step back. "I, um, don't like horses."

So the bravado had serious limits. Good to know. Izzy wasn't sure what to say or the best way to deal with the situation. They only had three days, which meant she couldn't outwait Heidi.

"How many horses have you met?"

Heidi cleared her throat and hunched over. "Not many."

"As in none?"

"Yes." The word was barely audible.

"Okay, then you're going to meet Flower because she's really nice. I think you'll get along. But if I'm wrong, we'll renegotiate. Sound fair?"

She took the heavy sigh as a yes and motioned for Heidi to follow her out of the house.

Minutes later they were in Flower's stall.

"Flower, this is Heidi," Izzy said as she patted the mare's neck. "It's okay, Heidi. Flower's a sweetie. She won't hurt you."

But Heidi stood in the doorway, unmoving, not speaking. Izzy couldn't read her expression so she wasn't sure what was wrong.

"Don't you want to pat her?"

"No."

"But you're a girl. Girls love horses."

"Not me. She's too big. She'll bite me. Or worse."

"I see," Izzy said. "Wait here."

Seconds later she was back with one of the barn cats in her arms. "This is Alfredo. Are you good with cats?"

"I like cats." Heidi moved toward her and gently stroked Alfredo.

"He's small." "He's still a kitten. He was born here in the barn. Now I think you're bigger than Alfredo."

Heidi actually giggled. "Well, yeah. He's a cat."

"Good. Now remember that." Izzy put Alfredo down.

"What are you doing?" Heidi shrieked. "He'll be killed."

"He'll be fine. Horses and cats usually get along. Watch."

Izzy couldn't see very much, but she'd grown up around barn cats and horses. She knew that Alfredo would be fearless in the stall. Sure enough, a few seconds later, Heidi gasped.

"Flower likes him. She's kind of petting him with her nose. He's drinking her *water.*"

"Really? So maybe now you're not so afraid of Flower?"

"Maybe. But I don't want to ride her. It's too high. What if I fall?"

"Then you lie on the ground feeling stupid. Trust me, I've done it a thousand times."

"I'm not riding. Why do you care if I ride?" Heidi's voice rose with her words until she was practically shouting.

"Because you can't be afraid all the time. Because you need to learn how to live again and this is a start."

"You don't know what you're talking about. You've never been set on fire. You can't know what I go through every day. Don't talk to me about being afraid. You don't know anything."

Izzy blocked the doorway, so Heidi couldn't get past her and Izzy had no plans to move. She felt bad about the girl's quiet crying, but she wasn't going to back down.

"I was in an explosion," she said. "Does that count?"

There was a sniff, then, "What do you mean?"

"I was on an oil rig that exploded. I don't remember what happened, mostly because I was busy being tossed up in the air, falling through fire and then landing in the water. I could have drowned. Huh. I never thought of that before. Anyway, I was in the explosion. I had a few cuts and bruises but the big thing is I'm blind. Well, I have thirty percent of my sight, which is pretty darned close."

"You're not blind."

Izzy laughed. "Tell that to my doctor."

"But you're so pretty."

"Thanks, but that doesn't matter. I get around, but I can't read or drive."

Heidi moved closer. "You can't see me?"

"I can see your shape and the light and dark of colors. Not details."

"So you don't know what my face looks like."

"No. Why? Is there something wrong with it?"

As soon as she asked the question, Izzy wanted to shoot herself. What a stupid thing to say. And here it had only been what? Twenty minutes?

"I'm hideous," Heidi said, turning away. "A freak. Children run screaming when they see me."

"So basically you never have to wait in line when you go to Disneyland."

For the second time in as many minutes Izzy spoke without thinking. But before she could bang her head into the side of the stall, she heard a faint giggle. She breathed a sigh of relief.

"It's not funny," Heidi said, even as she giggled harder.

"You're the one laughing, not me."

"I know." She cleared her throat, then chuckled again. "No one talks about how I look except my surgeon and his staff. And my therapist. We're all supposed to pretend I'm normal."

"Is that bad?"

"I don't know. I'm not normal. I've had

266

so many surgeries and I'm going to have more. I get scared because it hurts and I just want to be like everyone else."

"Not an option, kid. Sorry. You're going to have to be yourself. But you know what? That's not so bad."

"That's what my mom says."

Izzy winced. "So you're saying I'm old and mom-like? I'm crushed."

Heidi laughed again, then stepped toward Flower and patted her neck. "You're funny."

"Gee, thanks."

A loud bell sounded.

"Mealtime," Izzy said. "You are literally saved by the bell. By the time we're done with dinner, it will be too late to go riding, so first thing tomorrow, we're going to take this pony out and see what she can do."

"Really?"

"You'll love it. I promise. I'll be with you every step of the way."

"But you're blind."

"So?"

"You ride horses?"

"Honey, I do everything. Well, e-mail is a challenge. I need to get one of those talking programs."

"You're not like anyone I know."

"I'm going to take that as a compliment," Izzy said, grabbing Alfredo and walking out of the stall. She set the cat down, then waited until Heidi followed her before securing the low door. "See you tomorrow, Flower."

The horse neighed.

"Does she understand you?" Heidi asked, sounding intrigued.

"Most of the time. Horses are people, too."

Heidi laughed.

After dinner, Heidi followed Izzy into the living room while the other two kids went with Aaron to watch movies in the media room of the main guesthouse.

"Is your hair naturally curly?" Heidi asked as she bounced onto the sofa. "Do you like it?"

"It's natural and sometimes I like it. Sometimes I want really straight hair, but I've learned to live with it."

"I have straight hair," Heidi said.

Izzy reached out and touched the silky strands. "Nice. Very soft."

"My mom buys me this fancy conditioner that makes it shiny and stuff but . . ."

"But what?"

"No one's looking at my hair. The scars are all along one side of my face. I've got a patch of hair missing where the follicles burned away. My surgeon said we can talk about a transplant, but he says that's just minor stuff."

"He's not a twelve-year-old girl," Izzy said, aching for her.

"Yeah." Heidi sighed. "Sometimes I get scared about growing up. About being accepted and stuff."

"Me, too."

"What?"

"I have two brilliant and beautiful sisters. Lexi, the oldest, started her own business. It's a day spa and it's really successful. My other sister, Skye, runs a foundation. She inherited a bunch of money from our mom and is using most of it to feed hungry children."

"Wow."

"Exactly. I'm the screwup. I didn't go to college and I look for crazy jobs, like ski patrol. I was an underwater welder on an oil rig, which is where the explosion occurred. Now I'm blind and I don't know what to do with myself."

"Don't you work here?"

"Sort of. It's temporary. Until I can get my life back together."

"What do you want to do?" Heidi asked.

"I haven't a clue."

"Me, either."

"You're twelve. You get to be confused. I'm supposed to have figured it all out by now."

"You're good with the horses."

"I enjoy working with them." But she wanted something more. The question was what?

"You're easy to talk to," Heidi told her.

"Thanks. So are you."

Later that night, after Heidi had gone to bed, Izzy went looking for Nick. She found him in his office.

"If I didn't know better, I would say you were hiding," she told him as she entered.

"Sorry. I've been busy getting ready for the kids this weekend. There's a lot of paperwork."

For the thousandth time, she wished she could see his face. She wanted to know what he was really thinking. "Are you worried I'm going to get all girly because we slept together?"

"No. I never worry about that with you."

She sat down. "Good. Because I'm not. Are you?"

"No."

She heard the humor in his voice.

"I like Heidi," she said. "She's not what I expected. Things have got to be hard for her, but she's a great kid."

"Most of them are."

"She didn't deserve what happened to her. I guess no one does. I was scared of not knowing what to say or do, but she doesn't need me to make anything better. I'm just a friend."

"That's good."

Feelings welled up inside her. It took her a second to figure out her point.

"I'm not curing cancer or anything, but I think this helps. This experience. And I'm a part of that. I've never been a part of anything like this before. So I wanted to say thank-you."

"You're welcome."

She stood to leave, then turned back to him. "You don't get involved with the kids who come here?"

"I have other things I need to do."

"No, you don't. You should meet the people you help, Nick. You might just be surprised by how good that makes you feel."

"What kind of trees are those?" Heidi asked the next afternoon when they left the corral and started actually riding out in the open.

"Like I can see them?" Izzy asked with a laugh. "Did you get the whole blind thing?"

"Oh, right. Sorry. They're nice. I live in Southern California. Not so much on the

271

trees there. I thought Texas had lots of wildflowers. I don't see any."

"They happen in spring. It's too hot now."

Heidi provided a running commentary on everything they rode by, which could have been wearing but was actually nice. She was enthused, happy and acting just like a kid. And it had only been a day. What would she be like after a week or a month in a place like this?

She thought about the facilities already in place. Couldn't Nick host kids all summer and save the corporate stuff for the rest of the year? Maybe have families visit on weekends, but during the week, kids only? It could work. He would need a full-time staff of psychologists and maybe a couple of nurses, but that was all doable. If it was a summer program, they could hire school psychologists who were experienced with kids and still had the time off.

"Oh, look, Izzy," Heidi whispered. "Look."

"I can't," she whispered back.

"There's a deer. She's so beautiful. I've never seen a deer, except at the zoo. She's real and everything. Look how she walks. She's eating." Heidi's voice rose. "She's eating and, oh, look."

Izzy glanced around at the blurry world and waited until the deer had moved on.

Heidi urged Flower forward.

"That was so cool," the girl said, sounding excited. "I love riding. Can we go every day I'm here?"

"Of course. Flower would like that."

"I'm going to call my mom tonight and tell her I want to take lessons. I don't care if people stare. It's too much fun. I can't hide in my room forever, right?"

"Right." Izzy felt all bright and light inside, like she could float away on a bubble of happiness. "By the way, have you ever been rock climbing?"

"No."

"We'll have to try that when we get back."

"Is it fun?"

"I think you're going to love it."

Monday came too quickly, Izzy thought as she hugged Heidi goodbye.

"You'll call me?" the girl asked, tears thickening her voice.

"I'm going to have to. It's not like I can do e-mail."

Heidi hugged her again. "You're the best. I had such a good time. Thanks for everything."

"You're welcome." Izzy let go and straightened. She fought the burning in her eyes. There was no way she was going to cry. At least not in front of Heidi.

The girl climbed in the SUV and closed the door. Izzy waved and had no idea if Heidi was waving back. When the SUV pulled away, she turned and practically ran into Nick.

He caught her and held her in front of him. "You okay?"

"Yes. Just a little choked up. I didn't know it would be like this. She's amazing and tough and still sees the wonder in things. After what happened to her, how is that possible?"

"She's strong. You were good with her. I saw you two together."

"I hope I helped. I loved hanging out with her." She hesitated. "Whatever you went through, whatever you did, if it brought you here, then it's not as bad as you think. This is worth it, Nick. This is magic. You're helping children in a profound way. You're making them believe in themselves. It's amazing. Don't believe me. Ask their parents."

"None of this makes up for what I did."

"Maybe not, but did it ever occur to you that you had to make that mistake to get here? To make this kind of a difference? How many others are there like Heidi? How many others will you help?"

"Not enough."

He was so stubborn. "You won't be able to reach them all, but each child is a chance. Why can't you see the good you do?"

"This isn't about me. It's about them."

"Maybe it's about all of us." She touched his arm. "I want to have the surgery."

He didn't say anything.

She shrugged. "It's time. I get it. After spending the weekend with Heidi, how can I still be afraid?"

He touched her face with his fingertips, then pulled her close.

"Will you take me?" she asked, her words muffled against his shoulder. "I don't want my sisters to know until after the surgery. I don't want them to worry."

"Yes."

She waited. "That's it? No 'I told you so' or 'You should have done this weeks ago'?"

"No."

"Can I stay here while I recover?"

He kissed her. His mouth was warm and sexy and tempting. "If you tried to leave, I'd drag you back."

"Promise?"

"Yes."

CHAPTER THIRTEEN

The world was totally black. There wasn't a hint of light. Not a flicker or a shadow. The world was black and still and filled with terror.

Izzy told herself to breathe slowly. To focus. It had only been a day since her surgery. A single day. She had to survive a week. Which was seven days. And how many hours? She tried to do the math, then bumped into a table in the hallway and wanted to scream. Who was stupid enough to put tables in hallways? Didn't everyone know she couldn't see?

Except that table had been there since she first arrived at Nick's ranch and she'd learned all the rooms so she could walk through them easily. She knew about the table, just like she knew about the stairs and the doors and the walls.

Only it was different now. There was only darkness. She hadn't realized how much she'd depended on her faulty vision to help her figure out where she was and where she was going. She was going to have to relearn everything.

"I have a week," she said aloud, only to hear someone's footsteps.

"I'm pretty sure talking to yourself isn't good," Aaron said, as cheerful as ever. "And don't take this wrong, but a bandage wrapped around your head, covering your eyes? Not your best look."

"Gee, thanks."

"Honesty keeps us friends. I, for one, am wildly excited about you getting the surgery. Next week, when you can see, I want to have a serious conversation about my hair. I was thinking highlights. Steve gets them and I'm really tempted, but I wanted a second opinion."

Aaron casually took her arm. "It's nearly lunchtime. Do you remember the way?"

"Maybe," she said, grateful for the help. "I thought I'd already figured out the house. I guess I was wrong."

"You've only been back a couple of hours. Give it time."

"Thanks."

After her surgery, she'd spent the night at the hospital. Nick had checked on her frequently, then had brought her home this morning.

"Norma has made a special lunch of your favorites. BLT sandwiches with pudding." She felt him shudder. "Banana pudding."

She laughed. "What's wrong with that?"

"Everything. Can't you at least want a delicate sorbet or a nice chocolate-dipped strawberry?"

"I could go for the strawberry."

"Be sure to tell her."

"I will. Besides, I'm sure there's more for lunch than just sandwiches."

"Probably, but I would like to point out that she's never gone to this much trouble for me and I *rave* about her biscuits. I feel so unappreciated. Now there's a step, then another step."

She reached out to feel the doorway to the dining room, then couldn't remember how far to the table. The darkness was complete. What if this was how she had to live forever? What if there wasn't anything beyond touch and sound?

The panic swirled again, but she forced herself to keep breathing. Regular breathing and a prescription for Xanax if the anxiety got too bad, although Izzy was determined to tough it out. Dr. Greenspoon was the best. She trusted him. He'd done a good job and had been pleased with the outcome of the surgery.

"What are you thinking?" Aaron asked.

"That I'm strong and I'll work through this."

"It's a week, Izzy. I'm supposed to be the drama queen in the relationship."

"I meant if the surgery went bad."

He patted her arm. "It didn't. Nick told me. The doctor thinks you'll have your sight restored."

"But he's not sure. He can't be sure until the bandages come off."

"No, he can't. And aren't you a little ray of sunshine? Here's the chair. Can you feel it?"

She reached out and felt the familiar curve of the back of the chair, then managed to sit down. Norma bustled in seconds later.

"I made the BLTs," she said briskly. "And a few different salads. Oh, and the banana pudding."

Aaron groaned.

Izzy grinned. "Thanks, Norma. You really didn't have to."

"I know," the other woman said. "Now where's Nick? He knows how I feel about serving meals on time."

"I'm right here."

Izzy turned toward the sound of his voice. Normally she could see the shape of him but now there was nothing.

"How are you holding up?" he asked, lightly touching her shoulder.

"Fine."

"I caught her talking to herself," Aaron said. "That's never good."

"At least I know the conversation is going to be interesting," she said.

"I'm ignoring that," Aaron said.

She heard the sound of a chair being pulled out, then liquid being poured into glasses.

"What can I get you?" Aaron asked. "Because I live to serve."

"Maybe half a sandwich to start." She could hold it in her hand and keep track of it. That sounded better than chasing something around her plate.

"Don't think you're getting out of eating that damned pudding," he murmured in her ear. "Iced tea is on your right."

She reached in that direction but encountered warm fingers rather than cool glass.

"Here," Nick said, guiding her. He helped her find her drink.

The meal seemed to go on for hours. Izzy managed to eat part of her sandwich, but kept having trouble with her tea. Aaron and Nick talked, which should have been a nice distraction. Instead she kept thinking that they were watching her, not sure if they should help or not. She felt awkward and confused and afraid of spilling or dropping or missing her mouth and jamming her sandwich into her cheek.

"Maybe I could get a tray in my room from now on," she said abruptly.

"If she gets room service, I want it, too," Aaron said in a whine.

Despite the tension filling her, she smiled. "You act like you're two."

"So? What are you?"

She managed a laugh. "Point taken."

"It's okay, Izzy," Nick told her. "It's your first day. You'll get used to it."

"I don't want to get used to it," she snapped, her good humor fading. She stood, then realized she had no idea which direction to turn. Dread swept through her, making her sorry she'd eaten anything. She was trapped.

No, she told herself, breathing steadily. Not trapped. She was fine. She would be fine. She was tough. Compared to what Heidi had gone through, this was nothing.

Someone else rose and took her arm. She knew immediately it was Nick.

"You're killing my great exit here," she told him.

"You ready to stalk out on your own?"

"Not really."

He led her out of the dining room, toward the stairs. They climbed slowly and when they reached her room, she was shaking.

"I'm trying," she said as she sat on the bed and waited for the trembling to pass. "I'm just so damn scared."

"I know."

She heard the sound of movement, then felt him take both her hands in his. From the angle and the way he rested his forearms on her legs, she guessed he was kneeling.

"Usually guys who get in that position are proposing," she teased. "Gee, Nick. This is so sudden."

"Not bad. You're getting it."

"I'm not," she admitted. "Every other second, I'm terrified. I can't live like this. I can't."

"Yeah, you can. You're strong, Izzy. Stronger than you know. It's just the first day. Try to relax. I want you to lie down. I'm going to teach you some breathing techniques. When you're feeling better, you can call your sisters."

She didn't think breathing was going to be a whole lot of help. "Or we could just have sex."

Nick stilled. "As tempting as that is, I think you need to heal a little more."

"Are you trying to say the right thing or get out of doing it with me?"

Instead of answering in words, he leaned in and kissed her. His mouth was hot and hungry, claiming hers. She met him stroke for stroke, enjoying the wave of need and desire that crashed through her. Horny was a whole lot better than afraid.

He cupped her cheek with his hand, then sucked on her lower lip. Only when she was breathing hard did he pull back.

"What was the question?" he asked.

"I have no idea."

"Good. Now lie back on the bed and . . . Sorry. I was going to say close your eyes."

"Already doing that," she said, touching the bandage. "Next?"

"Hollister," Nick said into the phone, still studying the computer screen.

"You have a lot of explaining to do. What were you thinking? You didn't call us? Do you remember meeting our friend Dana? I swear to God, I want to have you arrested and your ass thrown in jail."

The voice was familiar, although he couldn't place it. "Just my ass? Not the rest of me."

"I see you've been hanging out with Izzy too much these days."

The information clicked into place. "Hello, Skye."

"She had the surgery."

"I know."

"She didn't tell us she was going to do it and you knew. And don't even think about saying it was her decision to make because even if I can't come close to beating you up, I'm engaged to a former Navy SEAL. He could kill you with a Q-tip."

Nick leaned back in his chair and smiled. While Izzy was his favorite, he liked all the Titan sisters. "Seems like a stupid plan to me. Why not use a gun?"

"Don't think you can charm me, because you can't. What were you thinking?"

"That it was Izzy's decision to make. She didn't want you to worry. She had the surgery and told you after. It happened and now you know."

"Oh, I see. You're going for rational. Tell me, Nick. Have you ever been in a relationship with a woman before? Did the rational approach ever work?"

"No."

"Then try something else."

"You've obviously spoken with her. You know she's fine, but you're always welcome to come to the ranch. You can see her for yourself." He shifted the phone to his other hand. "Besides, if I remember correctly, getting Izzy to the point where she wanted the surgery was the entire reason for having her here."

There was a long pause. "Okay. Yes. Maybe. Speaking of which, you need to bill me for the rest of her time there."

"We're good."

"But all I gave you is a small deposit. You were going to bill me weekly."

"I changed my mind." He wasn't taking money for having Izzy around. "She worked hard. She contributed." She dazzled, he thought, then frowned. He had no idea where that idea had come from.

"But we owe you —"

"Nothing," he said firmly. "Come by on Saturday. We'll have a barbecue. Bring everybody. You'll see your sister, you'll feel better."

"That sounds nice," Skye said slowly. "Okay. We'll be there."

"I'll tell Izzy."

"Thanks for everything. See you soon."

"Bye."

He hung up and shook his head. Women were a constant complication. Speaking of which . . .

He glanced up at the ceiling and then checked his watch. It was after nine. Izzy had said she was tired and wanted to go to bed early. The doctor had told her to take it easy for a few days. No strenuous physical activity. No riding. And while he hadn't specifically asked, Nick had already figured out that meant no sex.

Not his first choice, he thought, remembering what it had been like to spend the night with Izzy. She was responsive, interested and adventurous. A perfect storm. One he wouldn't be experiencing anytime soon.

Which was for the better, he told himself. He wasn't going to get involved with her. Neither of them needed the complication. Still, she'd been quiet at dinner. He saved his work, then headed upstairs.

Izzy sat in a chair in the corner, her legs pulled up to her chest, her head resting on her knees. For one gut-clenching second, he thought she was crying. Then she straightened and looked at him. There was tension in her face, but no tears that he could see. The bandage made it tough to be sure.

"Hey," he said.

"Hi."

Her mouth moved in what he guessed was an attempt to smile.

"You have all the lights on."

She shrugged. "I feel better knowing

they're on. It's not like I can see them. Or anything."

He crossed to her and took her hand. "Come on. You need to rest."

"I can't. Every time I lie down I freak. It's like I can't breathe or something. I'm better here in the chair."

"You need to rest so you can heal. Look, I'm bigger and stronger, so you can come quietly or I can force you. The forcing won't be pretty. It'll mess up your hair."

Slowly she lowered her feet to the floor. "Do you see me laughing? I'm not. You know why? It's not funny."

"I know."

She rose.

He drew her close and wrapped his arms around her. "I'm here. You're safe. You can breathe."

"You don't know that."

"I'm a guy. I know everything."

When she didn't respond to that, he knew she was more scared than he'd realized. He led her to the bed, then stretched out next to her.

"I'm going to stay right here," he told her. "All night. I'll keep you safe, Izzy. I promise."

"I can't cry. I keep reminding myself that. I'm not supposed to cry. Something about the tear ducts. But I want to. And I want to run so hard and so fast that there's light. But it's not possible, either."

She was right next to him. He could feel her shaking and didn't know what to do to make it better. Frustration made him want to hit something, but that wouldn't help Izzy. Instead he kept his arm around her, moving his hand up and down her back.

"Remember the breathing we practiced earlier today?"

"It was stupid."

"Maybe, but we're going to try it again."

"I can't."

"Yes, you can."

"No. I can't breathe." She inhaled sharply. "Something's wrong. I can't breathe."

"You're breathing just fine. If you couldn't breathe, you couldn't talk. Now roll on your back."

She didn't move.

"I'm going to stay here all night. You're not getting rid of me. But you need to relax and you need to sleep. Come on, Izzy. I've traveled the world and trained with professionals. I don't get to practice this much. Give me a break."

He waited, not sure which way it would go. Was she just on the edge of losing it or already falling?

She rolled onto her back and sighed. "Because it's all about you?"

The relief was instant. She was coming back. "Sure."

"You're just like Aaron."

"Hey. What does that mean?"

She managed a slight smile. "Nothing bad. I adore Aaron."

"Good. Now we're going to start breathing."

"Where's the we? I'm doing all the work."

He bent down and kissed her.

"What was that for?" she asked.

"I wanted to."

"Just so typical," she muttered.

But her smile was bigger and the shaking had stopped. Once again she'd proven that she could be knocked around, but she couldn't be broken. He could respect that. Maybe more than respect, but he wasn't going there. Not now, not ever.

The next morning, Izzy made her way to the barn. It was difficult, walking out into darkness with nothing but her memory and other senses to guide her. She worried about tripping over something or falling in a big hole — not that there were any on the ranch. The use of a cane suddenly made sense.

But as she got close, she could smell the hay and the horses. The quality of the dirt changed. She could feel it in her steps and knew it had been trampled by countless hoofs. She put her arm up to find the building and bumped her fingers against the wall three steps later.

"How do you do it?" she asked Rita as soon as she got to the barn. "How do you figure out where stuff is and where you are?"

"Practice. My other senses come into play."

"I'm scared nearly all the time," Izzy admitted, sitting on the bench by the door. "I had my first panic attack last night."

"How was it?"

"Not something I want to repeat."

Rita joined her on the bench. "It's a week, kid. You'll be fine. Think of this as a character-building exercise."

"I liked my character fine before."

"But it will be better now."

"Oh, joy."

She knew there was more at stake here than just her character. There was the possibility the surgery wouldn't work. That she would be lost in the darkness forever. Not a thought to perk up her mood, she reminded herself.

"I can't ride," she told the other woman.

"But I can still do the grooming and help out in other ways."

"Then that's what I'll use you for."

"I like working with the horses. Flower sure made a difference with Heidi."

"They usually do. Riding is an act of mutual trust. Kids who have been betrayed by someone who is supposed to love them aren't big on trust. We start with a horse. It builds confidence."

"Did you study this?"

Rita laughed. "I have a lot of common sense. Sometimes that's better than any fancy education, if you ask me."

Izzy was less sure about her common-sense profile. "I've done a lot of dumb things in my life."

"Who hasn't?"

"I went swimming with sharks."

"Then you *are* an idiot."

Izzy laughed. "So college would help me?"

"It's a must."

"I never went. I hated school and couldn't wait to be out. I bummed around Europe for a few months, then came back here and joined a ski patrol in Colorado. From there it was an easy downhill slide . . . no pun intended."

"I've never been skiing. I know they have programs for the blind, but I really hate the cold. So what do you want to study?"

Izzy hesitated. Not because she didn't know but because the idea was so new, so tender, it could easily be crushed.

"Psychology," she said at last. "Child psychology. Specifically childhood traumas. I want to help children like Heidi. But going back to school? I don't know if I can do it. School was never my thing."

"You were never motivated before. You are now. They say that returning women are the most successful students in college."

"Seriously?"

"Sure. Start small. Go to community college, then transfer. It's the same classes at a slower pace."

Community college? Izzy hadn't thought of that. "It makes the process seem more manageable," she admitted.

"Or you could just stay here and marry Nick."

Izzy was glad she was sitting down, but hated that she couldn't see Rita's expression. "What?"

"You heard me. I may be blind, but I can see what's going on between the two of you."

"But we . . . I . . . What?"

There was something going on, but it was just that they liked each other and were going through something intense. He had helped her last night, which she appreciated. But married?

"I don't do commitments. Never have." That would require trusting someone to be there, to take care of her. Not her strong suit. "And Nick isn't looking for anything permanent." Until he could at least start on the road to forgiving himself, he wasn't in a position to care about anyone.

"He's a good guy. I've known him a while now. And he's supposed to be decent eye candy."

Izzy tried to laugh and choked instead. "Less of an issue for me today," she said, touching the bandages. "We're just friends."

Rita snorted. "Sure. Like anyone believes that." She stood. "The horses aren't going to take care of themselves. Come on. We have work to do."

Work Izzy could handle. "You have some really strange ideas."

"Maybe. Maybe not. But if I'm right, I'll be the first one to say I told you so."

"Jed Titan's here to see you. He doesn't have an appointment."

Garth raised his eyebrows. Jed coming to see him? That could only be good. The winner in a war never bothered with personal visits.

He pushed the intercom button on his phone. "Send him in."

He'd barely had time to walk around his desk when the door opened and Jed strolled in.

His father was a tall man, fit, with only a hint of gray in his dark hair. Garth knew he looked a whole lot more like Jed than Kathy. He'd also inherited his father's ruthless nature, quest for dominance and business savvy. He had a feeling that any softer characteristics his mother might claim had long been burned out of him.

"Jed," he said, crossing the space between them and offering his hand.

"Garth."

They shook. Jed eyed him, as if assessing him.

"Nice office," the older man said. "You own the building?"

"Sure. Why pay rent when you can collect it?"

Jed nodded. "Good. That's what I like to hear." He crossed to the leather sofas and chairs in the corner and took a seat. "It's a little early for bourbon so I'll take coffee. Black."

Garth used the intercom to give his assistant the order, then settled in a club chair opposite Jed.

"Cowboys have a fair chance this year," Jed said. "You follow football?"

"Not especially. Work keeps me busy."

"It's the Cowboys. They're America's team."

"I'm not sure the rest of the country would agree with that."

"Screw 'em."

The coffee was delivered. When the door closed and they were alone again, Jed leaned toward him.

"Garth, I have a proposition for you."

Victory, Garth thought, feeling a bone-deep sense of satisfaction. If not today, then soon. Jed was running scared. His visit here was proof of that. The plan was working.

"Which is?"

"A partnership. This has been a good game. You've given me a run for my money and I respect that, but we're talking business. Why waste the resources?"

"Because I have money to burn."

Jed's gaze sharpened. "So do I, but it's not necessary. Here's what I'm offering. I'll bring you in as president of Titan World with a generous salary. I'll gift you a truck-load of shares. The rest you'll vest over time so that when I'm gone you'll have controlling interest in the company. I mean the whole company. Not just a piece here or there. I'll also cut my daughters out of my will. You'll get it all. You'll win."

It was an offer made of desperation, Garth thought, pleased and a little disappointed. He hadn't thought Jed would cave so easily and he sure wasn't ready for the game to be over.

"What makes you think I don't want your daughters to get anything?"

"You've gone after them plenty. Look, Garth. I'm impressed and proud as hell. This is a onetime offer. What do you say?"

"That I'm not interested in working for you. I've built my own business."

Jed glared at him. "It's nothing compared to Titan World."

"It's getting there. Give me another year. As for the stock, I already own nearly ten percent. I plan to take you down the old-fashioned way."

Jed visibly relaxed. He leaned back against the sofa. "You want to play rough."

"Absolutely."

"I respect you coming after me. You have a bone to pick and maybe I earned it. But my girls are different. What you did to Izzy is just plain wrong. It's also against the law."

"I didn't have anything to do with the

explosion. I might be interested in having a little fun with my sisters, but I've done nothing to hurt them. I don't know what happened on that rig, but it wasn't me."

Jed shook his head. "At least admit you did it."

"If I had, I would. But I didn't."

Which left the same question on the table. Who else was after Jed? Who else had so much on the line that he would blow up an oil rig?

His gaze returned to his father. Had he been set up by Jed? Would Jed do that to his own kid, just to make Garth the bad guy? Why not? Jed was ruthless.

Garth stood. "I appreciate the offer, but no thanks. I don't need to work for you to control Titan World."

Jed came to his feet. "You won't win, boy. I'll crush you."

"You'll try. There's a difference. But in the end, I'll have it all."

"Then I'll see you in hell."

Garth shrugged. "You first."

CHAPTER FOURTEEN

Izzy sat in the sun, taking in the chaos around her. She could smell the meat on the barbecue and the sweet scent of lemonade, hear the multiple conversations, the clink of ice in glasses and hum of insects. It was a perfect September Saturday and most everyone she cared about in the world was around her.

Lexi was there with Cruz and his daughter, Kendra. Skye had brought Mitch and Erin. Rita and her husband had come, as had Norma, whose "date" was an Australian Shepherd who kept trying to herd everyone into a central spot. Aaron had brought his boyfriend, Steve. Izzy felt the love and support all around her but the one person she was most interested in hadn't come out of the house yet.

She was annoyed both by his tardiness and by her desire to have him next to her. Being totally blind was hard and having Nick nearby made it easier.

Familiarity, she told herself. It had nothing to do with how she felt. It couldn't. Talk about a disaster.

"How are you doing?" Dana asked as she came and sat next to Izzy.

"Okay. Still blind."

"I can see that. The bandages are a nice reminder."

"You like them? I think they're going to be on all the spring runways."

"Like I'd know what that means," Dana grumbled.

"It's a fashion thing."

"I don't do fashion."

Izzy grinned. "Or the whole mani-pedi experience. Do you even own mascara?"

"I did. Once. Maybe."

Dana was a wonderful friend and a lot of fun, but she was the opposite of girly.

"It's probably best you didn't go into retail," Izzy teased.

"You think?" Dana sighed. "Everyone here has someone but me. Even Norma brought a dog."

"Do you want a dog?"

"No. I'm just saying."

"You want a guy."

"Maybe." Dana sounded almost angry. "Let's change the subject."

"Why? You could date."

"Thanks. I was waiting for your permission."

Izzy laughed. "At least now you have it. Look. You're great and pretty and sexy and guys love that. But you've always picked safe, boring men who don't challenge you. Then you dump them because they're safe and boring. You need to try a different type."

Dana didn't say anything. Izzy suspected it was because her friend was afraid to try a different type. She didn't want the challenge. Izzy suspected there were secrets in Dana's past she'd never talked about and it would be impossible to —

The skin on the back of her neck prickled. She couldn't say why — she hadn't heard anything. But the sensation wouldn't go away. Seconds later, a strong, warm hand settled on her shoulder.

"How are you holding up?" Nick asked.

"Good. This is nice. Thanks for having everyone over." She felt oddly nervous to be around Nick and most of her family. As if she were afraid they would figure something out.

This was all Rita's fault, Izzy thought grimly. If Rita hadn't made that stupid comment about marrying Nick, she would feel completely normal. But noooo.

Just as awkward was the conversation she'd had at her doctor's office the previous day. She'd been in for a bandage change. One done in a nearly totally dark room with her eyes closed, so she still didn't know if she could see or not. But Dr. Greenspoon had lifted her physical restrictions. Meaning she could now go riding. Or, more important, make love with Nick.

Only she hadn't told him. *Her!* A woman used to taking whatever she wanted. A woman who gave as good as she got in bed, as well as everywhere else in life. She'd felt awkward and shy. Almost confused. And she hadn't said a word.

"Sorry I'm late," Nick said. "I was talking to a social worker about a couple of kids."

"You didn't miss much," Dana told him. "Skye's daughter, Erin, and your friend Aaron can't get over the fact that they have the same name, only it's spelled differently. The joke is hilarious to them, but getting old for the rest of us."

Izzy laughed. "You'll have to forgive Dana. She's a little cynical."

"Sounds like your kind of people," Nick said.

"She is."

"I'm going to get a beer. Want anything?"

"I'm good," Izzy told him.

"Me, too," Dana said. A few seconds later, she added, "You're going to be pleasantly surprised when you get a look at him. Seen him naked yet?"

Izzy grinned. "Not seen. How about experienced?"

"That's my girl." She lowered her voice. "I've heard about some interesting leads on the explosion. I've made friends with a couple of guys on the team and they're keeping me informed. I hope it leads somewhere. The Dallas police are all over the guy who hacked into Skye's foundation. So far he's not talking, but I think it's just a matter of time until he cracks."

"I hope so," Izzy said. "I'm so ready for us to take Garth down."

"Me, too. I plan to do everything in my power to crush him like the bug he is."

"Can I watch?"

"Every second of it."

Nick looked at Izzy from across the yard. She sat with her sisters and they were all laughing about something. There were over a dozen people at the picnic — friends, not a corporate retreat. It was personal.

He didn't do personal. Didn't believe in it. He knew he had to keep himself apart — part of the ongoing punishment.

What would Izzy say if he told her that? Or did she already know? Had she guessed? Thinking about her made him wonder how long he had to pay, which was a stupid question. The payments never ended. There would never be atonement. He couldn't ever do enough.

He spotted a car heading up the driveway. He hadn't expected anyone else. The small import screamed rental car. He headed toward it, then stared at the young woman who climbed out.

She was petite, with red hair and too many freckles. He recognized her immediately. Her name was Denise and she'd been the first kid he'd ever had at the ranch.

Aaron rushed past him, shrieking like a girl. "You made it. I wasn't sure you would."

They hugged.

"Made it" as in she was invited? Nick looked at Aaron. "What's going on?"

"A nice surprise to help you remember you're one of the good guys." Aaron hopped in place as he beamed at Denise. "I haven't seen you in forever. You look fabulous."

Denise laughed. "So do you."

Nick moved toward them. "Hi."

"Hey, Nick." Denise smiled at him, then looked past him to the crowd. "No one said there was a party."

"Nothing big. It's a barbecue for friends."

Denise had been a sullen, withdrawn teenager whose mother had been in and out of her life for years. When Denise had been fourteen, her mother had taken her out on the streets to bring in money as a prostitute. Denise had endured for nearly six months, running away time and time again, until she was picked up by the police and turned over to foster care.

It wasn't the drinking and drugs that had made her caseworker nervous. It had been the cutting. When things got too bad, Denise cut herself.

She'd been in therapy about a year when she'd shown up as his first kid. He hadn't known what to do with her, but Rita had stuck her on a horse and Aaron had talked boys and fashion. She'd stayed a long weekend, then had returned half a dozen times. Nick had written her a letter of recommendation to college and paid her tuition. Scholarships had funded the rest.

"You have friends?" Denise teased. "What happened to solitary guy?"

"He's growing," Aaron said, hugging her again. "We're all so proud. And look at you. I love your haircut. It's perfect."

"I learned everything I know about fashion from you."

Aaron waved his hands in front of his eyes as if trying not to cry. "I need to get a glass of water." He moved away.

Nick turned toward Denise. "Everything okay?"

She grinned. "Better than okay. Aaron e-mailed me a couple of weeks ago, just to say hi. He suggested I stop by. I couldn't get the idea out of my head. Mostly because I should have come to see you before. I wanted you to see this." She pulled a small card out of her back pocket.

He took it and stared at the ID. It was for Denise, showing her to be a student at the UCLA medical school. He felt a flush of pride. "Good for you."

"I'm going to be a doctor. I'm leaning toward specializing in trauma. It's grueling and I should be back there studying, but I couldn't stop thinking about you, Nick. How you helped me."

He handed her the ID card. "You did this yourself."

She shook her head. "I don't just mean that you paid for most of my college. I never told you before, but that day you came and got me . . ." She looked down, then back at him. "I couldn't do it anymore. I couldn't stand hurting myself, but I didn't know another way to manage. I'd decided to kill myself. I'd figured out exactly how to do it. Then you showed up and made me come here and everything changed."

Her green eyes were bright with hope and promise. "I wanted you to know you saved my life."

Her praise made him uncomfortable. "Like I said, you saved yourself."

"Still not taking credit for what you do?" she asked. "Maybe I should go into psychiatry and figure out why."

"No, thanks."

"Typical guy." She stepped forward and hugged him.

He hugged her back. "You did good, kid. You earned your way out of hell. Don't ever look back."

"I won't. I just wanted to say thank-you. For the chance. For dragging me out here. You make a huge difference here. Aaron tells me you're still having kids out. Don't ever stop. You never know who you're going to save."

He didn't know what to say to that.

Denise giggled. "If you could see your face."

He desperately wanted to take a step back, turn and run. "That's really, ah, sweet of you. Do you need anything? Can I help pay for medical school?"

"I'm fine. I have grants and scholarships and if all goes well, I won't even need a student loan."

"Come to me before you get a loan. I want to help."

"I know. That's why you're one of the good guys." She glanced at her watch. "I need to head back to the airport soon. I'm doing a one-day turnaround and want to drop in on a few friends. I just couldn't stop thinking about you."

They hugged again, then she waved and left. Nick watched her go. When he turned back to the picnic, he saw Aaron talking to Izzy and her sisters. Skye and Lexi were staring at him with identical "that's so sweet" expressions. Izzy simply smiled.

He knew what they were thinking, but that was going to change just as soon as he told Izzy the truth about Garth. He'd already put it off too long — he knew that. But he'd wanted to wait until after the surgery. As soon as the bandages came off, he would tell her. Better to hear it from him than Garth. Because if the man he'd once thought of as his friend believed it would help his cause, he would tell Izzy himself. Former friendship be damned.

But however she heard it, she would be devastated. And not just her. Aaron, who was a better friend than he deserved, and Izzy's family would be hurt. The information would wound them all and there was nothing he could do to make it better or easier for anyone.

Izzy tried her best to keep still in the chair, but it was difficult. "Will I know right away? Is it going to hurt? Do I have to wear dark glasses?"

Dr. Greenspoon gently unwound the bandages from around her head. "We've dimmed the lights so don't worry if everything isn't as bright as you'd like. It will take a few minutes for your eyes to focus. Try to relax."

"You didn't tell me to stop talking."

"I didn't think that was possible."

Izzy tried to laugh at the joke, but she was too scared. The week was over, the moment was here. In a few seconds she would know if she could see or not. Her entire life would change based on the outcome of the surgery.

"I'm going to throw up," she whispered.

"No, you're not."

The last of the bandages fell away, as did the pads that had been pressed against her eyes.

She sat in the exam room, terrified of opening her eyes and learning the truth —

that she was blind forever. That she was going to have to learn to be strong and resourceful in ways she didn't know were possible.

She wasn't that kind of tough. She was . . .

Izzy realized she wasn't in total darkness anymore. There was a hint of light. Slowly she opened her eyes and blinked several times. There was a second of blurriness, then the room came into focus. She could see Dr. Greenspoon, the equipment and just beyond that, Lexi and Skye standing together, hands clutched, their faces locked in identical expressions of hope and dread.

Izzy's gaze dropped to the light tan Coach handbag Lexi had over one arm.

"Great bag," she said. "Is it new?"

Lexi and Skye both shrieked and rushed toward her. Izzy jumped to her feet as they grabbed each other.

"I can see! I can see!"

"I knew it would work," Skye said. "I knew it had to."

"I was so scared," Lexi admitted. "This is the best."

More than the best, Izzy thought, practically floating with happiness and relief. She could see. She could *see!*

The three of them turned to the doctor, a delightful man in his seventies, then took turns kissing him on the cheek.

"I don't know how to thank you," Izzy whispered as she hugged him. "You're a miracle worker."

He smiled at her. "That's what I like to hear."

Thirty minutes later, they stepped out into the sunny morning. Izzy had on sunglasses, but the light didn't bother her at all. In fact, it was amazing and the world was a beautiful place.

Okay, she was looking at a parking lot, but the sky was blue and the cars were so pretty. She could *see.*

"I didn't know if this was going to happen," she admitted as she walked next to her sisters. "I'm relieved."

"Us, too," Lexi told her.

"And happy," Skye added.

Izzy couldn't believe it. She had no restrictions. Just eye drops to use three times a day and a follow-up visit in a couple of weeks.

They turned down a row of cars. She came to a stop. A familiar red GT Mustang convertible was parked next to Skye's SUV.

"You brought my car," Izzy said, feeling her throat tighten.

"We weren't going to tell you if it hadn't gone well," Skye said. "I called the doctor's office a couple of days ago and they said you'd be able to drive so we wanted it here."

Izzy took the keys Lexi offered. "I have wheels."

"You have an engine and tires, too," Lexi said with a grin. "Oh, and I believe this is yours, too."

Izzy frowned as Lexi pulled something small from her pocket and held it out. Izzy took it, then laughed when she recognized the swirl of tiny diamonds.

"I still think piercing your belly button is beyond strange," Skye said with a sniff. "They took it out while you were unconscious at the hospital. I wanted to sell it at a pawn shop and donate the proceeds to charity."

"Of course you did." Izzy grinned. "But as I haven't had the benefit of your elegant finishing school education, I'm happy to have it back."

She would put it in later, then flash it at Nick.

Thinking about him made her both excited and nervous. She was finally going to see what he looked like. Would seeing him be okay? Would she feel weird about it? Would he?

"Want to get coffee?" Lexi asked. "There's a Starbucks around the corner."

"I'd love that," Skye said.

"Me, too." Izzy wanted to spend a little time with her sisters before going to the ranch.

When they'd ordered their lattes and were seated at a corner table, Izzy took a minute to simply look around. The store was just like all the others. Light and bright, full of delicious smells and friendly conversation. She could see the colorful labels on the bags of beans for sale. The fall shades of the mugs, the print on the newspaper left abandoned on the next table.

She turned back to her sisters and saw them both watching her.

"Sorry," she said with a laugh. "Just enjoying the miracle. I feel like Scrooge on Christmas morning. I've been given a second chance."

Skye's eyes filled with tears. "I'm so happy for you."

"Me, too," Lexi said, not nearly as emotional. "What are you going to do with it? Any big changes planned?"

"Like not piercing your belly button?" Skye asked.

"I won't get it pierced again," Izzy promised. "But if I can fit this back in . . ."

"That's tacky."

"I know. I've been given a second chance,

not a new personality."

The sisters smiled at each other.

Izzy sipped her latte. "I'm going to get a job and start saving for college."

Skye nearly choked on her coffee. Lexi's eyes widened. They both stared at her.

Lexi recovered first. "College?"

"Community college. I have to get my brain in working order. Then I'll transfer to a four year. I want to study psychology. Specifically for children. We've had a few at the ranch. There was this one girl, Heidi. She's been through a lot. I want to help and college seems like the place to start."

More tears filled Skye's eyes.

"Maybe you should go see Dr. Green-spoon," Izzy muttered. "I'm going to college, Skye. Not curing world hunger."

"But it's so great." Skye dabbed at her eyes. "Don't get a job. I'll release your trust money."

Izzy did her best not to react. The trust was from the money their mother had left Skye when Pru had died. Skye had taken a percentage of it and put it in trust for Izzy until she was thirty. It would more than pay for college, along with living expenses.

"You don't have to do that," Izzy told her. "I can work."

"But it will be easier to focus on your

studies. Izzy, that money was always for your future. Now you know what you want it to be."

Which all sounded great, as long as Izzy didn't think too much about the fact that her own mother hadn't bothered to mention her in the will.

"I appreciate that," she said at last. "Thanks."

"College," Lexi said. "You going out for cheerleading?"

"Very funny. I'm not the one who tried out for the Dallas Cowboy Cheerleaders."

Lexi winced. "We agreed not to talk about that again."

"You agreed," Izzy teased. "Me? Not so much."

Izzy spent an hour with her sisters, before heading back to the ranch. She put the top down on her convertible, cranked up the CD player and loved every second of the long drive.

There was so much to see. The sky, the other cars, the strip malls. Life was good and she planned to enjoy every minute of it.

She managed to keep her nerves at bay right until she turned off the highway and headed down the long road leading to the main house of the ranch. She slowed as she approached, taking in the large, white clapboard structure with the wide porch and flowerpots. Beyond the house was the barn and the corrals. In the distance she could just make out the shapes of the guest cottages.

Scared and jittery, she parked her car and climbed out. The front door opened. A thin man stepped out. He was only a few inches taller than her, with sandy brown hair and brown eyes. His shirt was lavender, his jeans tighter than hers and he wore bright red cowboy boots. She grinned.

"You're beyond fabulous," she yelled.

Aaron clapped his hands, then rushed toward her. "Seriously? You can see me? Don't you love my boots?"

"They're perfection!"

They hugged, then Aaron put his arm around her shoulders. "So, what do you think about Chez Nick?"

"Fancy."

"I've had to make a lot of changes. You should have seen it when I got here. It gave the word *institutional* a bad name. You're healed? All is well?"

"I'm healed and have nothing but eye drops to worry about. Oh, and no eye makeup for the next month."

"You don't need it." Aaron squeezed. "I'm

so happy for you. Come on in. You'll want to see the house. And Nick."

Izzy hung back. "I thought I'd go see Rita first."

"Chicken."

"Maybe. I need a few minutes."

"All right. When you're ready, he's in his office. I won't say a word."

"Thanks."

Aaron went back in the house and Izzy started toward the barn. Partway there, she paused and glanced back at the house. She really wanted to see Nick, to finally know what he looked like. But not just yet.

The barn was big and red, with crisp, white trim. As she walked in the large open door, she saw that everything was clean, the supplies neatly stacked. She followed the sound of soft words into the storeroom.

Rita stood patting a barn cat on a shelf. Izzy took in the petite woman's curly brown hair, her work-roughened hands and eyes that didn't track with her actions.

"Hi," Izzy said.

Rita turned toward her. "What happened?"

"I can see."

Rita smiled and moved toward her. "Good. I knew that's what would happen, but I'm happy all the same."

Izzy bit her lower lip. "Are you sure it's okay?" Because nothing changed for Rita.

The older woman cupped Izzy's face. "Never be sorry for what you have. Be grateful. But don't think this means you're going to stop working for me."

"I'd like to stay." For as long as Nick would let her. But she was only here to heal. Wouldn't everything be different now? Wasn't she supposed to leave?

"Then tell him that."

"Okay."

Rita dropped her hands to Izzy's shoulders, turned her and gave her a little shove. "Tell him now."

Izzy made her way back to the house. She went inside.

The huge living room was decorated in shades of green. The hardwood floors were covered with big rugs. There were comfortable sofas and chairs. She crossed to a couch and touched the fabric she'd never been able to see before. The fireplace was brick. She hadn't known there was one. Brass lamps sat on end tables. Everything was different than she'd imagined. Different, yet familiar.

She took a step, then stopped, not sure where to find Nick's office. Then she closed her eyes. The darkness was familiar. She got her bearings, opened her eyes and started down the hall.

A door stood open on her left. She heard him working on his computer. Izzy swallowed a couple of times, trying to ignore the butterflies in her stomach. She jumped out of planes without a second thought. Of course she could walk into a room and say hi to a guy. She stepped into the doorway.

"Hi, Nick."

He looked up, then stood.

Her first impression was of size. He was tall and muscled, which she'd figured out already, but knowing and seeing were very different. He had broad shoulders and long legs. He seemed to fill the room with his presence.

He had dark hair, which wasn't a surprise, but piercing green eyes that were. His mouth was perfect, nearly as good to look at as to kiss.

"Izzy."

She saw the questions in his eyes, the concern and something that might have been a little case of nerves. She smiled.

"You're very crush-worthy."

He gave her a slow, sexy smile that made the butterflies in her stomach sigh. He walked around the desk. "You can see."

"Everything. I'm healed and restored and

ready to swim with sharks. Oh. I can't go swimming for a month. No swimming, no eye makeup, but otherwise, it's back to nor—"

He silenced her with a kiss. That sensual mouth of his claimed her with lips and tongue. She hung on to him, feeling the shoulders she'd just seen, knowing what the muscled body now looked like.

Kissing him felt right, she thought, giving in to the experience. Better than right. It felt like something she would be very happy doing for the next five thousand years.

He broke the kiss and stared into her eyes. "Ready to hear I told you so?"

"You're one of *those* kind of guys. That's disappointing."

He kissed her again.

She let the desire wash through her. It mingled with happiness and elation and every good feeling she could imagine. Today was a very good day.

He straightened and rubbed his thumb against her mouth. "What am I going to do with you?"

A question she wasn't sure she wanted answered. "Whatever you want?"

The slow, sexy grin reappeared. "Works for me. But I was thinking about out of bed."

"Oh. That."

"We're busy for the next few weeks. Want to stay and help out with the corporate retreats? Aaron always needs staff."

She rested her hands on his chest. "You mean I wouldn't be in charge?"

"Not this time."

Stay here with Nick? It was the best offer she'd had all day. She would be doing work she enjoyed while getting ready to start the next phase of her life. And, hey, maybe figure out her feelings about Nick.

"I'd like that."

"Good. I've already talked to Aaron and he's giddy with excitement. He wants to meet with you this afternoon."

She wrinkled her nose. "Now I'll have to take notes and everything." She grinned. "Kinda cool, huh?"

"It works for me."

She started to leave, then turned back to face him. "Oh, I have wheels now. My sisters brought my car to the doctor's office. It's the red Mustang. If you ask real nice, I'll let you drive it."

"How nice?"

"You'll figure it out. And that's not the only thing that's new." She pulled up the hem of her T-shirt, exposing her belly button and the diamond bar nestled against her skin. "For later."

He swallowed. "Promise?"

"Oh, yeah."

CHAPTER FIFTEEN

"Are you paying attention?" Aaron asked.

"Yes." Izzy sat slumped at the kitchen table. "You're way bossier than I remember."

"You were gone a morning. How could you possibly forget anything?"

"I didn't have to take notes before."

"You couldn't see the paper before." He tapped on her yellow pad. "Chop-chop."

"You did *not* just say that to me."

"Want to arm wrestle for dominance, honey?"

Izzy laughed. "That's okay. Back to brainstorming."

They were talking about ways to make more use of the ranch.

"So far we've got renting out the facilities without staffing them," Aaron said. "I like that. Groups can come in and do their thing, then leave. Our expenses will be minimal. We'll charge them a cleaning fee, so there's the insurance issues and wear and tear. And I like your idea of expanding the obstacle course."

"I think we should talk about having kids here longer than a weekend," she said. "What about a week at a time?" Her plan was eventually kids would take over for the whole summer, but she doubted Nick was ready to hear that.

"What additional staff would we need?" Aaron asked. "A nurse? Counselor?"

"Maybe. What about a school counselor? They have the summer off. We could invite a counselor and his or her whole family. They'd get a free vacation, we'd get the expert we need?"

Aaron eyed her. "You've been thinking about this?"

"Some. I saw what the time here did for Heidi. That was only three days. In a week —"

"We're not doing weeks."

The statement came from behind her. Izzy turned and saw Nick standing in the kitchen.

"What are you two doing?" he asked, not sounding or looking happy. She'd never seen him frown before. Or the ice that seemed to invade his eyes. "You're supposed to be working on logistics for our fall retreats."

"We've done that," Aaron told him, unfazed by the obvious annoyance. "We're brainstorming ways to make your life better."

"My life is fine the way it is." He left.

Izzy rose and went after him.

"What's your problem?" she demanded as she hurried to catch up with him. "We're helping. You need to be starting the conversation with thank you."

He stopped in front of his office and faced her. "This doesn't concern you."

Had he been this much of a jerk when she'd been blind?

"Excuse me? I should just shut up and do my job? I don't think so. What's wrong with you?" She planted her hands on her hips and glared at him. "Getting the most use out of the facilities makes financial sense. Expanding what you offer will bring in more clients. The more corporate sessions you book, the more money for the real work with the kids. Although if you ask me, you need to completely change the schedule to do corporate stuff from fall to spring and have kids all summer. Aaron 231 and I were talking about having one-week sessions for them that —"

"No."

Nick didn't speak loudly or harshly, but there was a finality to the single word that silenced her.

They stared at each other.

"Just like that," she said. "Only you get to decide? There's no team here? What is going on with you? Why are you acting like this?"

"This is how it has to be."

She knew he had a gentle, caring side. She'd seen it. She'd experienced it firsthand. But apparently that part of him was on vacation.

"Is this about the guilt?" she asked.

The ice thickened. "I'm not having this conversation."

"Actually, you are. That's why we're both angry." She drew in a breath. "I understand you have issues."

"I don't have issues. I'm responsible for the death of three innocent people. That is fact, not emotional baggage."

"True, but because of those other people, *children* are getting a second chance. That girl who was here before. Denise. She's going to be a doctor. She'll spend her entire career saving lives. There are people who will still be living because of her. People who otherwise wouldn't make it. And she's doing that because of what you did."

"Nothing makes up for what I did before."

"All the more reason to have the kids here longer."

"No."

He stepped into his office and closed the door behind him.

There wasn't a lock. She could have followed him inside. But that wasn't the point. He was trying to shut her out and he was doing a heck of a job at it.

So much for the romantic homecoming, she thought sadly as she walked away. So much for thinking there was something between them. It was as if Nick was trying to push her away.

And he was doing a damn good job.

Nick stood in the center of his office and wanted to throw something. He knew he should go apologize to Izzy, but he couldn't. Not without telling her what was wrong. And to tell her that was to admit the truth about Garth.

He would have to tell her eventually. The longer he waited, the bigger the risk that she would find out from Garth directly, and Nick didn't want that.

But he also didn't want to lose her.

He knew the second she found out the

truth, she would stare at him as if she had no idea who he was. Because she would believe he'd betrayed her. That he'd sold her out from the beginning. And he wasn't sure he could explain well enough to change her mind. She wouldn't be able to forgive him just like he couldn't forgive Garth, despite the continued calls from his former friend.

Just another day, he thought. One more day. One more night. Then he'd tell her.

What tonight was supposed to have been, he thought grimly. Them together. He'd blown that.

He crossed to his desk, but couldn't relax enough to sit. If only he'd met her another way. If only they didn't have Garth between them. Would that have made a difference? And why did he care? It wasn't as if Izzy was a significant part of his life. She was a friend. He respected her, but in a few weeks she would be gone. He wasn't looking for anything permanent.

Connections were impossible. What if he got so happy he forgot what he'd done? What if he stopped making payments on his debt to society?

He'd never thought to ask the question before. Izzy claimed peace could be found, or maybe made. But he didn't believe her.

Life wasn't that easy. He'd been wrong and he had to pay. There was no way around it. However much he might want that to be different.

The early morning was cool and clear, with almost no humidity. Practically a miracle, Izzy thought happily as she drove with Aaron to the guesthouse to set up for their corporate retreat. Norma had spent most of the previous day working with the caterers on food prep, the housekeeping service had been through to get the rooms ready and boxes of folders, pens and notebooks had been delivered.

"I want to be outside," Izzy whined when they came to a stop in front of the large guesthouse building. "Don't make me stay inside."

"Work this morning, play this afternoon," Aaron told her.

"I want to play now."

He got out of the Jeep and looked at her. "You sound like you're five."

She got out, raised her arms so they were level with her shoulders and spun. "I want to see things, do things. I'm not blind anymore, Aaron. Give me a break."

"Putting together the notebooks is doing something. Don't make me use my stern voice. You won't like it."

Izzy slowed and looked at him. "If I'm bad, will you spank me?" she asked, mostly to make him squirm.

Aaron wrinkled his nose. "I am *so* the wrong person to have that conversation. Didn't Nick tire you out last night?"

"No. I slept alone."

"While I want to hear all the details, I have a very busy morning." He pointed to the back of the Jeep. "Take those boxes inside to the conference room and set everything up. We have thirty people due here at ten-thirty. We are going to be ready. Don't make me get crabby."

"All right." She sighed heavily, then started taking boxes into the conference room. At least she would spend the afternoon outside, demonstrating the rope bridge. She couldn't wait to see how it really was and what it would be like now that she could see everything.

She went inside the conference center. There were several smaller rooms and one large one with tables set up in a square so everyone could see everyone else.

"Very corporate," she murmured as she opened the boxes and began setting out a notebook filled with very technical financial information, a pen and a pad of paper on the desk in front of each chair.

When she was done, she went exploring. The so-called media room was more of a theater, with raised seating, an industrial-size popcorn maker, a huge fridge and a remote control to turn down the lights. Heaven forbid anyone should get up and actually *walk* to the switch on the wall.

She went upstairs and looked at the guest rooms. They were all beautifully decorated — a lush combination of upscale hotel and cozy B and B. The baths were spacious and well stocked and light filtered in from large windows.

She returned downstairs and made her way to the kitchen, where Norma was hard at work directing the catering staff.

"Nice place," Izzy said, glancing around the restaurant-size kitchen. "It inspires me to cook."

Norma barely looked up. "Don't even think about it. I'm having enough trouble as it is. Did you see what was delivered? They're not going to care if I serve them steak or dog food."

Izzy looked in the corner. Cases and cases of beer sat ready to go in the massive refrigerator.

"There's only thirty guys," she said. "They can't drink all that in three days."

"I guess they're going to give it a try. Can you put those in the refrigerator? At least as much as will fit on the bottom two shelves. We already have three cases on ice in the main living room and two more out back."

Izzy admired dedication to a cause, but this was too much even for her. "Somebody's going to be really sick by the end of the day," she said.

"Just what we need. A bunch of finance guys puking all over the furniture," Norma muttered. "Why didn't I become a plumber? That's what my mom always told me. People always need plumbers, you can overcharge folks who annoy you and are mostly out of the heat. But did I listen? Of course not."

Izzy hid a smile. "You're a fabulous cook. Aaron worships your biscuits."

"I know. He's a good boy."

Words that would make him shudder, Izzy thought.

When Izzy had finished with the beer, she went outside. It was after ten and cars were already pulling up in front of the main building.

There were three and four guys to a car. They were all in their twenties, most wore glasses. They looked smart and geeky and the first words out of their mouth were,

"Where's the beer?"

"What company is this?" she asked Aaron as he walked by looking nervous.

"One who won't be using these facilities again. They're already annoying me. Did you see how much beer there is? They'll be drunk by noon. I can only hope they all fall off the rope ladder." He waved toward the building. "Go be flirty. Keep them busy and away from me."

Izzy turned back, only to feel a prickling along the back of her neck. She searched until she found Nick by the back of the building. He was walking toward her, looking far too handsome and sexy in the sunlight.

She knew there were other guys around and under other circumstances she would be cruising the group to pick out any who interested her. But not right now. Maybe not for a long time. There was only one man who occupied her thoughts these days. Unfortunately, he was the most annoying person on the planet.

He walked up to her.

"You were a serious jackass yesterday," she said by way of a greeting. "We were only trying to help. I'll accept that everyone has issues, but we shouldn't have to pay for yours. And it's fine if you want to keep on punishing yourself for what happened in the past, but not having kids here more is punishing them and they don't deserve that."

He stared at her for a long time. His eyes were an impossible shade of green. Dark and rich and more appealing than she could have imagined. His mouth was even more tempting. Looking at it made her want to kiss him, which she couldn't. Not until he was done being a jerk. It violated her principles. Oh, but she was tempted.

"You about done?" he asked.

"Maybe. Are you willing to admit you were wrong?"

"Maybe."

She smiled. "Someone needs to beat you with a stick."

"It would take several someones."

"You think you're so tough?"

"I *know* I'm tough."

"Want to prove it?"

Fire flared in his eyes. "When and where?"

Here and now seemed like a good answer. Except . . . "You haven't said you were sorry or that Aaron and I were right."

"Do I have to?"

"Yes. Admit it. My point's a good one. It's one thing to beat up yourself, but keeping kids from getting better is not the road to recovery."

He didn't say anything, but then he didn't have to. She knew what he was thinking — that there was no road to recovery. But she didn't deal with that. Instead, she waited, hoping, believing he would see that she was right. That helping other kids, more kids, was the best thing to do.

"I'm sorry," he said slowly. "And having more kids here makes sense."

She grinned. "See? That wasn't hard. Just accept that you can't resist me and your life will be much easier."

"Thanks for the update."

His mouth twitched as he spoke. She had a feeling that he was doing his best not to smile.

"About that when and where," she said. "Tonight?"

"Your room or mine?"

"I'll come down to your room." She turned to leave, then glanced back at him. "Don't piss me off between now and then."

"I'll try not to."

"As you're a man, I guess that's the best I can hope for."

Izzy loved everything about the rope ladder, except the harness Ethan, Nick's mountain-climbing friend, had insisted she wear.

"But I'm not blind anymore," she whined.

Ethan, a fortysomething tanned hunk, shook his head. "Until you can prove you bounce when you fall, you're wearing a harness."

"But it takes away from the experience."

"What my seventeen-year-old son says about condoms. Do I look like I care?"

"Fine," she muttered and started to climb.

The afternoon was warm, there was a slight breeze and if she ignored the very drunk finance guys and their tacky comments, she was fine.

"Baby, I'll catch you if you fall," was acceptable, but "Nice ass" made her want to practice a nice knee-to-the-groin move.

She reached the ladder. Ethan was already on the other side, waiting for her.

"I can do this," she called, walking across without slowing. It was a whole lot easier with actual vision. She loved being level with the leaves on the trees and watching birds fly by.

"Can I go again?" she asked when she reached Ethan.

"I doubt it's going to be a problem. They're all too drunk to climb."

"Maybe they're afraid of heights and it was their plan."

"You're giving them too much credit."

Izzy made her way down the tree. Nick stood with the manager of the group, probably explaining they wouldn't be testing their courage anytime soon.

Sure enough, Ethan was already down and putting away harnesses.

She walked toward Nick.

". . . take them for an easy hike," he was saying. "They can burn off the alcohol."

"They work hard. They deserve to party."

"No one needs to party this much." Nick sounded frustrated.

Izzy moved closer. "I'll go on the hike with you," she said. "I can make sure there aren't any stragglers."

The manager looked unconvinced. "They're fine."

"For guys at a frat party," Nick said. "I want everyone out of here by sundown."

"What? We've paid for the whole weekend!"

"You'll get your money back. We don't want a group like this around." He glanced at his watch. "I'm cutting off the beer as of now. They have five hours to sober up, then get out of here."

The manager muttered something Izzy couldn't hear, then stalked off.

"Now what?" she asked.

"We wait until they stop acting like idiots.

If they want to continue without the beer, they can stay. Otherwise, I'm throwing them out. I need to go see Ethan. I want him to stick around and help me make sure no one does anything stupid."

"What are the odds of that?"

"Tell me about it. You okay?"

"I'm fine. They're harmless. I'll stay out, too. Maybe I can shame them into better behavior."

"Interesting plan."

He headed toward Ethan. Izzy did a quick head count to make sure everyone was still in the area, then frowned as she realized four guys were missing.

She hesitated, trying to figure out which way they'd gone. She heard male laughter off to her left and walked in that direction.

"Get it! Get it!"

"You get it. Man, look at it."

"It's pissed, bro. You are so dead."

Izzy couldn't begin to imagine what the four guys were up to and she didn't much care. She would herd them back to the main group and count the hours until they were gone.

She stepped around a bush, only to find four very drunk men had trapped a rattle-snake between a tree and a fallen log. They were taunting it by jabbing it with sticks.

The snake was fair-size, maybe six feet long, coiled, rattling its tail like mad and, from the crazed look in its little snake eyes, out for blood.

"Are you insane?" she yelled.

The guy closest to the snake dropped his stick and leaped back when the snake lunged.

"Jeez, lady," the guy complained. "You nearly made me drop my beer."

"And what a shame that would have been." Izzy kept her attention on the snake, telling herself not to panic. While she wasn't technically afraid of snakes, she didn't have any as close friends. "Step away from the rattler and head back to your group. No sudden moves, just a general easing back."

"We're not afraid," a guy said, poking the snake again.

"Then you're really stupid."

"I'm wearing boots. It can't bite through boots."

"Great. Did you know rattlers can jump nearly as far as they are long? Hmm, let me think. If that snake took a flying leap, by my calculations it would hit your balls. You wearing boots there, too?"

The men moved back.

She drew in a breath. Everything was going to be fine. She just had to stay calm and speak firmly. Pretend the guys were actually four-year-olds, although in her opinion the average four-year-old showed a whole lot more sense.

"All right, gentlemen. If you'll follow me."

"You think you're so smart," one of the guys said and grabbed her arm. "Let's see how you like the snake."

Before Izzy knew what was happening, the man was drawing her forward, between him and the snake. The creature's fury was palpable. It coiled tightly and lunged.

The next few seconds were a blur. Izzy screamed. Something hard slammed into her, pushing her out of the way. The snake made contact with someone, although she was pretty sure it wasn't her. Then she was falling.

The ground was as hard as it looked. All the air rushed out of her, but she forced herself to roll onto her side, gasping. Even as she sucked in air, she saw the snake slithering back into the underbrush, the guys scattering and Nick standing next to her, two clear bite marks on his left forearm.

Izzy scrambled to her feet. The phrase *blind panic* suddenly made perfect sense because it didn't matter if she could see. Nick was going to die, right here, in the semiwilderness and she didn't know what to do.

"Don't scream," she said as she rushed to him. "Don't scream."

"I wasn't planning on screaming," he told her.

"I was talking to myself."

"It's all right," he said calmly. "I'm going to move to this tree and lean against it. Send Ethan to get Aaron to drive the SUV as close as possible. Then bring back the first-aid kit."

Her heart pounded so fast, she thought she was going to pass out. The bite marks were deep. Blood oozed out of them. "There's antivenom serum in the first-aid kit?"

"No. A bandage. You're going to wrap my arm, then we'll drive to the hospital."

As he spoke, he walked to the tree, then leaned.

"Should you sit down? You need to sit down. How can you be so calm. Is it the venom? Is it already in your brain?"

"I don't want to move around. Lack of movement keeps the venom localized." He stared into her eyes. "Izzy, you can do this."

She wanted to run in a circle screaming. She wanted to wring her hands and beg the universe to fix him. She wanted to sit down and cry, then lose herself in panic. Instead she knew she had to take care of business.

"Okay," she said and took off to find Ethan.

Five minutes later she was back with the first-aid kit Ethan had handed her. She brought it to Nick, who told her to open it.

Easier said than done, she thought as her hands shook. "What kind of bandage?"

"Gauze to put over the bite marks, then an Ace bandage to wrap my arm. See if there's a sling."

She didn't bother reading the contents. Instead she dumped everything on the ground and rapidly searched through it until she found what she needed.

"I'm going to throw up," she muttered as she grabbed everything and raced to his side.

"Just don't get any on me."

"Shut up. Tell me what to do."

"I can't do both."

She looked at him. "I am hanging on by a thread, Nick. I swear, why couldn't you catch the damn snake like they do in the movies?"

"So this is my fault?"

There was actual humor in his voice. As if he thought the situation was funny. As if he wasn't going to die.

341

"Did I tell you not to piss me off?" she asked.

"I hate to disappoint you, Izzy, but we're not having sex tonight."

"Yeah, I got that. Tell me what to do."

He walked her through covering the wound, then wrapping his arm. The work was difficult, what with her fingers shaking and the sense of impending doom sending waves of panic through her. Knowing his life depended on her, she kept going. Slowly, carefully, she secured the sling around his arm and helped him anchor his arm against his chest, his wrist and hand higher than his elbow.

"Go wait for the car," he told her.

"I'm not leaving you."

"You're not leaving. You're checking on the car. Go on, Izzy. I'll be right here."

She hesitated a second, then raced to the clearing. The corporate guys were gone. She hoped Ethan had bullied the hell out of them and thrown in a few threats for good measure. She planned to call the sheriff just as soon as she knew Nick wasn't going to die, but right now she didn't care about anything but getting him to the hospital.

"Hurry," she said aloud. "Hurry."

Seconds later Nick's SUV raced down the road and slammed to a stop just beside her.

Aaron jumped out.

"Where is he?" he yelled, his arms waving. "Oh, God. A snake? A rattlesnake? Is he dead? He's dead, isn't he?"

"Not yet. Come on."

She grabbed Aaron's arm and led him back to Nick. He was still leaning against the tree, looking calm. But she saw the sweat on his forehead and noticed the tension in his jaw.

"You all right?" she asked.

"Fine. We're going to walk to the SUV. Aaron, I'll lean on you."

"Yes, yes." Aaron sounded as shaky as Izzy felt.

He looped Nick's free arm around his shoulder and they moved the few feet down the trail. Nick wanted to go slowly, stepping carefully. His breathing was steady. She told herself that was good. It had to be.

When they reached the SUV, she helped him slide into the backseat, then closed the door behind him.

"Are you driving?" she asked Aaron.

"Yes."

"Do you know where the hospital is?"

"Yes. I've already called and told them we're coming. They're ready."

"Good."

She climbed into the passenger seat,

343

buried her face in her hands and burst into tears.

Nick lay in the hospital bed. Morning light filtered in through the blinds. His arm hurt like a sonofabitch, but he could deal with the pain.

He glanced over at the woman curled up in the big chair in the corner. No matter how he'd ordered, yelled and pleaded, Izzy had refused to leave. She'd spent the night fussing over him, talking to him when he couldn't sleep and getting him ice for his water.

Slowly she stirred, then straightened and groaned. "Not exactly comfortable," she said as she stood and straightened. Then she looked at him. "How are you feeling?"

"Better."

"You sure?"

"You heard the doctor. I'm going to be fine."

"He said you were lucky. It was a big snake."

"I'm a big guy."

"And you knew what to do. I would have freaked and made everything worse."

He didn't want to think about her being hurt. The memory of seeing that guy dragging her toward the rattler would haunt him forever.

She crossed to the bed and put her hand on his forehead. "Not clammy anymore."

He grabbed her wrist. "You should go home. Get some sleep. Take a shower."

"Are you saying I'm not at my best?"

"I'm saying I'm okay. You don't have to monitor me."

"Maybe I like monitoring you."

There was a knock at the half-open door, then Lexi and Skye entered.

"Hi," they said together.

"How are you feeling?" Lexi asked as she hugged Izzy.

"You look pretty good for a guy who wrestled a snake," Skye told him.

"Thanks. I'm fine. I was telling your sister she can go. I don't need her hovering."

Lexi and Skye exchanged glances, then turned back to him.

"Poor man," Lexi said. "You don't actually think she'll listen, do you? Have you met our sister? She's fairly stubborn."

They were both carrying tote bags. As Lexi talked she pulled out a large plant and a colorful blanket she spread across his feet. Skye removed two big boxes from her tote.

"A robe," she said. "I got blue because it's a traditional guy color. And these are cookies. Erin and I made them last night."

Lexi put the plant by the window. "They're chocolate chip. I could smell them the whole way here. Torture."

There was another knock, then Dana entered with a tall, thin man.

"Hi," she said. "This is Sheriff Rogers. He's going to take your statement."

"We're pressing charges," Izzy told him. "At least I am."

"There's no law against being an idiot," the sheriff said as he shook Nick's hand. "But we draw a line when an idiot hurts someone else. How you doin', son?"

"Good," Nick said, a little stunned by the invasion.

Skye and Dana disappeared for a few minutes, then reappeared with more chairs. The sheriff was eating cookies and talking with Lexi. Izzy stood next to him, holding the hand on his uninjured arm. Apparently no one was leaving anytime soon.

"Oh, Aaron called while you were asleep," Izzy told him. "He's taking care of everything. Steve came by to help. The corporate guys are very subdued and following orders. The beer is locked away and everything is good. But we're still pressing charges."

He didn't know what to make of what was going on. He'd never had family before, and while Garth had been his friend for years, neither of them ever fussed over the other.

The Titan women fussed. Even as they spoke to him and each other, his blankets were straightened, his pillows fluffed. They discussed his meals, his color and asked him if he needed to use the bathroom. When the sheriff was ready to talk about what had happened, they sat in the corner with Dana, talking quietly, constantly glancing at him as if to make sure he was all right.

It felt good and at the same time made him feel like crap. Because Izzy wasn't going to be the only one hurt by the revelation about Garth. They would be devastated, as well.

He had to tell her, and quickly.

He looked at the women. He would tell Izzy as soon as they had a moment alone. He had no choice — he was running out of time.

CHAPTER SIXTEEN

"Have you tasted Skye's cookies?" Aaron asked as he followed Izzy down the hall. "Silly question. Of course you have. How could you grow up with cookies like that in the house and not weigh four hundred pounds? They're fabulous." He lowered his voice. "Don't tell Norma I said that. She'd cut me off her biscuits for weeks."

"I won't say a word," Izzy promised, staring at the half-closed door to Nick's bedroom.

She wanted to check on him. The doctor had let him out of the hospital that morning only after Nick had promised to take it easy, including staying in bed for a couple more days. She'd agreed to make sure he followed the doctor's orders. But she had a feeling he wasn't the type to do what he was told, which meant he was probably doing jumping jacks right this second.

She had to go make sure. The only problem was, she couldn't seem to bring herself to walk into his room.

"Would you look in on Nick and make sure he's resting?"

Aaron frowned at her. "Why? Aren't you two speaking?"

"We're fine. The man saved me from a rattlesnake. He gets a free pass for at least a month. I just don't want to hover too much."

"Okay."

Aaron poked his head in the room, then backed out. "He's either asleep or faking being asleep," he said in a low voice.

"Good. He's lying down, which is important."

They walked to the living room.

"Tell me what happened during the rest of the weekend," Izzy said. "The guys were gone when we brought Nick home."

"I kicked them out Sunday morning. They didn't seem all that upset to go."

"I'm sure they're sorry they ever signed up for the retreat in the first place," she said. "They were all morons. I just hope they aren't working on something important, like third-world financing."

"I'm with you on that," Aaron told her. "I don't know that Nick is going to go forward with wanting to press charges."

She looked at him. "He has to. He could have died."

"I think he's more concerned that you could have died and doesn't want to put you through that."

His words made her feel funny. All hot and squishy on the inside. And a little sick to her stomach. "We can talk about it later."

"Are you all right?" Aaron asked. "You're acting very strange."

"I'm fine. Just dealing with the stress of what happened."

He didn't look convinced. "Did something happen that I don't know about? You know I hate being the last to know anything."

"I'm not keeping secrets," she promised, knowing it was true. She couldn't keep a secret about something she wasn't willing to admit even to herself.

"What are you going to do now?" he asked.

"Take care of the horses."

"Not look after Nick?"

"I'll check in on him later. He's a big boy. He can survive a few hours by himself."

"A few minutes ago you said you were worried about hovering too much."

"Right. Well, I can't hover in the stable. I need to go or Rita will be screaming."

"Rita never screams. What's going on with you?"

"Nothing."

She made her escape and ducked outside. But once there, she didn't feel any more comfortable. The need to run, to hide, to move, to do something was as powerful as it was unexplained. She felt like jumping out of her skin.

It was the whole incident with the snake, she told herself as she walked toward the barn. It had been terrifying. Her delayed re-action made perfect sense. She'd never seen anything like that in her life. Nick could have died. She could have died. She would be better in a few days.

As she went into the barn and walked toward Jackson's stall, she felt both hot and cold, as if she were coming down with the flu. But it was also different. Uncomfort-able and scary and . . .

She stopped in the middle of the stable and stared into Jackson's big, brown eyes. Possibilities flashed through her mind, each more frightening than the one before. Would she? Had she?

She'd been terrified about Nick's snake bite. The drive to the hospital had seemed endless and she'd been unable to stop cry-ing, no matter how many times Nick calmly promised he would be fine. It was only after the doctor had sworn he was out of danger that she'd allowed herself to hope.

Nick was a friend, she told herself. Of course she would worry about him. Only she knew it was more than that. Much more. Losing Nick would have crushed her in ways she'd never experienced. The reason she was confused, the reason she didn't know how to act or what to say was that everything was suddenly different. At least from her end.

Love.

Sometime, when she wasn't paying attention, she'd fallen in love with him. She, who had never loved anyone. Who never got involved. She'd fallen for a man who had vowed to never let himself be happy or connect with anyone else. Which was pretty much just her luck.

Nick watched Izzy carry in his tray for dinner. She brought it over to the bed and set it on the low table Aaron had already settled across his lap.

"Thanks," he said, more interested in looking at her than the food. "I haven't seen you all day."

"I've been around," she said, not quite looking at him. "You know, busy. There's so much to do. Things to get caught up on. Despite appearances, you *are* more than a pretty face. I'm trying to pick up the slack."

She sounded fine, but something wasn't right. He could tell. "It's been three days. There isn't much slack to pick up."

"I like staying current," she murmured. "Anyway, here's your dinner. Norma made all your favorites, which you should really mention. *She* said it about three times. And she kept Aaron from eating all the biscuits. Here's my question. How does he eat so much and stay so damn skinny? It's annoying."

She gave him a tight smile that looked more pained than happy, then started backing out of the room. "I'll just let you eat in peace."

"Or you could keep me company."

She froze, momentarily looked trapped, then gave him the fake smile again. "Sure. If you'd like. That would be great. Really nice." She pulled over the armchair from the corner.

"Go ahead," she said. "Eat. I'll do the talking. I'm good at that." She paused as if searching for a topic. "I, ah, got the catalog from the community college. I missed the fall semester start by three weeks. Which is okay. I can take my time and figure out my major. Not that I have to declare right away."

He cut into the roast beef. "I thought you were studying psychology."

"I am, but there are a lot of choices in the field. Not at the community college level, of course, but you know, um, later."

"Izzy, what's wrong?"

"Nothing. I'm fine." She smiled again and this time did a better job of faking it. "You're getting tons of get-well cards. You're way more popular than I would have guessed. Aaron has them all. He'll bring them by later. I'm sure small but tasteful gifts will be arriving soon. Oh, look at the time."

She started to stand. He grabbed her arm and held her in place.

"You're not leaving until you tell me what's going on."

She stared at him, wide-eyed. "I have no idea what you're talking about."

"You're acting strange."

"No, I'm not. It's the snake bite, isn't it? Your brain is addled."

He frowned. "You don't say things like addled. What happened?"

"Nothing. Seriously, I'm good. And I really have to go. I'll see you later."

She slipped free of his grasp and walked

out of the room.

Nick thought about going after her, but wondered if she needed time to deal with whatever it was that had . . . What? Scared her? It would be his first guess, only very little scared Izzy. She was tough and gentle, an impossible combination.

He would give it time, but eventually he would figure it out. Something had happened. Something that had her running scared and he was going to find out what it was.

The knives came out of the darkness. Nick recognized the burning as the blades cut through him. It was always the same, he thought, doing his best to fight. Silence, then the burn, then the warm trickle of blood followed by the intense pain. They liked to cut in a place that had almost healed. It hurt more that way. Sometimes they jabbed under his fingernails or the bottom of his feet. He never knew where they would strike or when. Or how long it would last.

The burning continued and he waited for the agony. Only it wasn't there this time. And a part of him knew he was dreaming. This wasn't real. But it felt real, he told himself, even as he fought the bone-chilling fear. It felt more real than it had for years.

The venom, he remembered. The snake bite. That's what was different. He was weak — he who hadn't allowed himself to be weak since his escape.

He fought the memories, the heat and told himself he would escape again, as he had before. He knew the way. He could . . .

Something cold stroked his face. A soft voice whispered for him to come back. It promised safety. A hand held on to his, guiding him, drawing him up and up until he opened his eyes and saw Izzy leaning over him.

"You made it," she said. "You were dreaming. The jungle?"

He nodded. "What time is it?"

"Just after midnight."

"What are you doing here?" he asked.

"Watching over you."

Being around him was safe, or so Izzy had thought. While Nick was asleep she was at less risk of giving herself away. So she'd curled up in the big chair a couple of hours ago, prepared to spend the night. She'd nearly been asleep when she'd heard him moaning.

She dipped the washcloth in the basin of water, squeezed it, then placed it back on his forehead.

"I want to check for a fever," she said. "You feel hot."

"Not as good as looking hot," he teased.

"Someone's been hanging out with Aaron just a little too much."

"Is that possible?"

She smiled. "You certainly sound all right."

"I'm fine."

He looked better. The color had returned to his face. She dropped the washcloth into the basin and straightened.

"You should try to go back to sleep," she told him. "I'm sure the nightmare has passed."

His eyes were so green, she thought as she stared into them. She'd gotten used to everything about him except his eyes. They still startled her when she looked at him. Although not as much as the realization that she loved him. There was a piece of news designed to make her stagger from shock.

He cupped her face with his palm, then slid his fingers into her hair.

"You're so damn beautiful," he murmured.

Words that made her heart beat faster. Words that could make her want to believe.

"Yeah, yeah, I look the same as I did yesterday. Now go to sleep."

"Tell me what has you spooked."

She drew back. "I have no idea what you're talking about."

He kept looking at her. "Tell me. I can help."

"Actually you're the last person who can fix this problem," she said before she could stop herself, then wanted to scream. Talk about a stupid thing to say.

He was going to ask a thousand questions. She would bet her last breath on it. He would come after her, relentless, determined to know, to "help" without realizing he was most of the problem.

"Izzy," he began as he sat up in bed.

She panicked. Later she would even be able to admit it to herself. She panicked and did the only thing she could think of to distract him.

She kissed him.

At first he didn't respond. She kept her lips against his, mostly to keep him from talking, but after a couple of seconds because it felt good. Really good. Then his mouth moved against hers in a way that told her he wasn't interested in questions. Not when this was the alternative.

As he reached for her, she leaned in close. The night was around them, but the lamps in the room chased away the darkness. They were safe — maybe because she was always safe when she was with him.

He cupped the back of her head, then slid his hand down her back. She wore the same clothes she'd had on earlier that day and regretted not changing into something with less layers.

She tilted her head and felt the light stroke of his tongue against her lower lip. She parted for him, wanting to deepen the kiss, wanting to tease and arouse and get lost in what they were doing.

He plunged into her mouth, claiming her with an intensity that took her breath away. She remembered the last time they'd made love, how he'd reduced her to a puddle of satisfaction. The knowledge of how she would feel in a few minutes combined with the pleasure of his mouth on hers to make her whimper.

It was just a kiss, she thought as need shot through her. But that didn't seem to matter. Not when her breasts already ached and she could feel herself swelling in anticipation.

She clung to him, then wanted more and tugged at his T-shirt. He pulled back enough to pull it off. She did the same, then reached behind her for the hooks of her bra, only to freeze in place.

She'd never seen his chest before. She'd touched it, had stroked the scarred flesh, but she'd never seen the crisscross marks that were proof of all he'd suffered. There were thin scars and thick ones. They made a patchwork pattern of ugliness and pain. Of course the purpose had simply been to punish him. Francisco had done his job well.

"Don't," Nick said, touching her chin and forcing her to meet his gaze. "Don't get lost there. They don't hurt, Izzy. They don't matter."

He was wrong about both. Of course they still hurt. They haunted his dreams. But that was a conversation for another time.

As much as she wanted to press her mouth to each of the scars, perhaps to heal, perhaps just to tell him she cared, she knew it would be a mistake. He wouldn't understand what she meant and he would think she pitied him. So she reached behind her and unfastened her bra, then dropped it onto the chair next to the bed. She took his hands in hers and raised them to her breasts.

"These are for you."

One corner of his mouth tilted up. "Exactly what I wanted."

"Really? Because I can take them back if you don't like them."

"They're perfect."

"I'm glad you think so. They're —"

He leaned in and took her left nipple in his mouth. She'd had more that she planned to say, but suddenly none of it was important. She wanted to feel everything he was doing to her. Feel his body against hers. Feel him inside her. Yes, the pleasure would be great, but she wanted the intimacy — the connection, more than she ever had before.

He moved between her breasts, licking and sucking her nipples, making her squirm and wish she were more naked. She ran her hands up and down his back, feeling the scars, but doing her best not to think about how he got them. That was for later. Tonight was about them being together.

He raised his head and pressed his mouth to hers. Their tongues tangled. She loved kissing him, but there were more pressing matters. She pulled back enough to kick off her sandals, then pushed down her jeans and thong. He removed his sweatpants and briefs. When he reached for her, she shook her head and pointed to the bandage on his arm.

"I'll take charge," she told him. "You're not supposed to put any weight on that." She knelt over him, straddling his hips and smiled. "I'm going to boss you around."

"Or so you think."

"Try me."

She lowered her head so her hair teased his chest and belly, then kissed him. He cupped her face as he slid his tongue into her mouth. She clamped her lips around him and sucked. He groaned, dropped his hands to her hips and urged her back. She felt his erection flex against her.

He was already hard, which worked for her. She was already wet and ready. She lowered herself onto him. He squeezed his fingers into her hips.

"Not yet," he said. "I have plans for you."

"Excuse me, but who's in charge? I believe that person is me." She straightened and lowered herself onto him, taking all of him deep inside her.

His breath came out as a hiss.

Izzy loved the idea of controlling such a strong man. She had always believed that sex should be as much about play as it was about passion. So she locked her gaze with his and slowly raised her arms until they rested on top of her head. Then she moved up and down, watching him watch her, seeing what the sensation, not to mention the show, did to him.

He got harder. Muscles tensed in his jaw as if he were trying to get and keep control. Foolish man. Didn't he know this was about losing control? She moved up and down in a steady rhythm, stealing his ability to determine his fate.

There was only one flaw in her plan — she enjoyed it, too. He filled every part of her and each time she raised and lowered herself, he drove in deeper, arousing her, pushing her to the edge. Nothing in her body cooperated. Her skin was sensitized to every brush of his. Her heart pumped faster and faster. Her breasts bounced as if showing off and her muscles kept tensing in anticipation of a release she was determined to resist.

Nick moved his hand down her belly in a slow, sexy movement that mesmerized her. She knew where he was going but was less sure what he would do when he got there. She sucked in her breath, determined to be strong, then he cupped her center and pushed his middle finger between her curls to find that single spot of pleasure.

He circled it slowly, as if exploring, remembering. Around and around, never touching it exactly. She rocked her hips, hoping to push him onto the spot, resisting the need to guide his hand with her own. He knew exactly what he was looking for. If he wasn't touching it, it was on purpose.

She could do this, she told herself, moving a little faster. She could hold off just as long as he could. She wouldn't give in to the pleasure shooting through her.

Around and around. Up and down. Eyes locked, bodies straining, they moved in a sensual dance that left her gasping.

She tightened her muscles around him. He tensed but didn't surrender. She went faster, so did he. Then he shifted slightly so his fingers pressed directly on that knot of nerves.

Izzy came in an unexpected rush of ecstasy. The shudders started deep inside of her and worked their way out. It was beyond pleasure — it was a new plane of being, of feeling. Then Nick pushed up hard and groaned, losing himself in her. She knew because she could see it in his eyes. They continued to stare at each other all through their release, barely blinking, seeing all that was there and into each other's soul.

When they were done, she slid off him and started to climb off the bed. He pulled her down next to him, rolling onto his side so they faced each other. Once again she stared into his eyes. He touched her cheek, her bottom lip, then he kissed her.

It was just a kiss. Soft and gentle. Almost like a promise. They moved together, her leg over his hip, him entering her again. She didn't ask how he was already hard or why she was suddenly so close. He filled her, shorter strokes because of their position, but still satisfying.

Like before, they stared at each other. She knew she could get lost in his green eyes, possibly forever. And what would happen if she couldn't find her way back? This was the man she loved. Terrifying but true. But what would he do with her heart? Could she trust him? Then the pleasure swept through her and she couldn't think any-more. There was only the magic of being with this man. Maybe it was enough.

Izzy rubbed down Jackson. The horse stood in the sun, seeming to enjoy the attention. Every now and then he gave her a friendly head butt.

"You're getting sassy," she told him. "I'm not sure that's such a good thing."

He snorted.

"Of course you think it's fine. You already know you're a darned handsome horse, don't you. It's important to be all nice and clean for the weekend. We have three more kids coming."

Aaron had told her that morning. At least she was pretty sure that's what he'd said. It was hard to tell with the glow from last night still burning inside her.

For the first time in her life, she knew the difference between having sex and making love. It wasn't in the act itself. She'd enjoyed the physical part of what she and Nick had done. What had made it different, what had made it matter, was how she'd felt after. There had been a sense of belonging. Just as scary, she knew she'd exposed a part of herself to him. An intimate part she never showed anyone.

Love. It was terrifying. What did it mean? And more confusing, what was she supposed to do? Tell him?

"No," she said aloud. "That's not a good plan."

Because she knew in her gut Nick didn't want to hear the words. Not from her and not from anyone else. He wouldn't believe it was okay for him to love anyone and certainly wouldn't think he was someone who should be loved. There was a whole lifetime of punishment in his future. Or so he thought.

She had to figure out a way to make him see that he'd set himself on an impossible task. The rules were such that he couldn't win. Of course he'd made a mistake, but at some point didn't he get to have a life, too? Didn't the good outweigh the bad?

The problem was he was trying to earn forgiveness, which was yet another impossible task. Forgiveness was a state of grace. Like faith, it either existed or it didn't.

"Deep thoughts," she told Jackson. "And I've only had one cup of coffee. Impressive, huh? Okay. Back to those kids."

Aaron hadn't told her much about them, mostly because he hadn't been told either. She knew it was their first visit and that they'd been involved in domestic violence. The possible horrors were endless, but that wasn't her concern. She was going to help them learn to ride so they could have fun and forget about whatever bad thing existed.

She heard footsteps and turned, expecting either Aaron or Nick. Instead her visitor was Garth Duncan.

Izzy wouldn't have been more shocked to see a talking garden gnome, or the devil.

"What are you doing here?" she demanded, wishing she'd thought to bring a gun. Not that she knew if Nick kept any around. She was going to have to ask.

"So the operation was a success," he said.

"What?"

"You can see me."

"Better to be blind."

Garth smiled. "You're always a challenge, Izzy. I like that about you."

Righteous anger filled her, giving her strength. "Is that why you tried to kill me? To show your affection?"

His expression hardened. "That wasn't me. I had nothing to do with the explosion."

"Right. And of course I'll believe you."

He wore jeans, a long-sleeved shirt and boots. Despite his billions, he looked at home in the barn. Maybe he was one of those men who looked at home anywhere.

"Ask me about any of the other incidents," he said. "I'll tell the truth. I didn't have anything to do with what happened to you."

For a second she wanted to believe him. There was something in his dark eyes — the truth maybe? She wasn't sure. Then she shook her head. There was no way she was getting weak when it came to Garth.

"Are you saying that in the battle to ruin my family, you have limits? I don't think so."

"You're wrong," he said, "but that's not why I'm here. I wanted to check on Nick."

She frowned. "How do you know anything happened to him?"

Garth smiled. "We're old friends. Didn't he tell you?"

Despite the shock and pain that ripped through her, she refused to go for the bait. "Sell it somewhere else."

"You don't believe me?"

"Why should I? You're a known liar."

"I do many things, Izzy, but I don't lie. I know Nick. I have for years. We were roommates in college." He chuckled at the memory. "What a geek. He was fifteen or sixteen, clueless when it came to anything about girls. But he was smart. Scary smart, and a good kid. We became friends."

She didn't believe him. She repeated the words over and over because it was the only way to make them true. He had to be lying, because if he wasn't, then Nick had kept his relationship with Garth from her. Nick had known what was going on and not said a word. He'd betrayed her.

"After college he went to work for my company," Garth continued as he reached for the front of his shirt and started unbuttoning it. "Did he tell you about finding oil in South America? Did he tell you what happened next?"

She didn't want to look, didn't want to see the proof, but she couldn't turn her head. Garth pulled apart the fabric and exposed a network of scars eerily similar to the ones Nick carried.

Her legs nearly gave way. She leaned against Jackson to stay standing.

"No," she whispered, even though she

knew it was true. All of it.

"I kept him alive all those months, then he carried me out. Nick and I are like brothers. He's on my board of directors, Izzy. Why do you think you're here? I arranged it."

She couldn't breathe. Her throat had tightened to the point where she could barely speak.

"Nick knew I wanted you here, so he brought you."

"No," she whispered.

"He's known from the beginning. In the battle for Nick's soul, I'll always win." He buttoned his shirt and shrugged. "There are some things a person can't get over. You know Nick. Tell me — do you think there's anything you can say or do that compares to what he and I went through?"

She was going to pass out. The shock was too great. Everything she'd thought, everything she'd believed . . . She'd trusted him, cared about him, fallen in love with him.

"Nick works for me," Garth told her. "He always has. This is nothing but a game for him. I guess you didn't figure that out."

"Get out," she said weakly.

"Sure. No problem." He walked away a few feet, then turned back to her. "Ask him, Izzy. He'll confirm everything."

"Get the hell out!" she yelled.

"Right."

He walked around the barn. A few seconds later, she heard a car engine start.

Ask Nick, he'd said. But she didn't have to. She already knew the truth.

Chapter Seventeen

Izzy clung to Jackson, her arms around his neck, his warm body providing comfort. Her stomach churned, her hands and feet felt cold. She was sick to the very core of her.

"I don't believe it," Rita said from behind her. "I heard him and I don't believe it."

"I do," Izzy said, straightening and brushing the tears from her eyes. "He was with Nick in college and later in South America. I saw the scars."

Nick had always talked about the other guy he'd been held captive with, but had never mentioned his name. And she'd never thought to ask. It hadn't seemed important.

"I know Nick," Rita said. "He wouldn't do this."

Exactly what Izzy would have thought five minutes ago. "He was in on it from the beginning. He was working for Garth when he took me from my sisters."

She thought about all the times they'd talked, how he'd baited her and challenged her until she'd left her room and started living again. He'd kissed her, held her, made love with her, all the while knowing it was a game. He'd led her to believe that he'd opened his heart to her. But it had all been a lie.

She didn't know what to feel, what to think. Everything hurt. Her body was ice and fire and she just wanted to make it all go away. How could it be true? How could she have been so wrong?

She'd fallen in love with one of Garth's men. Nick had never cared about her. He'd been playing a part and she'd trusted him with her very soul.

"I'm so stupid," she murmured.

"You couldn't have known."

"I should have guessed. I was too easy. He was too perfect." She walked to Rita and hugged her. "I have to go."

"I know. I'm sorry. I wish there was something I could do."

"You did everything. You made me believe in myself again. Thank you."

Rita grasped her arms and stared into her face. Izzy knew the other woman couldn't see her, but that wasn't important. Rita saw to the heart of things.

"Be sure," Rita told her. "Be sure before you decide. This isn't the man I've known for years. He's better than this."

"I'll be sure," Izzy lied. She liked Rita enough to leave her with a few illusions intact, but she knew the truth. Once again Garth had struck where they were all most vulnerable. It was a gift. Maybe later she would be able to admire it, but right now she had to get out of here.

She hurried back to the house and made her way to her room. She couldn't think too much or the tears would start again and she wasn't going to give Nick the satisfaction of knowing he'd made her cry. She got her suitcases out of the closet and began packing. She worked quickly, shoving things in as fast as she could. Wrinkled clothes were the least of her problems. All she wanted was to get out before Nick showed up. Was it too much to ask?

She got her answer when she heard footsteps in the hallway.

"I've been looking for you," he said as he entered the room. "What are you doing?"

She kept packing, not wanting to look at him. "You're a smart guy. Figure it out."

"You're leaving?"

"And he gets it in one try."

"Izzy? What's going on? Why are you leaving?"

She braced herself for the impact of his face, his killer green eyes, and looked up. "You're good. One of the best. Anyone can pretend for a few days or even a week, but you've had it going on for what, two months? Impressive."

He leaned against the door frame and crossed his arms over his chest. "Are you going to explain what that means or do I have to guess?"

She walked to the dresser and collected her underwear, carried the armful to the bed, then tossed them in the smaller suitcase.

"I thought you were amazing," she said. "What you did here. I understood about the guilt and even tried to help you see it wasn't necessary. Not as much as you've wrestled with the past. Color me stupid."

Nick moved toward her. "Why are you saying this?"

She turned on him. "Stop right there. Don't you dare get any closer to me. I mean it, Nick. Back off."

He paused in the middle of the room. "Izzy, tell me what —"

He stopped talking and his expression seemed to shutter. As if he'd remembered something bad.

"Exactly," she said softly, resuming her packing. "Here I'd thought you were special. Someone I could admire and care about. I let myself fall in love with you, which means I get a plaque for being idiot of the year. You're not a regular guy trying to make something of your life. You're working for Garth. You've been friends for years. You were held captive together and tortured. You're on his fucking board of directors."

Her voice rose with each word until she was screaming.

"You knew," she yelled. "The whole time, you knew. You didn't bring me here because Skye wanted you to. You brought me here because Garth asked. This was all just a game to you. How thrilling it must have been for you, playing me like that. Playing all of us."

"No." He crossed to her and grabbed her arms. "It wasn't like that. I do know Garth, and I was on his board until I resigned. But when you first came here, I didn't know what was going on with you and his family. I didn't have a clue."

She pulled free and glared at him. "Because I'll believe that."

"It's true," he said. "I knew Garth was your brother and there was tension in the family. He asked me to help you and didn't want you to know he was behind it. Later I found out there was more going on than he'd told me. I didn't know how far things had gone."

She desperately wanted to believe the words, which just proved what she'd always known — love made women weak and ridiculous. Because the proof was all there.

"We trusted you," she said, zipping up her suitcase. "We came to you for help. I told you everything. You never said a word."

"I didn't want you to leave."

"All the easier to watch me here."

"I wanted you to have the surgery."

If only that were true, she thought sadly, defeated, but determined to stay strong.

"You wanted to spy for your friend."

She grabbed her suitcases and started for the door.

"Izzy, stop. You can't go like this."

"I can go however I want. You're nothing to me. Nothing. I don't even hate you because that would be wasting too much emotion. You have my contempt and disgust and that's all you deserve. He tried to kill me, Nick. He blew up an oil rig and I could have died." Her eyes burned, but she refused to cry. "But who am I kidding? You don't care about that either. Nothing matters except Garth. He's your real family, isn't he? He's the one you care about. I hope you'll be happy together."

She started down the stairs. Nick followed her, grabbing for the suitcase. She jerked it away from him.

"He didn't blow up the rig."

She reached the bottom and dropped her suitcases. "You know this how? Oh, let me guess. Garth told you."

"Yes, and I believe him."

"Big whoop. I don't. He has done everything in his power to destroy my family, and you're on his team."

"It wasn't like that."

If only he was telling the truth.

"You had so many chances to say something," she reminded him. "From the first time I told you about Garth. You could have said or done something. Anything. But you didn't. There wasn't a hint. You wanted me to trust you so you could use that against me and my sisters."

"No. I never did that. I asked Garth to stop his campaign. I didn't agree with him. We argued."

"More lies," she whispered, started to feel the ache in her heart. "I can't be here. I can't do this. You are the worst kind of person. I'm glad you have the nightmares. I hope you have them until you die and then I hope there's a special place for you in hell. Whatever Francisco did to you, wasn't enough. You deserved more."

She picked up her suitcases and started for the door. Aaron came in from the kitchen, saw her and frowned.

"What's going on?" he asked. "I could hear you yelling."

"I'm leaving," Izzy told him. "I'm sorry. I'll call you later."

"What happened?"

"Ask him," she said, jerking her head toward Nick, then walking out.

It only took her a few seconds to toss the suitcases in her trunk. Then she climbed in the car, started the engine and drove away. When she reached the main road, she headed toward Dallas only to realize she didn't have a home to go to. Not anymore. Just one more thing Nick and Garth had destroyed.

Nick stood in the middle of the living room, listening to the silence. This wasn't happening — it couldn't be. There had to be something he could say or do to make it right.

But what? Garth had done it — told Izzy before he'd had the chance. It was his own fault for waiting. Or maybe it was his own fault for trusting Garth in the first place.

"What was that?" Aaron asked. "Did Izzy just leave? As in forever?"

"Yes." Nick started for his office.

Aaron trailed after him. "No. She can't just walk out. I don't accept that. What's happening? Did you fight? Is this all your fault? Do you need to apologize?"

"It's too late for that." Nick reached his office. "I don't want to talk about it."

"You think I care what you want?" Aaron asked, following him inside and standing there with his hands on his hips. "Izzy was my friend. What did you do to her?"

"It doesn't matter."

"The hell it doesn't. Tell me."

Nick sat heavily in his chair. "Garth is Izzy's brother."

"What? Your Garth? The scary one you've known forever? He's a Titan?"

Nick nodded. "I didn't know until a couple of months ago. I overheard Izzy and her sisters talking about him and what he was doing to their family."

"Doing as in . . ." Aaron stared at him. "No way. All those rumors in the paper? The mad cow, the treason? It's been crazy. I mean sure, Jed Titan thinks he's God, but all this? It's Garth?"

Nick nodded.

"You can't let him do that."

"I can't stop him. Izzy and her sisters think he's responsible for blowing up the oil rig. Garth says he didn't do it."

"And you believe him?"

"He hasn't lied."

"Excuse me?" Aaron stood and looked down at Nick. "He's more than lied. Let me guess. He's the one who asked you to bring Izzy here, but he mentioned you shouldn't say anything to her. He's the one who told Izzy about your connection to him."

Enough of the numbness had lifted for him to be surprised.

Aaron must have read his expression. "I'm more than a pretty face," he snapped. "I don't understand how you let this happen. Why didn't you just tell her?"

"Garth and I have a history." One he'd never fully explained to Aaron.

"I don't care if you're twins separated at birth. What he's doing is wrong."

"He has his reasons."

"So did the jerks who tried to kill me. Every villain is the hero of his own story. So it came down to loyalty and you picked Garth."

"No. I resigned from the board. I'm selling my shares in his company. I don't have anything to do with him anymore."

"But you didn't tell Izzy."

He didn't have to answer that one, Aaron already guessed.

"Then Garth showed up and told her himself. That's really friendly of him. Izzy's crushed because she thinks you planned this whole thing. She thinks you hurt her on purpose."

Reality reduced to a few words, Nick thought grimly.

He couldn't stop thinking about the pain in her eyes. Pain he would have done anything to stop. She'd been so full of life and he'd hurt her.

"I only wanted to help her," he said, more to himself than Aaron. "Instead I broke her heart."

"You didn't break her, you arrogant moron," Aaron snapped. "She's stronger than that. She's a Titan. She's been to hell and back and did it with grace and style. She's tougher than you know and more woman than you deserve. When are you going after her?"

"I'm not."

"You're just going to let her walk away. And why is that, oh great leader?"

"It's done. It's over. She's gone."

Aaron stared at him as if he'd never seen him before. "That's it?" he asked with a shriek. "You're not even going to try? You're just going to let her go?"

"It's the best thing."

"For who? Her or you?"

"For Izzy. She doesn't belong here."

Despite what she'd said. That she'd fallen for him.

She hadn't meant the words, he told himself. She couldn't. She knew the worst about him. Knew the darkness inside of him. There was no way she could simply accept that.

Aaron glared at him. "In all the years I've known you, this is the first time I'm sorry you saved me because I don't want to have to owe you anything. You're not doing this for her, you're doing it for yourself. Because you like your dark little world where you're always the victim."

Nick stood. "You don't know what you're talking about."

"Want to bet? You like being alone. You like not having to care about anyone but yourself. Sure, you wrap it all up in your past and pretend you're being noble, punishing yourself, but the people you hurt are those who try to care about you. At least the guys who tried to kill me were honest about it. They hated me and that's all that mattered to them. But you pretend to be like everyone else. You let Izzy think you could care about her."

"I didn't." He'd been careful about that.

"You slept with her," Aaron insisted. "You acted like you had a heart. You led her on. You're just as bad as Garth — working from the shadows and hurting those who are supposed to be important to you. How could you?"

Aaron walked out of the room. Nick stared after him, surprised by the sudden silence. Then he sank into his chair and stared at his blank computer screen.

He told himself he preferred it this way. That he didn't need anyone. He would be fine on his own. It was better this way. They weren't important to him.

He'd finally gotten what he'd always wanted — he was truly alone.

Izzy lay curled up on the low bed in Dana's guest room.

"I'm sorry that's all I have," her friend said awkwardly. "I don't get much company."

"It's fine," Izzy told her, not caring that she lay on a futon. It was plenty comfortable and she didn't see a whole lot of sleep in her future. She hurt too much.

The pain was unfamiliar — not a sports injury or a hangover or even like the flu. It filled her body and made her feel sick to her stomach. Her chest was tight and even though she knew she was breathing fine, she couldn't seem to catch her breath. The thought of eating made her head swim, she wanted to sleep but couldn't relax and any optimism she'd ever possessed had long since died.

If this was heartache, she was never going to fall in love again. Not that she planned to. Ever. She'd fallen in love for the first time in her life and it had been a disaster. Worse than a disaster. It had been betrayal that cut to her heart.

"Can I get you anything?" Dana asked, hovering.

Izzy sat up and took her friend's hand. "You've given me a place to stay. I won't be here long, I promise. I need a couple of days to regroup, then I'll get a job and find a place of my own."

"You can stay as long as you want," Dana told her. "Seriously. You don't get on my nerves as much as other people."

"If the law enforcement thing doesn't work out for you, you could probably get a job writing greeting cards."

"I know. I'm pure sentiment." Dana sat next to her and stared into her eyes. "I shouldn't be saying this, but I can get someone to beat the shit out of him. I know, I know. It's breaking the law and I hate to do that, but I'd make an exception."

Nick physically hurt. Did she want that? She turned the idea over in her mind, then shook her head.

"Not today," she murmured. "I don't want him hurt. How stupid is that?"

"You love him."

"Which again brings the stupid thing to mind." Tears filled her eyes. She fought them, determined not to cry over him. He wasn't worth it.

The doorbell rang. Dana stood.

"You want them in here?"

"I'll come out," Izzy said.

She stood and followed Dana to the small living room of her apartment. Her friend opened the front door and Skye and Lexi spilled in.

"I can't believe it," Skye said as she rushed forward to hug Izzy. "I can't. He seemed so nice. Oh, Izzy. I'm sorry. This is my fault. I made you go there."

"Always the martyr," Lexi said, taking her turn hugging her sister. "We both decided sending Izzy to Nick was a good idea. You don't get all the guilt, Skye."

"But my former assistant is the one who recommended Nick."

Izzy held them both. "I'm sure if you do a little checking, you'll find she has some connection to Garth. It's nobody's fault but mine. You sent me there so I would find the courage to have the surgery. Which I did. The falling-in-love part shouldn't have been on the agenda."

Her sisters stepped back and stared at her with identical wary expressions.

"Real love?" Lexi asked quietly.

"As opposed to the fake kind? Yes. Real love. Stupid but true."

Skye twisted her hands together. "I'm glad you finally opened up to someone, but I'm sorry it was him."

"Cruz wants him dead," Lexi said. "If that helps. Or at the very least beaten and left on the side of the road." She glanced at Dana. "You didn't hear that."

"Hear what?"

Izzy sank onto the plain dark blue sofa in Dana's modestly furnished living room. "I'm fine," she said as Lexi sat on one side of her and Skye sat on the other. Thankfully Dana took the chair opposite. She couldn't handle them all crowding around her.

"You're not fine," Skye said.

"Thanks for the vote of confidence."

"You know what I mean. You must feel terrible. I know how I felt when I thought Mitch was working with Garth." She balled up her hands into fists. "But this is worse. It sounds like Nick is Garth's best friend. I hate them both. I've never hated anyone before but I really hate Garth the most."

"I know," Lexi muttered. "It's so damn personal. What is up with that? He can't just attack our businesses? No. He has to go for the heart."

"I'm going to get him," Dana told them. "I've been talking to my friends at the Dallas police department and they're getting close. I'm going to be the one bringing him in for questioning. I promise you all that he will pay."

Dana looked fierce, which Izzy appreciated. She had love and support. That was something. She would make a new life for herself. None of what had happened with Nick changed her mind about college or what she would study. Obviously the fantasy about working with him on his ranch was over, but she could still make a difference.

"Thanks," she told them all. "I'll get through this."

"You will," Lexi promised. "You're strong. Stronger than you know. In time, the pain will fade. Then you have to deal with the anger. Eventually you get back to normal."

Izzy couldn't imagine ever being normal again.

"You'll find someone else," Skye told her.

"Ever the romantic," Dana said, rolling her eyes.

"She will. She's opened her heart once. Now she knows how."

"Lucky me," Izzy murmured, thinking she would never fall in love again. It wasn't worth it. Love was pain. She'd learned that as a child and had only gotten into trouble when she'd allowed herself to forget the truth.

Loving and losing Nick had fundamentally changed her. It was like a loss of innocence. She doubted she would ever be able to trust anyone ever again.

CHAPTER EIGHTEEN

The next day Dana didn't want to leave Izzy alone, which Izzy knew in theory was very sweet but she didn't need one more person watching over her.

"Go to work," Izzy told her. "We need you to bring in Garth."

"Call me if you need anything."

"I promise."

"Don't start looking for a job. Not for a few more days."

Izzy ignored that and pulled out the paper as soon as her friend left.

The fastest way to earn money would be to go back on an oil rig. In three months she could save enough to support herself for at least a semester of college. But that felt too much like returning to who she'd been before. As if she hadn't changed at all. She didn't want that.

"Money or principle," she murmured to herself as she poured more coffee. "Is that always the question?"

There was a knock on the front door of Dana's condo. She looked at it, hating the swell of hope she felt inside. It wasn't Nick. He wasn't the type to come after anyone. But that statement didn't stop her heart from thudding hard in her chest as she walked to the door and pulled it open.

Standing there was possibly the last person she'd ever expected to see.

"You're not still blind, are you?" Jed asked as he pushed past her and walked inside. "I heard you could see. Is that true?"

"Morning, Dad," she said. "I'm fine. How are you?"

"Too busy for bullshit." He waved his hand in front of her face. "Well?"

"Very sensitive. Yes, I can see."

"Good. You're going to get a call from a man I work with. His name is Bill. Don't ask me anything ridiculous, like is he cute. How would I know? He's a business associate and I need him to be happy right about now. So when he asks, you're going to say yes. Understand?"

She wasn't even surprised. After all these years she was finally useful to her father.

"I understand," she said coolly, "but I won't be going out with him."

"Of course you will." Jed stood a full head

taller than her. He glared down at her. "I need this, Izzy. Things are bad and you owe me."

"For what? Being born? I don't think that was much of a hardship on you. So no. I don't owe you."

Jed puffed up like an irritated crow. "I raised you."

"You paid nannies to raise me and you've pretty much ignored me all my life." She pointed at the door. "Get out."

"I'm not leaving until you tell me you'll take Bill's call."

"That's not what you want. You want me to sleep with him."

"Why not? You've slept with everyone else."

Anger built up inside her. She knew some of it came from a lifetime of being ignored by her father but a lot of it grew out of finding out about Nick. There was betrayal in her, and outrage.

"I'm not your whore to sell," she told her father, practically spitting with rage. "I won't do it."

"The hell you won't. Don't push me, little girl. You won't like the consequences."

"Then stop threatening me."

"You're my daughter. I'll do whatever I want."

"I don't think so."

She reacted without thinking. Maybe it had been building for years. Maybe in her heart she believed he deserved it. Maybe it really was about Nick. Whatever the reason, she pulled back her arm and slapped Jed across the face.

The impact sent pain up her arm to her elbow, but it was worth it, she thought as he jumped back and yelped. Blood trickled down his face from a cut her ring had made.

"You bitch!"

"That's me," Izzy said, resisting the need to shake her hand. Instead she opened the front door. "You need to go."

He dug a handkerchief out of his slacks pocket and dabbed at his nose, then swore again. "That's it. You're dead to me, girly. You're not getting a penny out of my will."

"Was I ever?"

He didn't say anything. Instead he stalked outside and walked down the sidewalk.

Izzy closed the door behind him, then leaned against the hard surface. It took a few minutes for her heart rate to return to normal, but when it did, she was surprised to discover she was actually feeling much better about nearly everything. Apparently she should have hit her father years ago.

■ ■ ■ ■

Norma might not be talking to him, but at least she hadn't left, Nick thought gratefully as he walked from the kitchen to his office. Unlike Aaron, who hadn't been seen in days.

The kids due to arrive tomorrow would be fed, which was good, but he couldn't confirm much else. It had taken him longer than it should have to confirm the cleaning crew, mostly because he didn't understand Aaron's filing system and hadn't been able to find their phone number for nearly two hours. Rita wasn't speaking to him, but she would have the horses ready. That was something.

The house had never seemed bigger or more empty. He'd lived here alone for a couple of years before Aaron had arrived. He'd liked the silence and solitude. Not anymore. Now it weighed on him, dragging him into darkness even in the brightest part of the day.

Izzy would be pleased — her hope that the nightmares would haunt him forever had been realized. They came every night but were worse than before. Because now she was there, with him. Tied up, tortured. He wasn't blindfolded, either, but instead gagged. He could see them coming for her with their gleaming knives, could hear her screams and see the blood but he couldn't help her or even speak to her. He could only endure, hour after hour, waking soaked in sweat, writhing with agony, desperate to escape.

He couldn't take much more of it. For the first time in his life he understood why people escaped into madness. Nothing was worth nights like those.

But the nightmares weren't the worst of it. Being awake, missing her, wanting her and knowing he'd lost her forever, was even more torture. He breathed the ache and there was no relief.

He paused in the doorway to his office, not interested in facing the paperwork the visit required, then frowned as he heard a familiar car pulling up out front. Seconds later Aaron walked into the house.

"I thought you were gone for good," Nick told him. "You just left."

"I'm not back because of you," Aaron said, neither smiling nor looking happy to be there. "I'm here because three children are coming. They've been through enough and don't deserve anything less than a fabulous time. Now I suppose you're going to tell me you don't need any help."

"I can't do it without you," he said instead. "Thank you for being here."

Aaron stared at him. "I expected so much more of you, Nick. You're the guy who saved my life and I'll always be grateful. You were my hero."

Were being the operative word, Nick thought grimly, feeling like shit. "Aaron, I'm sorry."

"For what? Making me feel bad or what you did to Izzy? I trusted you. Imagine how ridiculous I feel, knowing what you did to Izzy. She didn't deserve it. You're not that guy."

There was no point in defending himself. "I know."

"She loves you."

More knives. These were the kind that cut to the bone but didn't make him bleed. "I don't know that she —"

"Just stop it," Aaron told him. "She loves you and you betrayed her. I'm sure you're telling yourself that it's for the best. That you could never be the man she needs. Whatever it takes to look at yourself in the mirror."

Aaron moved closer, his expression painfully sad. "Here's the part I don't get. She was good for you. She understood you and loved you, anyway. Do you know how rare that is? How special? But you don't care. All you want is to feel guilty. You like hiding in the past — it keeps you from having to take a chance on the future. You're not punishing yourself. You're not atoning. You're taking the easy way out."

Nick did his best to hold down his anger. "You don't know what you're talking about."

"Sure I do and that's what you can't stand. It's like the ranch. You want to do it all yourself, but you can't. You need us all. Just like you need Izzy. Only you'll never admit it. You think you're not allowed to love anyone or that it makes you weak. You know what? You're wrong. Love is the only thing that makes us strong. It's all that matters in the end. Who we love and who loves us."

He paused and drew in a breath. "I don't know all the secrets of your past. I don't know what you're running from. What I do know is you'll never escape by hiding. You'll never find what you need. You'll just destroy everyone around you. Heroes don't do that."

Nick stepped out of the way as Aaron pushed past him. Then he walked into his office and shut the door.

Aaron's words ripped through him, mostly

because they were true. He had been hiding. Because by not living he could make the past right? He'd always assumed he knew what he was doing — that if he didn't get involved, no one would get hurt.

He'd been wrong. Everyone he cared about had been hurt. So what did he do now?

"Izzy Titan," the stable manager said, looking over Izzy's application. "You're not related to those fancy, rich Titans are you?"

"Don't I wish," Izzy lied with a smile.

The old guy laughed. "Good point. If you were one of them, you wouldn't be looking for a job with me." He glanced at her letter of reference. "Me and Rita go back a long way. She's a fine woman. I guess if she says you're okay, I can trust you. You'll be responsible for a dozen horses and their gear. Get 'em up and ready in the morning. Get 'em saddled when they have a rider or a lesson. Saturday mornings are the worst. All the rich kids come in. Can you deal with that?"

Izzy nodded. "When can I start?"

"Tomorrow. Now you're going to college?"

"In January."

"We'll work around your hours. College

kids with bills to pay make motivated workers." He held out his hand. "You got yourself a job, little lady."

"Thanks. I'll see you in the morning."

Izzy walked back to her car. She'd already collected the paperwork she needed to start at community college and now she had a job. If she could just figure out a way to heal her broken heart, it would be a really good day.

Nick looked up from his computer to find Garth standing in his office. Garth looked tired and drawn, which should have made Nick feel better but didn't. Regrets weren't going to help anyone.

"What?" he asked, not really caring. Izzy thought she was the one who had been played, but she was wrong. He'd never wanted to hurt her or tried to get her. Garth, on the other hand, had played him like an old string guitar.

"I haven't told the rest of the board about you resigning," Garth said, moving to the chair on the other side of the desk and sitting down. "I wanted to see if you'd changed your mind."

"No."

"Nick. We're friends. We're more than that, we're practically brothers. She's just a girl. You can get a dozen more just like her."

Nick thought about Izzy's sense of humor, her fearlessness, the way she challenged him, how she cared about the kids and teased Aaron and made every part of life brighter just by being alive. He thought about how she listened, how she trusted and the way she stood her ground and did what she believed was right.

"No. I can't. Izzy's unique."

"All cats are gray in the dark."

"Izzy's not a cat and we're not going to talk about her."

Garth stared at him. "You're going to end our decades of friendship because she's pissed?"

Nick had thought a lot about everything that had happened. He'd tried to see everyone's point of view to figure out where it had all gone wrong.

"I never got it before," he said slowly. "When we were in South America, I was so sure I was right about the drilling. You had other reports telling you it couldn't be done the way I said and when you believed me instead of them, I was determined to prove your faith in me. But I was wrong and three people paid with their lives."

"We got the oil."

"Sure. At a price."

"There's always a price."

Nick nodded. "That's what I thought. I've been to hell and back because I was responsible for their deaths."

"You didn't pull the trigger. It was an accident. A mistake."

"My mistake."

Garth shook his head. "You spent years trying to get someone to punish you, buddy. I don't know why. You're doing a fine job all on your own."

"I'm trying. But you're not. You don't care. You weren't interested in making amends."

"Francisco and his brothers held us prisoner for months, torturing us every damn day."

Garth was angry now. Nick could see it in the tension around his mouth and the way he sat in his chair.

"He got his pound of flesh and then some," Garth continued. "Given the chance, he would have killed us. You made a mistake, Nick. One damn mistake. You're not God, you didn't know. You screwed up. And, hey, you're sorry. So get the fuck over it."

Interesting. It was almost the same thing Aaron had said, but for very different reasons.

"Are you really so much of a bastard that

you don't care? Or is it too inconvenient to deal with the past?" Nick said.

"What's to deal with? You went to the governments of both countries. No one wanted to do anything. You spent months trying to find Francisco and his family and you couldn't. You've funded a couple of orphanages, you're working with kids here. What else do you want?"

"From you? A little remorse. Some regret. Something other than business as usual."

Garth's eyes narrowed. "You don't know what I think or feel. You don't know what you're talking about."

"Maybe not, but I do know we were once like brothers. We nearly died together. And a week ago you sold me down the river. You knew Izzy was important to me. You knew I wasn't happy to be lying to her. And you knew I'd keep your secret for as long as I could. You used that information, you used me, then you screwed me. You were leaving messages, telling me you wanted to talk to me and then you told her everything."

Most people didn't have the balls to assess his character, Garth thought. Nick had never had a problem speaking his mind.

He'd never thought it would come to this — that a woman would come between him and Nick. Worse. A Titan. One of his sisters.

402

"You're letting them win," he said.

"I was never in a fight with them," Nick told him. "Izzy didn't deserve any of this."

"She had the surgery. That wouldn't have happened without her being here."

"You don't know that."

"Yes, I do."

Nick shrugged. "She would have gotten there eventually."

"After wasting how many years?"

"Don't try to make this better than it is. You weren't doing her a favor." Nick stared at him. "You've lost it. I don't know why you're doing what you're doing, but you've gone too far. This isn't a battle to win — it's a vendetta. You want to hurt someone, hurt the man who's responsible. Take on Jed Titan. But whatever you have going on with your sisters is wrong. What kind of a man bullies a woman? Are you that frightened of them?"

Garth held on to his temper. He'd come here to reason with his friend. Apparently Nick wasn't willing to listen.

"You won't come back to the board?" he asked, already knowing the answer.

"No. I've sold most of my shares in your company."

"Just like that?"

"This isn't what I wanted," Nick told him.

"You're right — you've been my family for years. But I can't be a part of what you're doing. You're going to have to figure the rest of it out alone."

Garth stood, then left. Fine. If Nick wanted to be led around by the nose, that was his problem. Garth didn't need him. He didn't need anyone.

But as he walked to his car, he had the sense of being totally alone. He had few friends, no one he really cared about. There was Kathy, but she was more like a child than an adult. His staff, who might respect him but little else. If he ceased to exist this very moment, who would mourn him? Worse, who would know?

He got in his car, then looked back at the house. Damn feelings. He had to get out of here and fast. Whatever had gotten Nick seemed to be contagious. Emotions. A conscience. He had no time for either.

There was nothing wrong with being alone. It meant he could move faster. Easier. He was close to winning. Soon he would have it all. Then he wouldn't give a rat's ass about Nick or anybody else. Then he would have won.

Chapter Nineteen

Nick had spent nearly two weeks being ignored by his staff, walking the hallways of the house at night and examining his life. It had taken him that long to figure out what was important and what he needed to do. He had a feeling if Izzy knew, she would inform him that the average woman would have realized the truth in about an hour.

He paused by the front window in the living room and watched an SUV drive up to the porch. It parked and two women climbed out.

Lexi and Skye didn't look anything like their sister, but seeing them reminded him of Izzy. There was both pleasure and pain at the thought of her. Pleasure because he'd finally come to see she was everything to him. Pain because he might have lost her forever.

He met the women at the front door.

"Thanks for coming," he said.

"We're not here for you," Lexi said briskly as she pushed past him and walked into the living room. "We're here because you made it clear we were having this conversation one way or another and we didn't want Izzy seeing you in Titanville."

He motioned for them to sit down.

They sat together on the sofa. Skye eyed him with a mixture of contempt and dislike.

"We're not interested in helping you," Skye said bluntly. "Just last week, Jed paid a visit to Izzy to try to convince her to date one of his business partners. Izzy slapped him in the face and threw him out. If she was willing to do that to her own father, imagine how little trouble I would have taking you on."

Nick held up both hands in a gesture of surrender. "No one is questioning your motivation or ability."

"Good. Now, what do you want?"

"If he says Izzy," Lexi told her sister. "Shoot him or I will."

Unfortunately that is what he'd been planning to say. He needed a new plan.

"How much do you know about my past?" he asked instead.

Skye and Lexi glanced at each other. Skye motioned for Lexi to talk.

"Foster kid, very smart, goes to college at

fifteen. You're a total geek, you don't fit in, Garth saves you, becomes your friend. Flash forward seven or eight years, you're working for him. Another eight years, you screw our sister." Lexi gave him a cold smile. "Did I miss any highlights?"

"No."

Izzy had told them about him, but hadn't mentioned his guilty secret. He knew in his gut it was because she knew it was the part of him that shamed him the most. Even in her pain and heartbreak, she'd protected him.

"What Izzy didn't tell you is about my time in South America."

He spoke quickly, giving them a brief synopsis of what had happened there. He didn't spare himself the blame, taking full responsibility for what had gone wrong.

When he was done, the sisters again exchanged another look — this one he couldn't read.

"You paid for what you did," Skye said. "And maybe you suffered. That doesn't excuse what you did to Izzy. Garth is trying to destroy our entire family. You don't seem to get that. He nearly killed Izzy."

Risking their wrath, he said, "Garth has admitted to all his actions, except the explosion. He claims he had nothing to do with it."

"And you believe him?" Lexi asked, sounding outraged.

"Yeah, I do. I don't agree with what he's doing to you and your sister. If he had a problem with Jed, fine. Jed ignored his own son when he begged for Kathy's life. Jed deserves whatever happens to him. But you two and Izzy are innocent. Garth was wrong. His vengeance is misplaced. He's used us all."

His best friend. He still had trouble wrapping his mind around that truth. His own family had betrayed him.

"I've severed my financial and personal ties with Garth," he continued. "I've resigned from his board, sold my shares in his company. He's out of my life."

"Too little, too late," Lexi snapped. "You knew Garth was behind bringing Izzy here and you didn't say anything."

"The way he told it, he wanted Izzy helped out of concern. He said you wouldn't accept his help. I believed him because I didn't have any reason not to."

"But when you found out what he was doing," Skye said. "You could have said something."

"I know." He drew in a breath. "It was

too late, then. If I'd told Izzy the truth, she would have left and not had the surgery. At first that's what I wanted — her to see again. She's so full of life. So tough and sweet and honest. She leads with her heart. She's fearless. I've never known anyone like her. She needed more than half a life."

"The surgery could have left her blind," Lexi said, studying him.

"She needed to know." He shrugged. "If things had gone badly, she would have been all right. She would have found a way. That's what she does. I couldn't tell her about Garth because she had to have the surgery."

"And after?" Skye asked.

"I didn't want to lose her. If she knew, she would be gone. I . . . I liked having her around."

For the third time, the sisters shared a look. He'd given up trying to figure out what they were thinking.

"Why should we believe you?" Lexi asked.

"I don't know. I can't prove it. I could show you my letter of resignation from Garth's board, but so what? He could reinstate me in a second. He was my friend and I trusted him. That's my mistake and I have to live with it. I trusted a man I'd known for years, who had saved me and been like family. I don't know where everything went wrong for him, but it did."

Lexi leaned toward him. "Knowing everything you know, having lost Izzy, you still believe Garth didn't blow up the oil rig?"

"Yes."

"That's crazy."

"Maybe, but why lie about only that? Garth's proud of what he's doing to your family. He wouldn't deny something that big."

"Fine," Skye said. "To go back to my original question, what do you want?"

He smiled. "Izzy. You want to shoot me here or should I stand?"

"We're not going to help you get her," Lexi said.

Apparently they'd already discussed that because she didn't have to look at her sister for confirmation.

"You hurt her," Skye said. "She didn't ever want to fall in love. She didn't want to take the chance. But she did and you devastated her."

"I know. I'm not saying I deserve her, just that I love her. I'm not asking for your help. I'm asking you not to get in the way."

"What could we do?" Lexi asked. "Izzy is her own person."

"You're the people she loves and respects

most in the world. If you told her not to trust me, that I wasn't worth it, she'd listen."

"Then you don't know Izzy. She never listens," Skye told him.

"You're wrong. She listens to both of you."

"Interesting that you've figured that out," Lexi said. "I'm not sure even Izzy is aware our opinion matters to her. At least not on a conscious level."

"Even a blind squirrel finds an acorn now and then," he said.

Lexi smiled. "Meaning guys aren't inherently insightful?"

"Something like that."

Skye nodded slowly. "We won't help, but we won't get in the way."

Tension eased. The bands around his chest loosened for the first time in days. "Thank you."

The sisters stood.

"She won't be easy," Lexi said. "You're going to have to convince her."

"I'm willing to do whatever it takes."

"Try bleeding," Skye told him. "That will get her attention."

Kathy took the coffee and sipped. "Nice," she said with a smile. "You always remember."

"It's your favorite," Garth said.

411

He didn't have time to be here. He had meetings and was due to fly out to Germany in the morning. But he'd been unable to concentrate and had decided to visit Kathy before he left.

She frowned. "You're sad."

"I'm fine."

She didn't look convinced and touched his arm. "You're sad," she repeated.

Sometimes she surprised him. Most of the time Kathy was in her own happy little world, but every now and then she seemed to see more.

"I hurt a friend," he admitted. "I didn't mean to. Or maybe I did. I don't know. I'm doing something and . . ."

He trailed off as her expression changed from concerned to confusion.

He gave her a smile. "I'm sad because of a friend."

"Did you say you're sorry?"

"No."

"Say you're sorry. You have to say you're sorry."

There was no point in having this conversation. What ever moment had occurred was now gone. "I will," he said, not meaning it.

"We have new kittens," Kathy told him. "Five. I need to check on them."

"Okay." He kissed her cheek. "I'll be back

next week."

"Bye."

She turned and walked away. He watched her go. Did she remember him after he left or did he cease to exist? What did she think about during her day? Did she recall the person she'd been before?

Knowing he would never get any answers, he left the pet store and headed for his car. But before he could reach it, he saw Izzy Titan walking toward Bronco Billy's. She seemed to be alone.

Garth dropped his coffee container in a nearby trash can and hurried across the street, following her into the restaurant.

She was just being shown a table. He hesitated for a second, then walked toward her.

She saw him. Her face tightened and her eyes turned to ice. "Don't even think about sitting here," she snapped as she sat down.

He pulled a handkerchief out of his slacks pocket and set the white square on the table in front of her. "Truce?"

Izzy stared from the fabric to Garth and back. "I won't pretend to understand the game," she told him, wondering if she could slap him in the face the same way she'd hit her father. Something told her Garth would move a lot faster and she'd only end up hitting the back of the seat or something and hurting her hand.

"No game. I want to talk."

"And I should believe you why?"

"Please, Izzy. Give me fifteen minutes. I didn't blow up the oil rig. I did the rest of it. Sure. I was the investor in Lexi's spa, I arranged for Jed's horses to get doped. I tipped off the D.A. about Skye's foundation, had a guy hack into her records and plant false information. The illegal arms being shipped? That was me, too. All of it."

"I could so throw your ass in jail over this."

"I'll deny it all. But I didn't blow up the oil rig. I had nothing to do with that." He sat across from her in the booth.

"You just admitted you'd lie about talking to me."

"That's different."

"Degrees of evil? Do you have a chart so I can follow along?"

"No chart. You don't even have to talk, just listen."

"Not talk? Have we met?"

He smiled. "I meant you don't have to participate in the conversation."

She stared at him. The smile was gone already, but she'd recognized it. It was the carefree smile Jed had used often when she'd been younger. She hadn't seen it in years. It reminded her that Garth might be the devil, but he was also her brother. Perhaps only a half brother, but then Lexi was only her half sister. He was still family.

Somehow she'd forgotten that. They had a connection.

"Fifteen minutes," she said, glancing at her watch. "Starting now."

"Nick wasn't a part of it. I told him I wanted to help you without taking credit." He shrugged. "Nick used to think I was actually a nice guy and he believed me."

"There's a stunner," she muttered, wondering if any of this was true.

"When he found out there was more going on, he was pissed. He told me to back off. I wouldn't. He faced a real dilemma . . . tell you the truth and have you walk, or keep quiet until you had the surgery. You know what he chose."

Izzy didn't want to think about that — didn't want to think about Nick or the secrets he'd kept from her. How he'd hurt her.

"He picked his friend," she said.

"He picked what was right. If you'd known, you would have left in a snit and who knows when you would have gotten the surgery."

She didn't want to agree with that, but

knew he was right. "He could have told me later."

"When? While you were still in bandages? Afterward when he was falling for you? What would have been the best time, Izzy? When would it have been okay?"

She didn't have an answer for that, either. There was no good time. She knew that, but so what? Nick had still betrayed her. Given the circumstances and all Garth had done to her family, she would guess that decision should make Garth a happy guy. So why was he taking Nick's side? Was it another round in the sick game of crush the Titans?

"Why are you defending him?" she asked, figuring there was no point in avoiding the obvious. "You're the one who told me he was working for you. You're the one who came between us. You knew what was going to happen, so none of this is a surprise."

"Yeah, but I didn't count on Nick." He leaned back in the booth and stared past her. "He never gets involved. I didn't think you mattered that much to him. He told me to stop going after you and your sisters. I didn't listen." He returned his gaze to her. "Maybe I should have. He's gone. We're not friends anymore. He's angry and disgusted with me."

Garth actually sounded surprised and a little sad, she thought, refusing to pity him.

"Gee, you used your only friend to hurt people and you're shocked he's judging you. What an unfortunate time to be you."

"Thanks for the sympathy."

"You're welcome."

He picked up the handkerchief and stuck it in his pocket. "Give him a chance, Izzy."

"Why?"

"Because we both love him."

She blinked. "You can't love anyone. You're a cold, empty, ruthless bastard."

"He was the only family I had. I played and lost. Our friendship is a casualty of war. I don't like it but I can't change it. It's up to you. Take care of him."

Oh, please. Was he serious? She was about to tell him exactly what she thought of him when she remembered Nick talking about his friend in South America. The one who had kept him alive. The man who had been like his brother. The one who shared Nick's scars.

They had been tortured together and nearly died together. Nick had trusted Garth with more than his life and yet had rejected Garth's current actions. That had to mean something. Even more confusing, what had happened to the man who had saved Nick from those frat bullies all those years ago? Where was the young man who had explained how to get the girl and fit in? Where was that Garth Duncan? When had he changed and why?

"You want me to take care of Nick while you still plan to go after me and my sisters?" she asked.

"I mostly want to take down Jed, but sure, you girls can come along for the ride."

"That's insane. You're giving me advice and at the same time promising to ruin my family."

"I have layers."

"You have a desperate need for therapy." She stared at him. "Nick's your only friend, isn't he? You don't have anyone left."

Garth shifted on his seat. "We're talking about you and Nick."

"We were and now we're talking about you. What happens when you win? Who will you celebrate with?" Not Kathy. His mother wouldn't understand. So who was left? Staff?

"I should go," he said.

"No. Wait."

What he'd done was unforgivable. She knew that, knew he had to be stopped. And yet there were hints of an actual person inside the dark, angry facade. Someone who was part of her family. Someone who might be worth saving.

"Don't do this," she said, reaching across the table and touching his hand. "Stop now, Garth. Come talk to Lexi and Skye. We can try to work something else out. We're family, for better or worse."

He pulled back and stood. "It's too late, sis. Jed has to pay for what he did."

"Agreed, but let us in. You don't have to be alone in this."

"Thanks for the offer, but I'm good."

"You're not. You've lost everyone."

He gave her that smile again. "I like to travel light."

He was lying, she thought. Lying to cover being hurt and alone. He was so close to winning and knew he would end up with an empty victory. Only it was too late to stop playing now.

Without thinking, she scrambled to her feet and hugged him. He stiffened with surprise and didn't hug her back. She stared up into his dark eyes, knowing in her gut this was the right thing to do.

"I'm going to save you."

He took a step back. "What the hell? I don't need saving. I'm winning."

"I know. That's why you need saving. Don't worry, it won't hurt too much."

"I don't worry. I get things done."

She smiled. "Tough talk, big brother. Your life has just changed forever. You're not going to know what hit you. But it's okay. I'm going to do it with love. Lexi and Skye will take some convincing and Dana wants to introduce you to her favorite gun, but she'll come around, too. This is going to be great."

For the first time since entering the restaurant, Garth looked wary. "You don't know what you're talking about."

"You're wrong and it won't be the first time. It's late September. We need this resolved by early December so we can have Christmas together. That's a lot of healing to get done. I'm not a great planner, but my sisters are." She smiled again. "Thanks for coming by. I'm glad we talked."

Garth frowned, then left. When he reached the door, he glanced back at her, as if trying to figure out what was going on. She waved at him.

She wasn't sure why she hadn't seen it before. The solution was simple — Garth needed to be a part of the family. Then he wouldn't want to hurt them anymore. Just as important, he had to be stopped before he did something that really got him in trouble.

She wasn't sure exactly how they were going to make this all happen, but they would figure out something. Poor Garth — he wasn't going to know what hit him.

"Save Garth?" Dana scowled. "No. I'm throwing his ass in jail. Whenever I get tense, I picture that and get all tingly inside."

"I'm serious," Izzy told her. "I talked to him. He's worth saving. We have to figure out how."

"You figure out how. You'll have plenty of time after your sisters have you committed."

Izzy waved the comment aside. "Don't be crabby. This is the right thing to do. Think of how smug we can all feel when we're together."

"And smug is a goal?"

Izzy grinned. "Sometimes." Since meeting with Garth, she'd known this was the only way to win. She'd never been so sure of anything. "I'm going to talk to Lexi and Skye later."

"I can't wait to see that explosion."

"They're going to love my idea."

"Uh-huh. Are you on drugs?"

"I'm right and eventually you're going to have to admit it. That's enough of a high for me."

There was a knock on the door. She stood

to answer it.

"Besides," she continued as she reached for the doorknob and turned it, "what's the worst that could happen?"

She turned to face the visitor and nearly fainted when she saw Nick.

It had been over two weeks since she'd left his ranch. Two weeks of feeling as if the best part of her had died. She ached for him, had trouble sleeping and had known she would bear the scars of his betrayal forever.

Still, she couldn't help wanting to touch him now, to reassure herself that he was real. She saw the dark circles under his eyes, the drawn hollows in his cheeks. She wanted to hold him and ask if he was okay. She wanted to kiss him and have him kiss her back. She wanted to hear the sound of his voice.

"Should I get my gun?" Dana asked.

"You women are quick with the weapons," Nick said, staring at Izzy. "Shoot me if you want, I'm not going anywhere."

Izzy stepped back to let him in the condo. "Have it handy. I may need it later."

"Sure." Dana backed out of the room. "I'll be close by. Yell if you need anything."

Seconds later, Izzy heard the bedroom door close.

Nick continued to study her. "You look good."

"You look like shit."

"That's how I feel."

"Good. What do you want?"

He gave her a faint smile. "To tell you how much I love you, Izzy. I probably have from the first moment we met."

"You kidnapped me."

"I'm a helluva guy."

She turned away and walked to the window. She *desperately* wanted to know his words were true, but how could she trust him? She folded her arms across her chest and told herself to keep breathing. That the pain in her stomach would eventually go away. That hope was for someone else, not her.

He came up behind her, but didn't touch her, which was good. If he did, she would probably shatter.

"You changed everything," he said. "I can't stop thinking about you. Please, give me a chance to prove myself to you."

"You have Stockholm Syndrome," she said, closing her eyes tight. "That's all this is."

"That's when the prisoner falls for the person holding him hostage."

"Okay. You have something else then.

What you're feeling isn't real and even if it is, I don't care. You lied to me."

"I know. I kept my relationship with Garth a secret. I was stupid and wrong and, worse, I hurt you. I'm sorry, Izzy. God knows you deserve better than I gave you and you deserve better than me. I live with guilt every day. I can never make the past right. You should be with someone who isn't so damn scarred."

She spun to face him. "I never minded the scars."

"I meant the ones on the inside." His green eyes burned with a fire she'd never seen before. "But I can't help it. You're the one. I never thought I'd love someone. I never thought I deserved it. But here we are. I know I screwed up. I know I need to prove myself and I want to. Just give me the chance. Please. I love you."

He reached up his hand as if he was going to touch her, then dropped it to his side. For the first time since she'd known him, he looked unsure.

She thought about all the rejections in her life. How neither of her parents ever cared about her. How she hid behind crazy adventures. Facing death was a whole lot easier than facing the fact that she had no one of her own.

She, too, had never thought she would fall in love. Be willing to risk it all. Nick was everything she wanted, everything she needed. Not perfect . . . just perfect for her.

"I've decided to save Garth," she said. "It's the only way to resolve whatever issues he has. It won't be easy."

Nick blinked. "Save Garth, as in . . ."

"Drown him in love. Pull him into the family. Comfort his bruised and tattered heart."

"Garth Duncan?"

"He's a person, too."

"Don't you hate him?"

"Not anymore." She tilted her head. "He talked to me the other day. Said I shouldn't give up on you."

Nick looked confused. "Garth?"

"You keep saying his name as if there are three different men we could be talking about. So are you going to help me save him?"

"Uh, sure. If that's what you want."

"Good. We have to convince Dana first. She won't be easy. Then Lexi. Skye's all mushy inside, so I think she'll get on board right away. We need a plan and that's not my strong suit. Maybe we could ask Aaron to help."

He grabbed her upper arms. "Izzy, while I

appreciate you wanting to save Garth, that's not what I came here to talk about."

She smiled. "I know."

"I love you."

"You keep saying that, but don't people in love kiss? Or plan for the future? There's a lot of talk here, but not a lot of action. I have to tell you, it's fairly disappointing."

She had more to say but was cut off when he leaned in and kissed her.

She welcomed his mouth on hers, wrapped her arms around him and melted into his body. He pulled her even closer, holding her as if he would never let her go. They kissed until she thought she might drown from the joy of it all.

After several intense minutes, he pulled back. "Isadora Titan, will you marry me?"

She grinned. "Maybe."

He laughed, bent down and pressed his shoulder against her midsection, then straightened, lifting her off her feet.

She shrieked. "What are you doing?"

"Kidnapping you. I'm going to keep you at my ranch until you come to your senses and say yes. It worked before."

All the blood rushed to her head, but she didn't struggle too hard. A door opened and she saw the lower half of Dana enter the room.

"Do I want to know what's going on?" her friend asked, sounding both amused and appalled. "Is this what you do for fun?"

"Sometimes," Izzy said. "He's kidnapping me because I didn't accept his proposal."

"Should I be packing up your things?"

"That would be nice."

"You going to say yes?" Dana asked.

"Eventually, but he's going to have to work for it."

"That's my girl."

Suddenly she was on her feet again. The room spun as her blood rushed elsewhere. Nick held her, his expression fierce.

"You're going to say yes?"

Love filled her. The hot, bright emotion gave her strength and healed the last few cracks in her heart. "I love you. What else would I say?"

They reached for each other.

"Take it outside, children," Dana said. "I just got the sofa cleaned."

Izzy giggled. "She's so romantic. We have to find her someone."

"Not in this lifetime," Dana grumbled. "I mean it, Nick. Don't listen to her."

Izzy led him outside. Dana closed the door behind them. Izzy stared into his green eyes and knew she'd found home at last.

"Thank you," he said. "For giving me

another chance. I love you, Izzy."

"I love you more."

He touched her cheek. "Something for us to argue about for the next fifty years."

"As long as you're clear on the fact that I'll be the one who wins."

He kissed her. "We're both going to win."

"True," she whispered against his lips. Which made it a very good day.

ABOUT THE AUTHOR

Susan Mallery is a *New York Times* best-selling author of more than ninety romances. Her combination of humor, emotion and just-plain-sexy has made her a reader favorite. Susan makes her home in the Pacific Northwest with her handsome husband and possibly the world's cutes dog. Visit her Web site at www.SusanMallery.com.

We hope you have enjoyed this Large Print book. Other Thorndike, Wheeler, Kennebec, and Chivers Press Large Print books are available at your library or directly from the publishers.

For information about current and upcoming titles, please call or write, without obligation, to:

Publisher
Thorndike Press
295 Kennedy Memorial Drive
Waterville, ME 04901
Tel. (800) 223-1244

or visit our Web site at:

http://gale.cengage.com/thorndike

OR

Chivers Large Print
published by BBC Audiobooks Ltd
St James House, The Square
Lower Bristol Road
Bath BA2 3SB
England
Tel. +44(0) 800 136919
email: bbcaudiobooks@bbc.co.uk
www.bbcaudiobooks.co.uk

All our Large Print titles are designed for easy reading, and all our books are made to last.